UNCHAINED

USA TODAY BESTSELLING AUTHOR

J.L. WEIL

ALSO BY J. L. WEIL

ELITE OF ELMWOOD ACADEMY
(New Adult Dark High School Romance)
Turmoil
Disorder
Revenge
Rival
Unchained

DIVISA HUNTRESS
(New Adult Paranormal Romance)
Crown of Darkness
Inferno of Darkness
Eternity of Darkness

DRAGON DESCENDANTS SERIES
(Upper Teen Reverse Harem Fantasy)
Stealing Tranquility
Absorbing Poison
Taming Fire

Thawing Frost

THE DIVISA SERIES
(Full series completed – Teen Paranormal Romance)
Losing Emma: A Divisa novella
Saving Angel
Hunting Angel
Breaking Emma: A Divisa novella
Chasing Angel
Loving Angel
Redeeming Angel

LUMINESCENCE TRILOGY
(Full series completed – Teen Paranormal Romance)
Luminescence
Amethyst Tears
Moondust
Darkmist – A Luminescence novella

RAVEN SERIES
(Full series completed – Teen Paranormal Romance)
White Raven
Black Crow
Soul Symmetry

BEAUTY NEVER DIES CHRONICLES
(Teen Dystopian Romance)
Slumber
Entangled
Forsaken

NINE TAILS SERIES
(Teen Paranormal Romance)
First Shift

Storm Shift
Flame Shift
Time Shift
Void Shift
Spirit Shift
Tide Shift
Wind Shift
Celestial Shift

HAVENWOOD FALLS HIGH
(Teen Paranormal Romance)
Falling Deep
Ascending Darkness

SINGLE NOVELS
Starbound
(Teen Paranormal Romance)
Casting Dreams
(New Adult Paranormal Romance)
Ancient Tides
(New Adult Paranormal Romance)

For an updated list of my books, please visit my website:
www.jlweil.com

Join my VIP email list and I'll personally send you an email reminder as soon as my next book is out! Click here to sign up: www.jlweil.com

PROLOGUE

AINSLEY
JUNIOR HIGH

Some people have a shine to them like gold glittering in the sun. Bright. Breathtaking. Beautiful. That was how the Elite looked the first time I laid eyes on them—golden gods sparkling in a beam of sunlight.

My jaw dropped to the ground. I stood stunned motionless, the clicking of keys, the buzzing of timers, the smell of spilled pop, and the jingle of victory all whirling around me. And yet, I gaped like a fool among the other girls who also stared as the Elite walked by, heading into the arcade.

Even in middle school, they didn't look or act like their peers.

Pretty wasn't the right adjective, but at fourteen years old, it was all I could come up with. Flawless. Intimidating. Popular. Demanding. They drew eyes, even from the workers. Whether it was out of curiosity or suspicion, they had everyone's attention.

Brock Taylor.

Micah Bradford.

Fynn Dupree.

And Grayson Edwards.

The Elite of Elmwood.

They were a crew.

They were untouchable.

My gaze followed them as they wound through the packed arcade, talking and snickering among themselves. Just by looking, you could see they were a unit—a pack—outsiders not allowed. Their bodies carried that do-not-approach factor.

I knew their names. Everyone at Public High School and the Elmwood Academy knew the Elite, but I'd never seen their faces, and yet, just from what I'd heard, I could distinguish who was who.

Brock Taylor led the crew. Messy, dark hair fell over the side of his right eye, and as he shoved it out of the way, those piercing aqua eyes assessed the room.

Micah Bradford and Fynn Dupree followed behind side by side. Micah's lopsided smirk and platinum-blond hair distinguished him as the Elite rogue. He bumped shoulders with Fynn, the tallest boy in the arcade. Besides long legs, Fynn had the greenest eyes I'd ever seen and envious deep-golden skin. A runway model came to mind at the sight of him in person. If he wasn't destined to spend his adult years on the football field, I wouldn't be surprised to see him on magazine covers or in commercials.

Grayson Edwards trailed behind—the one with the twin sister—the one with a single facial expression. Grumpy. For a boy of fourteen, his eyes held a swarm of distrust. Everyone in the arcade was a potential enemy. Those rich brown eyes were sharp enough to cut a person with a sole glance. He made me instinctually want to back up and step out of his path.

But another part of me wanted to do the opposite and force him to go around me or right through me if he dared. My chin lifted despite the flutters in my belly. They might be the Elite, but I bowed for no one.

As they came closer, I reminded myself they were just freaking boys like every other douchebag at school, except...they weren't.

Did the arcade hush?

Yes.

Did heads turn?

Again, yes.

The four of them came my way, and I leaned back against a machine, holding my breath.

They didn't normally slum it on this side of town. Even at Public where I went to school, the four of them had a reputation, and seeing them up close for the first time, I got the full *Elite effect*. What an effect it was. I might be permanently damaged for life. No other guys at my school or any other could live up to them. The hype was real. So. Very. Real.

The nerd at the pinball machine behind me spun toward his friends, hands lifting in the air as he bumped into me. My lack of attention had me stumbling forward, completely unaware of what happened until I hit something.

Or someone.

A dozen curse words went through my head as I squeezed my eyes close, praying it wasn't who I thought. *My luck can't be that shitty. Can it?*

A pair of firm hands landed on my arms, and my nose planted into a flat chest, far too close to an armpit, which I hated to admit smelled fantastic. If I hadn't been so freaking enamored by the Elite, I might have maintained my balance instead of flailing like I didn't know how to stand on two feet.

My cheeks warming, I glanced up into the face of...

Grayson goddamn Edwards.

Screw luck.

The expression on his handsome face soured, somehow making him more attractive and making me feel like a troll with bright neon green hair and a massive pimple on my chin that had appeared this morning when I woke.

His dark eyes flicked over my face, judging me in two seconds. I couldn't remember the last time anyone looked at me with such disdain like I was a wad of chewed-up gum he stepped on, ruining his five-hundred-dollar pair of sneakers.

"Watch it, Public scum," he sneered, shoving me off him.

I stumbled back into the pinball machine. A few kids close enough to hear him snickered. They went to Public and were supposed to be on *my* side. Not theirs.

Micah and Fynn turned around to see why Grayson grumbled. I'd heard the four of them always had each other's backs. No questions asked. Another rumor that seemed to be true. Micah grinned, not in a friendly way, flashing a set of dimples. "Is it fucking Halloween?"

I flinched but wasn't altogether surprised. I'd grown used to people making fun of the way I dressed or looked and had almost become immune. Almost. My young heart could still be hurt, was still impressionable, and for reasons unbeknownst to me, I thought maybe the Elite would be more mature than the boys at my school.

I was wrong.

Fynn stared at me with straight lips.

Micah scrunched his nose. "What's up with the costume?" the playboy asked, eyeing me up and down with startling light-blue eyes that only made the flush staining my cheeks deepen.

"What's up with your face?" I countered, finally finding my voice through a swell of embarrassment.

"Other than perfection," Micah proclaimed, grinning like he owned the damn world. His eyes glittered with mocking amusement, finding himself funny.

Arrogant ass.

I blinked, doing my best to pretend as if we hadn't drawn numerous eyes in the arcade. "Are you lost?" I asked in a dry voice. "You seem to have stumbled into the wrong side of town."

He chuckled, and his three friends regarded me with equal frowns of annoyance as if I intentionally interrupted their day. Micah stepped closer to me, past Grayson, forcing my back to sink deeper into the machine, but I had nowhere to go. Although the smile never left his face, the change in his light-blue eyes froze the air around me as if I'd just been transported to the Antarctic. A shudder rolled through me. Not the pleasant kind that would have made me giddy or sweat.

Micah reached his hand out toward me, and I flinched, my eyes squeezing shut as I braced myself—an instinctual reaction for someone who lived with a parent who liked to use their fists. When the blow didn't come, my lashes batted open. His fingers attached to a strand of my badly dyed green hair and tugged.

He chuckled, shaking his head at me. "No wonder all the guys at Public are constantly trying to hit on our girls."

Please. We were in middle school. The dating scene just really started at our age. These were the beginning years of our sexual exploration. Most of the guys I knew at Public didn't know a dick from a vagina or were still too fascinated with their own parts to be ogling the opposite sex.

But that wasn't his point. He was trying to cut me down. It worked. I refused to admit it or show that his words mattered.

I will not cry. I will not shed a single tear over those rich pricks.

My bottom lip trembled. I bit down on it, focusing on the physical pain instead of the mental anguish. The physical pain I could handle.

"Micah," Brock barked. "Let's go."

Grayson and Fynn turned their backs, quickly dismissing me. Only Micah lingered for another few seconds. "Playtime is over," he said with a wink, giving my strand of hair another little yank before letting it go.

Every illusion I had about the Elite popped like an iridescent bubble. They were dicks then, and they grew up to be even bigger assholes.

That was the day I decided to never let anyone treat me like I was less.

1

AINSLEY

PRESENT DAY

I shouldn't have had that last shot or the beer that followed.

My father would be so disappointed. Not in the fact that I was drunk off my ass and stumbling down a dark street. No. He would be upset that his little girl couldn't hold her liquor. *"A Fisher knew how to drink. We weren't pussies. We were cut from a different cloth."*

The sound of his gruff voice in my head rolled the sour liquor in my stomach.

Fuck you, Dad.

I didn't want to be anything like Jett Fisher. A poor drunk with no job, no future, and a temper as quick as a strike of a match. I learned long ago how to read my father with a single glance. It was in the eyes. He had mossy-green eyes much like my own, but they wavered between mean, disinterested, and sad. I never knew which one I would get when I walked through the door.

The irony that I loved to party and drink wasn't lost on me, and yet despite my penchant for a good time, I refused to be anything like my old man.

When I got drunk, I didn't have random outbursts of violence. I didn't hit, blame other people for my behavior, beg for forgiveness the next day, or make promises I had no intention of keeping.

Going away to college was both a blessing and a burden. Although I was happy to be out of that house, it made me feel extraordinarily guilty because I left behind my mother—the only person I loved other than my best friend Josie.

I reminded myself daily that my mom chose to stay with him, to stay in that house. I gave up long ago trying to convince her otherwise. For reasons that escaped me, she loved the man who hurt her. My entire childhood wasn't awful, but those dark times seemed to overshadow any good my father might have done.

I am not my father.

I am smart.

I am driven.

I am thoughtful.

I deserve happiness.

I went through the affirmations my therapist recommended I recite when shit got gloomy inside my head. When I couldn't breathe from the heaviness of the world—of my life. Or when the dark pressed in around me so tight I lost myself.

Clenching my stomach, I fought against the churning that spun, threatening to come up at any second. I hated vomiting.

My eyes lifted, scanning the dark street. Cars lined the road, their headlights on dim, engines idly running. Night surrounded me, but unlike the stuff in my head, the physical darkness comforted me; it wasn't something I wanted to run or hide from.

As I drew in a deep breath, my lungs took in the crisp December air. Winter break had just started, and this was my last weekend at college before heading back home to Elmwood. What better way to kick off the season than a little street racing party?

Technically not my idea, but if booze, people, and music were involved, I was there. Grayson raced for a hobby, and the real reason we were here was to support and watch the daredevil speed down the road for pleasure.

I didn't snub my nose at a little thrill-seeking fun. I was just annoyed the jerk refused to let me ride shotgun. And now it seemed as if I'd lost my friends in the crowd.

Perfect.

An engine revved as a group of girls shoved past me. Giggling and murmuring, they made their way to the curb. The race looked close to starting. Six or seven expensive cars, most modified, moved into position on the abandoned back road. The fact that hardly anyone used the mile stretch made it the perfect place for some illegal racing and betting.

I leaned against the broken streetlight, wondering where Josie and the others had gone. I faintly remembered muttering something about not wanting to leave and declaring I needed another drink. I might have also told her that if she intended to suck Brock's face off all night to go back to his place.

The memories of the night were fuzzy.

Fuck.

Had I really been that bitchy?

Sober Ainsley was happy her best friend had found a guy who loved her like crazy and who she loved equally as madly. Drunk Ains was jealous. It wasn't just Josie and Brock. Now it was also Micah and Mads. Everywhere I looked, couples were forming, and here I was alone and about to puke. A clear sign it was time for me to go home.

Searching for Grayson's Bugatti among the cars on the road, I shook my head again, recalling the amount of money he handed over without blinking to buy into the race. As if his car alone wasn't worth more money than I'd ever seen.

Money was a sensitive topic for me. I found that people who grew up chasing their next dollar thought about money every waking moment, from needing a few gallons of gas to get to work or counting change for a bag of chips at lunch.

And for someone like Grayson Edwards, money was a fleeting thought. It didn't factor into his every decision. Money was an afterthought if a thought at all.

The parking lot went silent for a second. The music playing from someone's speakers switched to the intro of drums from a car parked on the side of the road. Not a racer, but a spectator or an organizer. A heavy metal song blared. Something about bodies hitting the floor. I was more of a K-pop girl myself, but I could get down with this. It fit with the drumming in my head as my thoughts turned back to the race.

Maybe I should sit down...or get another beer.

Another drink might shove back the queasy feeling that overcame me watching the headlights on the road spin, but the cars were not moving. Such a bad idea. I should just go home. I took a step and another.

There was just one problem.

I didn't know which way would take me back to my dorm.

Shoving a hand through my chestnut hair, I clamped down on my bottom lip, a curse popping off in my head. I'd just call someone. Surely, one of my friends was still around.

I patted my back pocket for my phone.

"Ainsley?"

I whirled at the sound of my name, but I whirled too damn fast. A pair of hands flanked my arms as I stumbled. I'd heard my name spoken in that gruff voice only a few times. Usually, he didn't bother to speak to me, but his tone still zapped through my body like lightning.

Grayson Edwards was a stunning guy. His attractiveness could blind me at times, not to mention the number of times he took my breath away. It was a wonder I hadn't yet fainted in his presence from lack of oxygen getting to my brain. His dark windblown hair was a little longer than it was at the beginning of the semester. A deep-gray sweater pulled against his broad chest and thick arms as he stopped in front of me, his sharp, rich-brown eyes scrutinizing me in that disapproving way. I didn't think there was a single time Grayson ever smiled at me or didn't make me feel as if he wanted to chastise me for breathing.

He was also my best friend's brother. And an asshole on his best days. On his worst... I shuddered.

God, why can't he be ugly?

Why are the hot ones always dickheads?

Was it a written law upstairs when the big guy filled out our bio sheets that gorgeous and nice didn't mix? Except for maybe in Fynn Dupree's case. Perhaps God only created the perfect male specimen once in a blue moon.

Fynn, like Grayson, was an Elite. Grayson sat on the polar opposite personality spectrum to that of Fynn. Like night and day the two were and yet thick as thieves.

It was a damn good thing Grayson held me up. Confusion worked its way into my swimming head. Wait. Why is he standing in front of me? "I thought you were racing," I grumbled, narrowing my eyes as I tried to get my vision to merge the two figures of Grayson scowling at me.

"I am," he answered snappily, which was how he normally spoke to me. That was when he spoke to me, of course.

My fingers pressed to my stomach, each word an effort to keep all that damn liquor from surging back up. "Shouldn't you be in your car then?" Seemed obvious even in my inhibited state.

"I was," he said through gritted teeth. "And then you stumbled into the road."

I was in the road? When did that happen?

Someone honked their horn, followed by a voice screaming to get out of the way. Wavering, I leaned into his solid frame. Hell, he was so damn warm, and I was so cold. "I-I don't know—"

Bang!

Startled, I froze. And then I moved too fast for my mind to keep up with what the fuck happened. I was falling. No. Grayson was holding me. He had yanked me against his chest, taking us to the ground as he tucked me into his arms. The sinful scent of him, warm and fresh like the Mediterranean Sea with hints of tangerine, surrounded me along with the hard press of his body.

Pop. Pop. Pop.

The sound came again, going off in rapid succession.

Either an engine backfired or someone was shooting off fireworks.

Grayson cocooned himself closer around me as another three shots rang out. My heart hammered in my chest. Someone screamed. Or it could have been multiple screams. The voices in the street were muffled by the high-pitched ringing in my ears that made me wince.

Holy shit.

Those were...gunshots.

The realization sobered me like a splash of cold water. Adrenaline pumped in my veins.

Grayson's fingers went under my arms, tugging me to my feet. There was no gentleness in his movements, not with our survival at stake. "Are you hurt?" he asked. Under the hardness of his eyes, a speck of fear gleamed, something he rarely displayed.

I didn't know if I'd ever seen him afraid of anything. This was real.

There was an active shooter in the dark.

I vomited. All over Grayson Edwards's pristine white sneakers. Tonight was probably the first time he'd worn them. And the last.

He stepped back, eyeing the mess on his shoes. "Christ. Your timing is impeccable as always."

Wiping my mouth with the back of my sleeve, I glanced up into a set of hard, dark eyes. I might go to a fancy school, but there was nothing fancy about me.

"You owe me a pair of new shoes, little devil," he said gruffly.

Why? Why did it have to be my best friend's fraternal triplet brother I hurled on?

There were dozens of other guys in and around the bar. Why couldn't it have been one of them? Hell, I would have even settled for Micah or Fynn. Just not Grayson.

Bile coated the back of my throat. I should probably apologize or something, but my mouth stopped working.

Panic erupted on the streets. More screams. People began to run, pushing and shoving, to find safety.

"Someone's been shot!" someone yelled.

Fingers pressed into my arm as Grayson hauled me through the crowd. "We need to move," he ordered over his shoulder.

I stayed close. His fingers ran down my arm to lace with mine. Several more shots went off behind us. They sounded closer than before, and my horror swelled.

I couldn't believe this was happening. We might be in a rural part of town, but it was still a thousand times nicer than where I grew up in. Shootings didn't happen here.

The flash of something in Grayson's other hand drew my attention as we jogged toward his car. A glint of moonlight reflected off steel. "You brought a knife to a gun show?"

A fight broke out in the spot where we'd been a few seconds ago. Grayson spared the two guys nothing more than a fleeting look. "Would you rather be defenseless?"

"I'm more concerned about you cutting yourself or me," I added, praying my feet and legs remained underneath me. The last thing I needed in the middle of a stampede was to fall. Yet the fear of being shot disconnected the working parts of my body. They weren't talking to each other, or they weren't listening. My movements felt clumsy at best, but a part of me knew Grayson wouldn't let me fall.

That should have made me feel better—safer. It did. And it didn't.

Grayson and I didn't exactly get along. We tolerated each other for Josie's sake while also throwing barbs, dirty looks, and general disdain. My favorite way to communicate with him was through hand gestures.

Irritation flared in his features at my last comment. "Don't worry. I know how to use it."

And that was what scared me. The blade looked too comfortable in his hands, like it belonged, an extension of him instead of an addition.

Just when I thought I knew what Grayson was all about, he pulled shit like this, making me feel as if I didn't know him at all.

Even as we ran for safety, he kept his body in front of me like a shield, protecting me.

Grayson flung open the Bugatti's door and deposited me inside the passenger seat before stalking around the car to the driver's side. He kicked off his puke-covered sneakers and slid behind the wheel in just white socks. "Buckle up. Or do you need me to do that too?"

Fucker.

My fingers fumbled with the strap, finally pulling it across my chest as he threw the car into drive and slammed his foot on the gas. The Bugatti lurched forward, tossing my head back against the seat. The sudden movement caused my stomach to flip, churning what liquor lingered inside. Swallowing, I vowed to not vomit in his car. Not only would it be embarrassing, which I'd done enough of, but the price of the cleaning bill would set me back for years. I couldn't afford any mistakes for the next two and a half years. Each penny mattered. Sure, I could skip a few meals, but if I lost my stomach in here, I wouldn't eat for the rest of college.

We had only driven a few feet when Grayson hit the brakes hard. The back end of the Bugatti fishtailed before coming to a jerky halt. Under a curtain of wispy strands of my hair, I watched a stream of frantic people run across the road.

Bang. Bang. Bang.

Another round of shots peppered into the side of a car two in front of us. One of the bullets went into the tire, flattening it on impact.

"Shit. Get down," Grayson hissed, his hand flying across the car to the back of my head, shoving me forward. I felt the car inching ahead a little at a time until a break occurred, and then we were through, speeding down the somber road. I lifted my head, but it took a mile before my heart even began to slow. The darkness of night blurred by.

"Holy fuck," I whispered, unable to believe what happened *and* that we got away. I interlocked my fingers on my lap, staring at my feet as my body trembled. Aftershocks. "Where's everyone else? Did they get out?" I asked, breaking the silence.

He shook his head, his fingers flexing over the leather steering wheel. "I don't know. Why aren't you with them?" Anger laced his question. I had no idea if it was directed at me or the situation. Probably both.

My lips stayed pressed together.

The interior lights illuminated a cool aqua glow over Grayson's scowling face. "Let me guess. You refused to leave. Or you picked a fight."

Oh, he thinks he knows me so well. "Does it matter?" I snapped.

He let out an irritated little guffaw. "Text Josie and find out where they are."

I scrambled to find my phone, leaning to the left as I fished it out of my back pocket. The closed space gave little room to move. Strands of my hair brushed against Grayson's shoulder before I settled back into my seat and glanced at my phone. A dozen notifications from Josie lit up my home screen.

Where are you?

Hello?

Don't ignore me. I shouldn't have let you go off on your own. I'm sorry.

Just let me know that you're okay.

The texts transitioned from worried to stressed, coming in back-to-back rapid order.

Okay, I'm super freaked out now.

Ainsley, please text me back!!

I'm coming to get you.

"Fuck." The swear breezed through my lips.

"What's wrong?" Grayson demanded, his body instantly

stiffening.

The last message had been sent three minutes ago. Knowing Josie, she would run straight into a hostile situation with no thought of herself to save me. She was my ride or die. "I need to call Josie before she goes back there to look for me."

Swiftly hitting Josie's picture on my phone, I waited for her to pick up, the repeated ringing in my ear torture. *Pick up. Pick up. Pick up,* I chanted in my head.

Of all the horrible things that could happen in the world, losing Josie was at the very top of my list. I couldn't live in a world without her. She anchored me through all the crap life tossed my way. I don't know how many times she talked me down from some of the worst panic attacks I'd experienced. They didn't happen often, but when they did, I felt like I was dying.

"Ains." Her voice came through the speaker, shaky and pitched higher than usual.

My back sunk against the seat. "Holy fuck, Josie. I nearly had a heart attack. Are you okay? Where are you? There's a shooter at Route Extinct." Or better known as Route X. "Oh God, Josie, I was so afraid I'd never hear your voice again," I continued to ramble, something I did when I was either excited or utterly freaked out.

"Let her fucking talk already," Grayson grumbled, ripping the phone from my hand. "Tell me where you are," he ordered into my phone as I scowled at him.

"I'm with Brock," she informed, and I could hear the quiet music of his car playing in the background.

"And the others?" Grayson inquired, his brows furrowing. Grayson had two sisters. Josie and Kenna. The three of them were triplets. Josie was Kenna and Grayson's once-thought-dead sister. Turned out she'd just been kidnapped for almost eighteen years.

I cracked the window, needing air. Frost flurried through the parted glass, kissing my cheeks, but I welcomed the sting of cold. It was refreshing against the warmth blowing on my feet from the car's heater.

"They're with us. We're heading back to the dorms now," she said, her tone stronger and steadier now.

"We'll meet you at Brock's," Grayson stated, ending the call. Silence followed as he turned to me, holding out my phone for me to take. "Was that so hard?"

I snatched my phone back. "Yes," I snorted sharply. The tension pressing down on my chest eased after hearing Josie's voice. "And I wasn't done talking to her."

The car's smoothness made it impossible for me to tell how fast we were going, but it was fast enough I didn't want to know. Grayson whipped the car at the first turn, handling the power of the Bugatti one-handed. I chewed on the inside of my lip. *You do not find that hot,* I reprimanded myself.

Except I did. Well, when my head wasn't spinning and my stomach didn't pitch at the turning movements of the car I did.

Guiding the steering wheel straight again, Grayson eyed me for a second. "Whatever endless chatter you have to say can wait until we get to the dorms," he mumbled.

I lay the back of my head against the cold window, staring at the shadows darkening his face. "Are you always this pleasant after a near-death experience?"

His brows arched. "You did vomit on me. This is as pleasant as you're going to get."

The emphasis on *you're* had my spine stiffening, implying he was only rude to me, which I knew was utter bullshit. I twisted in my seat, my mouth opening, but the question that burned on my tongue didn't come out.

Why do you hate me so much?

Over the last two years, I had held back from asking him.

"You suck," I said instead. Turning forward, I crossed my arms and glared at the dashboard.

He blew through a stop sign and grumbled, "You're welcome."

Gah! Why did he get under my skin so easily? His voice. The permanent frown on his lips. The cold chips of his eyes. They all grated on my nerves. It was just him. Everything about him pissed me off.

Ever since our first encounter, I'd never been able to shake the dislike. I didn't know what his excuse was. I was pretty damn sure Grayson didn't remember how we met, regardless of how I longed to forget.

I never imagined we would ever cross paths again. Let alone my best friend falling in love with the goddamn Elite king. Or that her cousin would entangle herself with the Elite playboy. And here I was, sitting inside Grayson Edwards's car, indebted to the bastard.

A part of me wanted to thank him, but the devil inside of me won. She usually did. "Do you expect me to kiss your feet?" I bit out.

"How much?" he asked, stone-faced in a serial killer kind of voice.

"What?" I replied, blinking.

Tight and humorless, his lips curved. "How much will it cost for you to kiss my feet?"

He was not seriously offering to pay me to put my lips anywhere near his sweaty-ass, stinky feet. The worst part was, I couldn't tell if he was kidding or not. Shooting him the evil eyes, I lifted my middle finger.

It wasn't until a few minutes later that I realized his stupid question had taken the edge off. He managed to distract me and bring what had been an extremely intense situation to a familiarly normal one.

Was that Grayson's way of talking me off a ledge? To keep the panic from consuming me?

Nah. It couldn't be. He literally just wanted to irritate me.

Mission accomplished.

Grayson was not that compassionate of a human being.

But regardless of his motives, the prick had saved me, protected me even, and he made sure I got out safe.

I guess I should be thankful no one got shot.

2

———

GRAYSON

Ainsley fucking Fisher.

With her eyes closed, her head fell to the side toward me. Long lashes fluttered over her pale cheeks. She always wore heavy makeup, hiding her face with smoky shadows, thick eyeliner, and enough mascara to kill a man. Not to mention the deep shades of lipstick.

Fuck. Don't think about her lips. Don't even look at them.

But the deep-cherry, almost black lips drew my eyes despite the warnings popping off in my head. I was a sucker for a plump glossy mouth, and hers might be perfect to fantasize about, but the shit that came out of that mouth soured the illusion.

Nothing about this girl tempted me.

So I continued to tell myself.

It was mostly true. There might only be a tiny fraction of curiosity that wondered what it would be like if I took full possession of those lips.

Not tonight though.

Not after she ruined my shoes.

Although, I didn't give a shit about the shoes. It wasn't the first, and surely wouldn't be the last, time someone puked on me. Went with the territory when you had a sister. Correction. Sisters.

Two years later, it still blew my mind Josie was my sister.

I shook my head to keep my thoughts from going down a rabbit hole. My past was complicated, and it seemed like the fates thought my present life was a little too quiet lately. I was no stranger to guns or even being shot at, but the feeling never failed to jump-start my heart, reminding me that I cared for only a handful of people.

When I saw Ainsley drunkenly stagger into the middle of a street race, my concern hadn't been that she would get hurt. I thought of Josie losing a friend. It was stupid, but I felt as if I had eighteen years to make up for as her brother. She was technically the baby of the family, and even after two years, a part of her still felt like an outsider —a fraud. Thinking about all the time we'd been apart and what it had done to my parents instantly instilled rage in my heart.

It was difficult to not think about how all of us might be different if Josephine James had never come stumbling into our lives.

Josie would probably be a different person. Although, I had to admit I admired and liked the tough girl she'd become. Kenna too, which in her case might not be a bad thing. And my brother, Sawyer, might still be here. This could be a far-fetched assumption. I doubted his love for street racing would have changed, but I wanted to cling to the idea that maybe, just maybe, he wouldn't have entered Burnout Bridge. His car wouldn't have sideswiped another racer, spinning out of control and slamming into the bridge where he and his car tumbled over the edge.

Burnout Bridge was known as the deadliest section of road in the state.

Was it screwed up I started racing because of Sawyer?

I didn't just want to keep his memory alive, but I'd looked up to him, and racing made me feel as if he rode in the car alongside me.

At the time of his accident, I couldn't really understand why he put his life on the line like that, but after my first race, I got it. The rush and exhilaration. The speed and power of the machine under my control. The thrill of winning. Money never posed as the driving factor. I needed the release it gave me. Racing became an outlet to burn through heavy emotions, stresses, and frustrations.

And because of some idiot with a gun, I'd been robbed of the escape I'd been looking for tonight. Now I was stuck driving home the one girl I tended to avoid.

It was about a ten-minute drive back to Brock's house on campus, and Ainsley passed out five minutes before I pulled into Greek Row. Probably a good thing. Ruining a pair of shoes was one thing, but getting the stench and stain of beer vomit out of the Bugatti's leather seats would suck.

Parking on the side of the street in front of the rowhouse, I killed the engine and glanced at the girl beside me. Honey strands of hair fell over the side of her pale face, and I lifted a hand to brush them away but stopped myself midway.

What the fuck am I doing?

How this girl's hair fell over her face did not concern me. She wasn't mine to take care of. Nor was I the type of guy who was overly touchy. No one would call me a cuddler. I also wasn't a coldhearted asshole everyone assumed I was unless they deserved it or fucked with someone I loved.

Then all bets were off.

Dropping my hand, I thought about leaving her in the car and letting Ainsley sleep it off, but the night's temperatures plummeted colder each day the closer we got to Christmas.

I unfolded my legs from the car, walked to the other side in just my socks, and opened the passenger door. Her eyes didn't open, but her head twisted toward me, a soft sigh escaping her parted lips as a gust of icy air caressed her skin. I scooted an arm under those soft thighs, the other behind her back, and lifted Ainsley out of the car.

In her half-asleep state, her arms went instinctually around my neck, resting loosely as her head snuggled close to my face against my shoulder. I tried not to inhale, the smell of vomited beer on her breath drudging up too many unpleasant personal memories.

I could handle hangovers, but of all the common illnesses a person could have, throwing up was the worst. It took too many damn parties in high school for me to figure out the ideal tolerance that got me buzzed enough without being sick.

Ignoring the cold under my feet, I strode down the sidewalk to the front door, kicking it with my toes. The wind hit my back as I waited for someone to let us in. From the other side of the door, the muffled chatter of my friends grew louder. A few moments later, the lock flung open, and Josie stood in the doorway. Her gaze widened at the sight of Ainsley in my arms, and her brows creased with worry.

Josie's brown eyes darted from Ainsley to me. "What did you do to her?" she accused, taking her bottom lip between her teeth while surveying her friend.

Careful not to hit Ainsley's head on a wall, I strutted past Josie into the house. The girl needed all the brain cells she had. "I knocked her out to keep her from throwing herself in front of a bullet."

"Grayson!" Josie shrieked, closing the door and following behind me.

"Do you honestly believe that I would hit your friend?" I replied, walking into the main room where my friends were gathered. They were all here and accounted for. Brock met my eyes and gave me a short nod.

Josie dashed in front of me with a stern look.

Kenna gave a short laugh from where she lounged in front of the TV beside Mads and Micah. "You hit me all the time," she interjected, her commentary unappreciated.

"Yeah, when we were like ten," I muttered, searching for an open seat to drop my extra baggage on. There were none. The barstools didn't seem like an optimal location considering I wasn't sure Ainsley would be able to hold herself upright.

Kenna sent me a bratty grin. "What's the difference? You still act like a boy."

And this was what it was like having two sisters the same age. They ganged up on me.

Fynn and Micah snickered. They were lucky I had my hands full right now, or I'd be smacking them on the back of the head.

"Where do you want her?" I asked Josie, ignoring my other sister.

Her gaze spanned the room before shifting past the kitchen. They had one of the larger rowhouses on campus. The main floor had an open concept with a single bedroom off the kitchen. Upstairs were the remaining bedrooms and bathrooms. "Her room is fine," she said after a moment of thought. "Someone should probably stay with her."

Freshman year, the four girls had all roomed together at the dorms. This year, as Josie promised Brock, they were living together in one of the campus houses with Micah, Mads, Kenna, and Ainsley.

I still didn't know how I felt about my sister and cousin living with my best friends. Everything seemed to be progressing quickly. My mind, even after two years, had barely accepted they were dating. At least I didn't have to listen to the mattress squeaking every night. Fuck no. Just thinking about either Brock or Micah banging Josie or Mads brought feelings that wavered between punching a hole in the wall or, much like Ainsley's current state, being sick off my ass.

Kenna hung her arm over the back of the couch as Micah stood up. "You're not sticking me with the drunk again. Last time, she almost puked in my hair."

As I adjusted the girl in my arms, she made a breathy moan of protest. "So she has a habit of throwing up on people. Wonderful."

Josie's shoulders went lax. "She threw up? That's good."

"My shoes beg to differ," I complained, thinking about the custom Pradas I'd ditched on the road. *They're just shoes*, I reminded myself.

"Damn, bro. Not the kicks." Micah grinned, slapping me on the back. If I didn't already have my hands full, I would have hit him back. Harder. Anything to knock that smirk off his pretty-boy face. And I didn't give two shits that his girlfriend, my fucking cousin, mind you, was in the room.

Good thing I had only one friend left and one sister. If they even thought about hooking up, I swear to God, I would raise hell. Kenna was too much for Fynn to handle. They would never fit, and out of all my friends, those two were the last I'd expect to have any chemistry. They'd known each other too long. I wasn't even going to think it. Not happening.

My friends were dropping like flies. Only Fynn and I were left. And I had no intention of settling down anytime soon. A commitment was not in my future.

No matter how warm Ainsley's body was curled against me, I wasn't touching her. I wasn't some creep who took advantage of drunk girls. I'd dealt with assholes like that in my past, and I constantly carried a slice of guilt and remorse within me from not being able to protect both my sisters from douchebags who abused women, who thought they were owed more than a female was willing to give, or who asserted control without consent.

Fuck them.

The sooner I deposited Ainsley somewhere that wasn't in my arms, the better for both of us.

Leaving everyone else in the family room, I strolled through the kitchen to the small hallway. Her room had the basics, a bed, a desk, a closet, and an adjoining bathroom. I'd never been inside her room, but the sultry scent of her perfume was ingrained into the walls and hit me as I entered.

The bulge in my pants instantly responded.

Laying her on the bed, I abolished the urge to drop her and run from the room. What was it about this particular girl that made me feel like I'd just walked into a witch's lair and she was about to cast a spell on me?

Ainsley snuggled into the pillow as I stood over the bed, debating if I should cover her up or leave her. Why did I give a shit if she was comfortable or not?

I didn't.

When I turned abruptly away from the bed, soft fingers grabbed my hand. "Don't leave me," she whispered, her voice faint.

I pivoted slightly, glancing down at Ainsley. Her eyes were still closed, and the black sweater she wore hung off one shoulder, exposing creamy skin. Unlike the females in my family who were golden tan, Ainsley's skin always remained lighter no matter how much sun she absorbed. Perhaps she was partly a zombie or vampire. Explained why she stayed out so late and constantly flashed her fangs.

I ignored the uncomfortable arousal growing in my jeans.

Christ, it's been too long since I last had sex. Well, long for me. A few months was pushing it.

I peeled her fingers away from my arm and set her hand on the bed, leaving her to sleep it off. Forking my fingers through my hair, I walked out of the room and gently shut the door behind me.

Going straight for the fridge, I took out a beer and twisted off the top. I had the bottle to my lips when Brock's level voice carried over the TV.

"What happened tonight?" he asked.

I carried my drink into the family room and sunk down into a recliner. Josie joined Brock in the chair opposite mine, sitting on his lap. My fingers scrubbed over my face before I met Brock's, Fynn's, and Micah's eyes. "I hoped one of you might have seen something."

Fynn and Micah shook their heads. "We were at the edge of the lot when the first shot went off," Fynn informed, his long legs stretched out on top of the coffee table.

Mads dropped her head on Micah's shoulder, and he squeezed her knee. "We grabbed the girls and got the hell out," Micah added.

I nodded. It was exactly what I expected from him, from all of them. Family came first, and these girls had become part of our family despite them actually being my blood relatives.

Brock made a rough, irritating sound in the back of his throat. "I wasn't about to take any chances." It might have been awkward at first knowing he had a thing for Josie, but there wasn't a better guy who could protect my sister than Brock. But being Brock Taylor also meant he had more enemies than the average Joe. There were pros and cons to every situation.

Holding my beer between my legs, I leaned forward. "Why am I getting a bad feeling about this?"

Mads lifted her head, gray eyes narrowing. A shadow fell over the side of her cheek, concealing the scar. It lightened over the last year, but my cousin still struggled with gaining back the confidence she lost. She'd been hurt by someone who had a vendetta against Micah, and even more than a year later, he still continued to blame himself. At least he loved her. I never thought I would see the day the Elite playboy got tamed. "You think it wasn't a random incident?" Mads speculated.

Brock and I shared a silent glance. For as long as we could remember, we had this ability to read each other's thoughts. Perhaps it was because the two of us were too similar. "No. I just hope that it has nothing to do with us," he said grimly.

Kenna tucked her legs underneath her, hugging the end of the couch. "Was anyone hurt?"

"How about we find out," I said, digging out my phone. I scrolled through my contacts, stopping at a guy named Rusty. He organized the race tonight. After pressing the call button, I switched the phone to speaker, and he picked up on the third ring.

"Gray, shit, man, you made it out." In the background, voices and music boomed. Rusty must have gone straight to a party.

I spoke louder, clearly letting him know I was pissed. "What the hell was that?"

"We had nothing to do with it," he quickly defended, the pitch of his voice going up. Guys like Rusty were weasels. They sucked up to whoever flashed the most money or posed the biggest threat. He had no balls. I had no idea how he became an organizer.

Brock leaned on the chair's arm, the back of his knuckles pressed to his chin, frowning. He didn't believe a word Rusty spewed.

"Who the fuck brought a gun tonight?" I pressed.

"I don't know. I swear, Gray. I'm in the dark on this one, man." That was what they always said.

Micah loosed a curse.

"Did anyone get hurt?" I demanded, staring hard at the phone. Rusty was damn lucky this wasn't a conversation I insisted we had in person. He wouldn't have liked what he saw on my face.

"I-I haven't heard yet," he stammered, an uneasiness moving into his tone. "We bolted before the cops came."

I'm sure he did.

Fynn cleared his throat, and I could tell that, like Brock and Micah, he suspected everything out of Rusty's fast mouth was a lie. Our gazes held for a moment, and Fynn nodded. If anyone got shot tonight, he would find out. Fynn was a whiz when it came to unearthing shit. The crap you could do with a phone or a computer. Scary shit.

"You better hope not. I don't want my name anywhere on the cops' radar. Is that clear?" My warning drenched with the promise of violence if I found he lied.

The party seemed to be ramping up. "What kind of operation do you think I run?" Rusty asked, ignoring the whooping of some idiot.

"I'm not sure anymore after what happened tonight," I replied.

"I told you, Gray. That was not my doing," Rusty insisted.

"Then you need to do a better job screening who you let into your events, or I'll find someone else who can." I let those be our parting words and hung up, having said all I had to say.

My phone buzzed before I had the chance to put it away. But it wasn't just my phone. Fynn, Brock, and Micah all reached for theirs at the same time, and then we glanced at each other, knowing something was up.

It was a text.

Bang. Bang. Count your blessings, for the next time, it won't be just a warning.

The four of us shared another long, silent look, each thinking the same thing. The shooting wasn't a random act. It was a message.

But from who?

Collectively and individually, we had our fair share of enemies, people who would love to hurt us, blackmail us, or seek revenge. We were known to compile dirt on people in our little black book that could destroy careers, end marriages, and convict corrupt politicians, civil servants, and men in power.

When someone came at us, we hit back harder.

Emptying the bottle, I stood up, irritated the drink had done little to quiet the energy buzzing within me. I had to get out of here. What I needed was a race. I needed power and speed. And I needed it like hours ago.

"Where are you going?" Kenna asked, her eyes trailing me.

"To get laid," I stated unashamedly. Sex was the next best thing to racing.

"Gross," Kenna said, wrinkling her face. "Keep that shit to yourself."

"Next time, don't ask," I shot back, dropping my empty beer bottle into the kitchen waste bin.

"You plan on getting your dick sucked barefoot?" Micah lifted his brows at me.

"Shit," I muttered, forgetting about the shoes I'd left in the middle of the road. "Micah, I need to borrow a pair of shoes."

3

AINSLEY

The next morning, I woke up in bed with no recollection of how I got there, but I had a guess. Grayson. Fuzziness clouded my head, the aftereffects of having too much fun last night, and the pieces were slow to click together.

A quick jolt of fear hit my heart.

The shooting.

Not the way I liked to end a night—running scared for my life.

If it hadn't been for Grayson, I'm not sure what would have happened.

Sitting on the edge of my bed with my feet hanging over the side, I pressed a hand to my temples, willing the dull throb to cease. How easy it would be to fall back onto the mattress and throw the covers over my head. Yet no matter how much I wanted to stay in bed all day and nurse this wicked headache, I couldn't.

Today I went home for winter break.

The joy inside me at the idea of going home was comparable to eating burnt toast.

I should stay a school, but I would be the only one here. All my friends were eager to go home because they actually liked their families. I did want to check up on my mom. That was the *only* reason I'd step foot inside my house again.

Before I left for college, things had gotten bad with my father's drinking. Worse than it ever was growing up, and I worried about how Mom fared without me. Despite our weekly chats on the phone, she would put a brave face on and tell me things were fine even when they weren't. She would sacrifice herself for me and my happiness.

Plus, I told my employer from when I was in high school I would be returning for breaks. Bea and Ralph, the owners of Pa's Place, expected me to show up on Tuesday for my shift.

I scanned the messy state of my room wondering if half the clothes on my floor were clean or dirty. I decided after a moment that it didn't matter. As long as I hadn't puked on them, they were fine, and I'd pack only what I needed. The rest could wait until I returned in January.

But before I started sorting out my room, I needed fuel. And a few pills. Nothing like knocking back a cocktail of caffeine and aspirin to start the morning off right. Breakfast of fucking champions.

Stripping out of last night's clothes, I tossed on a semi-clean hoodie and a pair of leggings before throwing my hair up into a haphazard bun. I made a quick trip to the bathroom, freshening up and taking two pills. Now all I needed was coffee.

I slipped on my boots and groaned. A flashback of Grayson's face and me hurling all over his shoes streaked through my memory.

Holy shit.

Had I really thrown up on him?

My face dropped into my hands. Like he needed another reason to scowl and grumble at me. Was it too much to hope he and Fynn already left? I'd rather avoid confrontation this early in the morning.

I stared at my closed door. Perhaps they were still sleeping?

The desire for coffee was too strong to ignore, so I stood up and cracked open my bedroom door, peeking into the hallway. Nothing but silence greeted me, and I took it as a good sign.

Being as quiet as possible, I tiptoed past the kitchen and glanced into the family room. I sighed with relief. The couches were vacant, save for a few discarded wrinkly blankets.

I stepped outside, the sunlight instantly killing my eyes. Who said the sun could be this cheery in the morning despite the frigid air? My sensitive eyeballs would have to make do for a few minutes. Luckily, the café, which I walked briskly to, sat only a block from our house.

I took shelter from the cold inside the small building and ordered my usual, caffè mocha and blueberry lemon muffin to go. When my name came up, I grabbed my coffee and muffin, happily walking to the exit. Except something blocked my path.

Correction. Someone.

Grayson God forbid Edwards.

Dread became a rock in my gut. Had it been too much to hope that I'd be able to avoid seeing him at all? Or that he had left campus?

The universe was out to punish me.

I lifted my gaze from his chest, not needing to see his face. Grayson had a presence about him. It could also be the way my body reacted around him. And his scent. Damn, if the smell of him didn't screw with my head and other parts of my body I refused to acknowledge.

Flinching under the dark gaze that captured mine, I said the first thing that popped into my head. Such a bad habit I needed to break. "I thought you left."

His hand held the door over my head, a blast of cold hitting my cheeks. "We're grabbing coffee on the way out," he said, his eyes flicking toward the café before landing back on me.

Fynn and Grayson didn't attend Kingsley University like the rest of us. They went to the University of Dalton two hours away, but at least once a month, they either came to KU or Brock and Micah went to Dalton. The four of them, despite being separated, remained almost as close as they had in high school. The distance took a slight toll on their friendship, as did the girlfriends, but the bond and the foundation of the Elite were very much intact. It had just gotten a little wider.

I shifted forward as the person behind me got their coffee and moved past us. We were sort of blocking the doorway, but this was as close as I was willing to get to him. "I'm sorry about last night. And your shoes," I added, deciding to get the embarrassing crap out of the way. No point in beating around the bush and making us both uncomfortable.

Grayson let the door shut, and a breath of cold air blew out of his mouth. "You should probably get home before you freeze to death."

The hoodie I'd thrown on didn't offer much protection against the December temperature. "Would you care if I did?"

His glare cut right through me, as icy as the wind. "For Josie's sake, I might."

Two girls walked into the café giggling and eyeing Grayson. Annoyance flared inside me, and I rolled my eyes. "Looks like your fan club has arrived."

His brows bunched in confusion.

How can he be so oblivious?

Holding my coffee between my hands, I let the warmth soak into my fingers. "Never mind," I mumbled.

He continued to scowl.

My feet took a step away from him, my irritation growing. "Since you're clearly annoyed with me, let's not run into each other again."

Jaw rigid, he replied, "Fine by me."

I wanted to dump my drink on him, but wasting the coffee was unthinkable. "Nice shoes, by the way." I couldn't stop myself from saying something snarky as he disappeared inside the café.

God, he is the most frustrating man ever. How the hell can he be related to my best friend? Not just related, but their damn DNA was practically copied.

Triplets.

Unreal.

I shook my head, turned, and left.

Back home, I took another look at my room and did what I did best.

Procrastinated.

Hopping on my phone while I finished sipping my coffee and eating my muffin, I scrolled through my social media. My eyes halted on the first post, the words **_shooting_** and **_dead_** popping out at me. A horrible feeling crept into my stomach, my heart sinking.

Post after post, all anyone talked about on campus was the shooting on Route X. I'd been wrong last night.

Someone had gotten shot.

A sophomore girl. And she didn't make it.

* * *

Her name had been Misty Reynolds.

I couldn't get the picture of her face out of my head. The whole drive home, I thought about her. She could've just as easily been me slapped all over the local news today.

The police didn't believe she'd been targeted but was the victim of a stray bullet. Wrong place. Wrong fucking time.

I lived on the less-than-desirable side of Elmwood, and last night hadn't been the first time I'd heard gunshots, but compared to cities like New York and Chicago, Elmwood was a safe town. Even the shady parts didn't compare. We weren't without crime, but we were far from a city that had drive-by shootings daily. Honestly, I was more afraid of the upper side of Elmwood than I was of where Josie and I had grown up.

I'd never faced more danger than I had since the Elite came into Josie's life and, as a byproduct of being her best friend, into mine as well. I'd been drugged, kidnapped, and now shot at. The other girls had suffered too. Each had their own nightmarish experience with internal and external scars to prove it.

What's next?

Not that I thought the shooting was Grayson's or any of the

Elite's fault, but I also couldn't completely rule it out either. Trouble followed those boys. Or perhaps they provoked it. Tomayto. Tomahto.

In a way, I was partially glad to be going home and having a little space from the crew. I just wished I had a different home to go to sometimes.

My piece-of-shit Honda Accord chugged down Maple Street, pulling up to 1357. Well, the address on the mailbox read 357 due to the one having fallen off many winters back and my father being too lazy to buy a new number.

A flood of memories waved through me. So many highs and lows. I gazed at the small run-down ranch in dire need of more than a fresh coat of paint to liven the place up. It needed to be burned to the ground. Planks were missing from the once country-blue siding, the color faded to a dull gray, and a few boards hung by a nail. Chipped white trim framed the windows and front door. A small, sad-looking porch sat in front of the door. Nothing grandiose like Brock's or Grayson's impressive verandas.

I glanced at the car's digital clock and heaved a heavy sigh. Mom would still be at work for another two hours.

My eyes drifted to the last window on the right side—my bedroom window. A mature maple tree sat close to the house. Its branches were barren and tapped against the glass. I'd had many spooky nights watching movies and being completely freaked out by the random rapping. Trimming trees and bushes was also not in my dad's skill set.

There was a time growing up that I'd been embarrassed by where I lived. My mother did everything she could to make the inside a cozy home while also working herself to exhaustion.

Mom was the epitome of hardworking.

Getting out of the car, I slung my duffel bag over my shoulder and headed up the rocky pathway, each step my feet growing heavier. The front door was unlocked when I turned the handle and walked inside. I slipped my shoes off on the worn rug placed past the threshold. Under the scent of lemon from the cleaning products Mom used, I detected traces of beer.

Laughter from the TV greeted me. Not my dad. He stayed in his mismatched recliner with a case of his favorite beer on the floor beside him. His feet were stretched out, and the hissing of a new brewsky opened under his fat thumb. My eyes counted the cans discarded on the ground. Nearly an entire case.

Fuck.

The urge to immediately turn around and leave rose like a soaring jet in my throat.

This was a picture I'd seen a dozen times coming home from school while Mom worked. In elementary school, he was supposed to meet me at the bus stop. He never once showed up to my relief. I didn't want him there, stumbling and slurring, in front of my peers and the other parents.

Not that they didn't know. The whispers about the poor girl moved through the neighborhood, and over the years, those mutterings turned into white trash among other colorful phrases. It was hard to grow up being the talk of the block and not develop thick skin. I stopped caring what others thought, and having Josie as my friend, I accepted my weirdness.

Or perhaps a part of me had thought if they were going to talk I might as well give them something to talk about. Hence, I embraced my love for black. Due to the constant fighting, I escaped in K-pop music and anime. I would crank the small TV in my room and drown out everything outside my four walls.

Nothing good ever came from taking a stroll down memory lane.

Hauling my bag, I moved farther into the house, finally drawing his attention away from the show and the beer in his hand. No sparkle graced his green eyes. No happiness on his leathery face. The years hadn't been kind to Jett Fisher, and the miles were really starting to show. His dark hair had signs of gray, and the full beard under his chin sported the salt-and-pepper effect. The pooch of his belly was not just good for holding his beer but also made him look seven months pregnant. "Oh, Miss Bigshot College has finally graced us with her presence. Did they kick you out already?"

I hadn't expected an emotional welcome from him, but would it have been too much for him to say something nice? "Hardly," I scoffed, eyeing my dad warily. "It's winter break. I came home for the holiday."

His gaze returned to the TV as he said, "I'm sure your mother will appreciate the help."

Or you can get off your lazy ass and do something. I kept my thoughts to myself. Perhaps the reason my mouth was so loose outside this house was because I spent the entire time here biting my tongue.

I hated it.

The feeling of constantly watching what I said or the tone I used stifled me, and I was always unsure what might set off the beast. The less interaction with Dad, the better. I avoided him. That hadn't changed.

Padding down the hallway that branched off the right side of the house, I headed to my bedroom. I tossed my bag on the bed and immediately went to the small window, flinging it open. The frosty air burned my lungs as I drew in a handful of deep breaths, but I didn't care. I wanted to feel something. Anything. Even the cold.

How am I going to survive three weeks at home?

It didn't sound that long on paper, but now that I was here, fuck... It seemed like a lifetime.

Leaving the window slightly ajar, I plopped onto my old bed and kicked the bag onto the floor. The day caught up to me, and I closed my eyes, only meaning to rest for a few minutes, but the next thing I knew, my father's gruff voice hollered through the house.

"Bree!" he yelled.

I rubbed my eyes and sat up in the dark room, glancing at the clock's red lights atop my nightstand. I slept for nearly two hours.

"Bree!" he called again, but this time, he stumbled into something. The wall by the sound of it.

Heavy footsteps clamored down the hall as I pulled myself out of bed and threw open the door. "Mom's at work," I said, raising my voice loud enough that he could hear me at the end of the hall.

There were only two rooms on this side of the house. Mine and a guest room my mother used as her craft space. My parents' bedroom was on the other end of the house.

The light flipped on, splashing the small hallway with a bright yellow glow. I squinted, my eyes annoyed at the sudden dose of brightness.

Leaning half of his body on the wall, Dad turned his focus to me in the doorway. I couldn't tell if those glassy eyes registered what I said. "Bree? What are you doing in there?" He'd never mistaken me for my mother before, and the longer he watched me with an expression of confusion and unwarranted anger, the faster the trickles of fear dripped into my blood like a rusty faucet.

"Dad, it's me. Ainsley," I said, putting grains of firmness into my tone. Not that I thought I'd have much hope of reasoning with him like this.

"Where'sss my dinner?" he demanded, taking a few more ungraceful, lumbering steps toward me. "You're late. Wh-where have you been? Out with some guy?"

My fingers clutched the doorknob as my blood pressure shot up. Temper licked in my veins for all the times my mom worked extra shifts so I would have a roof over my head, food on the table, and a warm bed. "How about you get off your ass and make it yourself. Or better yet, make dinner for Mom instead of having her slave in the kitchen after working a ten-hour shit."

I didn't see his hand until it hit me across the face.

My head snapped to the side, and I staggered against the doorframe, my fingers catching me. The sting came next, swift and painfully.

Holy shit.

My hand pressed to my face, strands of honey hair falling over my face. With malice in my eyes, I lifted to meet my father's gaze.

"Don't you ever lay a hand on me again, or I'll kill you." Despite the steely sass coating my words, inside I quivered. He could hit me again and probably would for talking back. Mom rarely engaged. It only made things worse.

But I wouldn't pacify him. Or shrink. I wouldn't let him make me feel like I was less of a person or that it was my fault he got so angry.

Fuck that.

"How dare you speak to me like—"

I shoved him before he could land another blow, but the man was solid as fuck. He latched on to my arm, his large fingers digging into my flesh.

For someone who could barely stand, his aim, speed, and accuracy were unfortunately on point. Ripping my arm from under his clutch, I shoved past him, going straight for the front door.

I snatched my purse off the hook, hearing him rambling and blundering behind me. Urgency screamed at me to get the hell out of the house. I slammed the door shut behind me, jogging down the driveway. A bottle crashed against wood a second later. His slurring voice followed, swearing crudely as he hollered, "Don't you ever come back!"

I fucking didn't plan on it.

Welcome home, Ainsley.

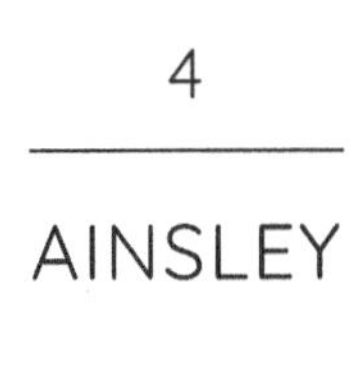

4

AINSLEY

Smearing away tears gathering in my eyes, I jumped into my car with just the clothes on my back. I fumbled with the keys, my fingers shaking as I rammed the right one into the starter. My car was too old for a push start but damn, if that wouldn't have been handy right now.

I glanced over my shoulder to check the road before backing out. My eyes were muddied with tears, and when I faced forward, my father stood in the doorway. The sight of him knocked my heart against my ribs. I pressed my foot on the gas, sending the car rolling out of the driveway.

I drove. No notable place in mind, just aimlessly caught in my head. So many emotions and thoughts crowded up there. Things had gotten worse since I went to college. So much worse. How many times had he told my mother not to come back? Only to beg on his knees for forgiveness the next day. An endless cycle of abuse. And I didn't know how to break it for my mother, short of kidnapping her.

But I vowed I would never live in that house again.

Yanking my car off to the side of the road, I slammed it into park.

My hands hit the steering wheel. "Fuck!" I cried in a half sob, half growl.

I let the waterworks bubbling up inside my chest and into my throat break free. Hot, wet drops fell from my eyes, streaking down my cheeks as I sat in my car. It was the only damn possession I owned, thanks to me working my ass off after school and during summer through high school. My car might not be much or as flashy as the cars the Elite drove, but it was mine.

In all the years growing up, I'd witnessed my father do a lot of things, but not once had he ever hit me. Not even a spanking when I'd been little. I don't know what it was about my mother that made him turn into a violent bastard. He'd never mistaken me for her before.

The messed-up part was he probably wouldn't remember tomorrow.

But I would.

It was difficult to remember the good memories of him and so much easier to cling to the bad. Particularly when the bad was so fresh and stung like a bitch.

I pulled down the visor and looked into the small square mirror at my reflection. My shoulders shook as I cried a little harder at the sight staring back at me. Angling my face slightly to the side, I examined the bright red mark, my cheek starting to swell. It would leave a pretty, purple bruise and probably turn nasty shades of yellow and green.

I searched the car for a tissue to blow the snot from my nose. *Time to collect yourself and figure shit out. You can do this.* Nothing like a little pep talk in the car to regain my composure.

Would I benefit from therapy?

Hell yes.

But first I had to solve the minor problem of where I'd be sleeping.

My glassy eyes stared out the windshield. I could go back to the dorm, but commuting to my job at Pa's Place would be a heck of an inconvenience. I failed to see what other choice I had.

My pocket vibrated. I ignored my phone. Whoever it was would have to wait.

I chewed on my lip, reflecting on how screwed up my life had gotten in one damn day.

My phone went off again. It was probably my mom calling. I wasn't ready to talk to her yet because I wasn't sure what I would say. I should tell her what happened. However, I also didn't want to.

I hated the shame. I had nothing to be embarrassed about, and yet the emotion sat inside me like a dirty stain growing.

The buzzing continued. I pulled it out of my back pocket, seeing Josie's picture flash across the screen. Emotion tugged on my heart. I wanted my best friend. She was the only person I wanted I realized. Clearing my throat, I answered her call.

"Hey, you home?" she asked after my raspy hello. Her voice was so familiar and comforting.

I swallowed hard. "Sort of," I admitted, unable to stop the catch in my voice. I was two seconds away from losing it again.

Her tone changed. "What happened?" she demanded softly, immediately recognizing something was wrong. That was what best friends did.

A long sigh left my lips as I rested the side of my head against the chilled window. "Nothing I can't handle."

Josie was never easily pushed off, and deep down, I knew that. "That's not what I asked. I know that you can handle any situation. Come over." It wasn't an offer but a command. Brock and his assertive attitude were rubbing off on her.

I didn't want to mix her up in my mess. She had a great life and didn't need my problems. "It's fine. I'm fine," I insisted. Josie had already done so much for me. I couldn't ask for anything else. I didn't like handouts or sympathy. I wasn't a charity case. It was hard enough for me to accept that Brock had gotten me the scholarship that paid not just for my tuition but also for room, board, and food. Without him *suggesting* a candidate to the school board, I would be working full-time at Pa's Place and paying my way through community college while slumming it at home. And that would have worked out so well considering my current predicament.

Josie pulled out the threats. "Get your ass over here now, or I'll send out the Elite to collect you."

I could picture her hands flying to her hips. The last thing I wanted was to involve multiple people. "You wouldn't dare."

"Try me."

I shook my head, a small smile cracking on my wet lips. "I love you."

"Not as much as I love you," she replied.

"Doubtful."

"Hurry up. I mean it."

The heaviness in my chest lifted, and I sunk into the seat. "Thanks for letting me stay. It will only be for a few days until I figure shit out."

I quickly called Mom after hanging up with Josie to warn her of the situation and let her know that I wouldn't be home. She was upset, but I promised I would swing by her work tomorrow for lunch to see her.

* * *

When I arrived at the Edwardses's huge house, I hadn't expected Liana, Josie's birth mom to answer the door. Unprepared to see anyone but Josie, I immediately wished I'd slapped some makeup on to cover my cheek. Perhaps she would mistake it for the cold weather pinkening my face. Hell, the tip of my nose was red.

Dressed casually for her in a pair of black trousers and a cream knitted sweater, Liana smiled brightly at me. Her onyx hair was knotted in a low, sophisticated bun. "Quick, let's get you inside and warmed up." She gave me a quick hug as I walked over the threshold into the foyer. "I'm so happy to see you." Liana reminded me a bit of my mother. Friendly and welcoming to everyone. Not a mean bone in her body, the kind of woman who took in strangers and strays. No questions asked.

"Thank you. I hope I'm not intruding. I know they just got back today," I said, fumbling with the bracelets dangling from my wrist.

She waved an airy hand. "Nonsense. We love having you."

I saw the moment she noticed my cheek, the chandelier above our heads bestowing light down on my face. I immediately cast my head down without thinking, staring at my boots.

She gently touched a hand to my chin, tilting my face just a fraction, and her gray eyes darkened for a brief moment. "Let's get you some ice." No questions. Only warm smiles, welcoming hospitality, and security. None of which were available in my home.

As much as I didn't want to feel humiliated, I did. No judgment filled Liana's eyes as I followed her into the kitchen nearly as big as my house, and still, my cheeks burned hot. I wanted her to think I was a good friend for her daughter, not some trailer trash. Sometimes, even as an adult, my station in life embarrassed me.

Liana went to the freezer and pulled out an ice pack. "Tell me how your semester went?" she asked, making pleasant conversation to put me at ease.

I sat on one of the counter stools, taking the reusable cold pack. "Good. I really enjoyed all my classes, and my professors were great." My shoulders relaxed, a sense of relief weaving through me at talking about something normal. It put my mind at ease as she intended.

Josie's real parents were amazing, like poster ad parents, the ones you see on TV. If anyone deserved love, acceptance, and security, it was Josie, and as happy as I was that she found out the truth and found her true family, I was also green with envy because that fairy-tale ending wasn't in the cards for me.

My parents were mine. There would be no stranger knocking on my door claiming he was my biological father from an affair my mother had twenty years ago.

"I still want a sample of your first perfume," Liana said, leaning her elbows on top of the counter.

As a chemist major, I was studying to be a perfumer. Liana had said time and time again that she wanted to be my first customer. Her support encouraged me.

"You're here," Josie said from behind me.

I whirled my head in her direction.

The smile on Josie's lips faded fast, turning into a deep scowl. Her chocolate eyes darkened, reminding me too much of Grayson. "Ainsley."

I shook my head, feeling the swell of emotions again. I didn't want to cry. With the ice pack clutched in my hand, I firmed my bottom lip before it trembled. "It's not a big deal." What I was actually telling her was *please don't make this a big deal.*

"I'll leave the two of you to catch up." Liana excused herself.

Josie came to sit on the stool beside me, her storming eyes studying my face with concern. "Your mom?" she asked.

I pressed the ice to my cheek and replied, "She wasn't home."

"Bastard," she hissed under her breath. "I'll kill him if he touches you again."

"Get in line," I muttered, leaning back against the chair.

Josie crossed her legs, worry etched in her expression. "What happened?"

Between the shooting, passing out last night, and both of us packing up to come home, we hadn't seen much of each other or talked. I gave her a quick rundown. Not that there was much to tell. The whole thing happened so fast. I'd only been home for two hours.

Josie and I both suffered different forms of abuse. She understood me and my situation like no one else could. Unlike my father who preferred to use his fists, Josie's abductor, whatever the proper term was for Angie, had used words and manipulation.

Both were forms of abuse. Both hurt. Both left scars. Both instilled fear, anger, confusion, bitterness, and basically fucked you up inside.

It was a whole nother level of pain to also witness someone you loved suffering at the hands of a man who vowed to love her.

Fuck marriage.

Fuck those vows.

Fuck love.

Swinging her feet to the side, Josie jumped off the chair and strolled to the fridge. "You're staying here," she said so casually, grabbing two sodas.

I set aside the ice pack and took the can she handed me, realizing I hadn't eaten in hours. "I appreciate the offer, but that's not why I came. I just really needed my best friend."

She sat back on the stool again, popping the metal ring. "And your best friend isn't taking no."

My nail tapped over the top of my drink. "I planned on going back to the dorm." At least that's what I decided on the spot.

"Nope." A stubborn gleam of inflexibility shone in her eyes. Once Josie got an idea stuck in her, there was no stopping the girl. I admired that about her except in this instance. "You're staying here. And that's settled. Besides, aren't you working at Pa's Place during the break?"

I nodded, still planning to argue. "I don't want to be an inconvenience."

Josie snorted. "As if. Mom will be thrilled to have you. We have more than enough space. You can take the extra room next to Grayson's."

Grayson. Ugh. Staying here meant I would run into the one Elite I wanted to avoid. It also meant he would see me like this. But did I really care? I puked on him last night. How much worse could my embarrassment get? "Speaking of your brother. Where is he? Kenna too?" I added so she wouldn't think I cared only about Grayson. A part of me worried about living under the same roof as Josie's sister. Kenna and I were growing on each other, but we were far from BFFs. Their cousin, Mads, was another story. I loved that girl.

Josie shrugged, taking a sip of her pop. "Beats the shit out of me. Brock dropped me off earlier. Grayson and Kenna got home before we did, but I haven't seen them yet."

"And Brock?"

She frowned. "Probably doing some Elite crap that he's hiding from me in some ultra-masculine attempt at keeping me safe."

"At least you have someone who cares about your safety." My voice softened and tinged with a tad of sadness and sprinkles of jealousy. I'd never had a serious boyfriend, and it hadn't been until seeing my best friend with Brock Taylor I thought I might like something more than random hookups. They were so damn good together. She moved. He moved. Sometimes the way they were synced up could be eerie. But I also couldn't help wondering what it would be like to have that.

Although, I wasn't sure what Josie and Brock had could be duplicated. They might have a rare relationship.

"So do you. Me. I love you, Ains." She grinned. "Come here." Her arms opened.

Shaking my head, I leaned over and hugged her, Josie's arms wrapping around me.

"He puts a hand on you again, and I'm siccing the Elite on him," she muttered. Most people might brush off a threat like that, especially from a girl. Not me. And not from Josie. She meant it. She'd gotten a taste for revenge a few years ago when she had a hand in putting her stepbrother's punk ass in jail where he belonged. And still resided.

I eased back in my chair. "I never wanted to hit someone as much as I did today."

"You should have," she encouraged. "Give the bastard a taste of his own medicine."

"Next time," I said, habitually toying with the diamond stud pierced at the corner of my lip. It was just one of many pieces I subjected my body to.

Josie being Josie straightened up and asked, "You hungry? How about I make us something to eat and then show you to your room." She brightened her voice, attempting to change the mood.

"Thanks, Josie. Are you sure this is okay?" I asked, rotating the can of pop on the counter.

"Yeah. I promise. Besides, there's no way Liana is going to let you leave now," she warned. "She might not know the details, but she'll insist you stay."

Shame crawled back inside me, and I hated it. "Is it wrong that I don't want her to know what happened?"

She shook her head, pink hair swaying with the movements. "No, but she's smart. I'm sure she put the pieces together."

It was no secret in my neighborhood or at Public, where I attended high school, that my father was a drunk. He made a name for himself at all the local bars and was picked up by the cops more times than I could remember. The Edwardses were involved in the community. It was foolish to hope they hadn't heard.

Josie made us grilled cheese sandwiches and bowls of hot tomato soup. Nothing fancy and just what I needed. Afterward, the two of us went upstairs so Josie could show me the spare room a door down from hers and across from Grayson's bedroom. My proximity to him could be worrisome. I hoped we could avoid each other. I refused to disrespect the Edwardses's hospitality by fighting with their son.

I cast an anxious glance at the closed door before entering a room that looked as if it were straight from an interior designer's Pinterest board. My sock-clad feet padded over glossy, rich wooden floors. A circular rug was nestled under a queen-sized bed, softening the sharply angled corners. Warm bedding and throw blankets covered the mattress, inviting me to jump right in and mess up the neatly made bed. In one corner sat a small dresser, and in the other, a half-height bookshelf styled with books, artwork, a vase, and other random pieces of decor.

Josie went to the lamp and flipped on the added light. "I think you should have everything you need in here. The bathroom is stocked with extra toothbrushes and stuff that Liana keeps for guests. It's like a hotel minus the room service, but I'm sure the days Elise is here she would probably make you whatever you asked for."

Elise was the Edwardses's cook-slash-housekeeper.

"I still feel weird asking her for anything," Josie admitted, wrinkling her nose.

"It's perfect," I said, dropping my purse, the only thing other than my car I'd brought with me, on the dresser.

For the next hour, Josie and I hung out in the room, sitting on the bed and talking about anything but my father. She was always good at distractions, and running to her house when shit got bad at mine wasn't a new concept. We'd been doing this since we were little, supporting each other. Didn't matter if it was my father or Angie, I could count on her, and she knew I'd do anything for her.

After making sure I was settled, Josie scooted off the bed. "If you want to talk more, you know where I am. And I mean it, Ainsley. Don't deal with this shit alone. I'm your best friend for a reason. I know things are different now with the Elite, but I'm not leaving you behind. Never."

I hugged a pillow to my chest and nodded. I watched her walk to the door but stopped her before she went into the hallway. "Josie."

She paused at the door and glanced over her shoulder, dark brows lifting in question.

"I didn't grab any of my stuff. Think I could borrow something to sleep in tonight?" I made a mental note to text my mom and see if she could bring my duffel bag with her tomorrow to work.

The corners of Josie's mouth curled. "I got you. Just like old times, swapping clothes as long as it's black."

The tightness in my chest lightened. "I don't think there's anyone else in the world who gets me."

"Ditto."

It wasn't exceptionally late, but exhaustion nagged at my body. My cheek still stung, yet not nearly as much as my pride hurt. I opted for a hot shower before crawling into bed.

It wouldn't wash away the memory stamped in my head, but at least it would drown out the tears.

5

———

GRAYSON

Why is nothing ever where it's supposed to be when I come home?

I swore my mother spent her days rearranging shit for no other reason than to occupy her time. With all her kids off to college, I guess she needed something to do. First, the kitchen had been reorganized. As if the pantry and fridge needed a hundred baskets and containers all perfectly lined. And now I was running late and couldn't find a damn tube of toothpaste to save my life.

Then I remembered the spare room across the hallway was always fully stocked with travel-sized products. I shut the bathroom drawer and grabbed my towel, wrapping it around my waist before stalking across the hall. I threw open the closed door and made it two feet inside when I noticed the space wasn't empty.

What the hell?

In the dimly lit room, a figure stood at the bed, her back to me. The figure was easily female. Long strands of deep-chestnut hair fell down the dark-gray shirt. A streak of a rainbow peeped from under the waterfall of hair.

Is that my shirt?

Regardless, it was the only thing she had on, and the hem of the material barely covered her ass, giving me a peek of black lace underwear, a sight I could have done without.

It was a fine ass. And I didn't need any distractions. I was already late.

My cock didn't seem to give a shit I was on a deadline. Or that a stranger stood in our guest room.

Her head whirled in my direction, finally sensing she wasn't alone. Something knocked inside my chest. Surprise? Confusion? Irritation? Desire? I couldn't decipher. Or perhaps I was too afraid to figure it out in the span of seconds.

Ainsley?

I blinked, my eyes doing precisely what I didn't want them to do —giving her another glance. "What the hell are you doing here?" I asked when my gaze returned to her face.

The shock in her expression at seeing me faded away and was replaced with annoyance. "Why are you naked in my room?"

To be fair, I wasn't naked. I had on a towel, but underneath that terry cloth fabric... "Your room?" I countered, a brow lifting.

Something dark flickered through her mossy-green eyes. "I guess you hadn't heard, sunshine? I'm spending winter break here."

The room smelled of peaches and apples. Steam came from the bathroom, warming the area. "Why? What's wrong—?" My voice halted as my gaze narrowed. The nightstand light hit the side of her face, and unless I was mistaken, her cheek looked eerily like it had been hit. I reached her in three strides, my fingers darting out and taking hold of her chin. I tilted her head slightly to the side for a better look. "Did you walk into a wall?"

"Funny," she snapped tartly.

I no longer gave a shit why she was here or that we were both half naked. "Who hit you?" I growled, my voice dropping. Why did I give a shit? Why did seeing the mark and the shadow descending into her eyes bother me? It shouldn't.

But then again, everything about this girl rubbed me the wrong way.

I groaned internally. *Why did I use the word rub?* Poor word choice when I stood in nothing but a towel and I could see her damn nipples hardening through the cotton material. Couldn't she have worn something less revealing? Two more seconds of these thoughts, and I'd be pitching a damn tent under this towel. No matter my distaste for this girl, she was still a girl with all the necessary parts. And I was a guy.

I could appreciate women in all shapes and sizes. Just not this one. Ainsley was not my type, yet her damn ample body tempted me.

Too damn much in fact, and I regretted not hooking up with someone last night. The midnight walk in the cold was a temporary solution for the restlessness howling within me. I hadn't factored in unknown variables like Ainsley Fisher staying in the room across from mine for three weeks.

Fuck me.

She's Josie's friend, I reminded myself. That right there drew a definite line in our relationship, which was no relationship. Nada. Nothing.

It was a good thing just the sight of her irritated me, making the whole hands-off rule easier.

Then why was I still in the room, staring into her face, holding her chin between my fingers?

Why had my heart started to race?

If there was one thing I hated, it was a hypocrite. Hadn't I hated when Brock and Micah both started to show interest in Josie and Mads? Hadn't I thought it was so damn cliché that my best friend hooked up with my sister?

And here I was having naughty thoughts about Ainsley.

Her chin jerked out from under my fingers. "It's none of your business."

"Whether you like it or not, it is. You're in *my* house, and you're friends with *my* sister. That makes it *my* business," I snarled.

Her gaze drifted down my chest before dashing back to my face as if she caught herself ogling. "Did you need something? Or do you plan to stand there and watch me dress?" she snapped.

The snark on this one. I thought Josie and Kenna were sassy. This one made my blood rage. "You would like that, wouldn't you?" What possessed me to move closer? We were already too close. I needed to get my head checked.

I needed to leave the room and get goddamn drunk.

A disgusted snort breezed through her nose, which should have annoyed me, and it did, but in all the wrong ways. "Go fly a kite."

The low chuckle slipping through my lips mimicked my sinister grin. I didn't hurt girls. Threaten them, yes, but I never laid a hand one. I'd done some pretty shitty things in the past, but this was one issue I stood firm on. "Stop deflecting. If you won't tell me, then I'll find out another way."

Her lips puckered, and her eyes glared with venom. "Why does it matter?"

I held her gaze. "I want to make sure whatever trouble you're in doesn't blow back on my family."

Her arms crossed over her chest, brushing slightly over my midsection. Ainsley might be a short thing, but her height played no part in the amount of spunk and grit she possessed. "It's condonable how much you care about them. No one but Josie knows I'm here."

Like that was supposed to somehow comfort me. It didn't. "It wouldn't take a genius to figure out the first place you'd run and hide would be to your best friend."

She toyed with the diamond on the side of her lip, a habit I noticed she did whenever she was stressed or in thought. "I see your point, but you don't have to worry. No one is looking for me. Trust me."

I angled my head to the side, regarding her. A sadness she definitely wanted to conceal flickered over her expression. She wasn't fooling me. Whoever hurt her had done more damage than a slap across the cheek. I was no stranger to internal wounds and the scars they left behind. How many did Ainsley have? And were they all inflicted by the same person?

Again, why did I give a fuck?

She was not my problem.

"The moment this comes to my doorstep, you and I are going to have words," I warned, making sure she understood my warning bordered on threatening.

Her tone was like acid as she replied, "If it comes anywhere near Josie, I'll leave. I would never put her in danger."

"That's the first thing out of your mouth I actually believe. At least we have something in common."

"Protecting Josie."

I nodded. "She's been through enough."

A spark of anger zapped through her eyes, her lips tightening as if to say *and I haven't been through any shit?*

Oh, I knew all about Ainsley's hard life and the shitty hand she'd been dealt. Not everyone hit the parental jackpot. She might not have come out and told me who laid a hand on her, but I had my suspicions. Her father was at the top of the list.

Unless she had a meeting with some shady drug dealer, the timeline of when she'd arrived home and showed up here didn't give her a lot of time to *walk* into trouble.

"Now that that's settled..." Her eyes shifted to the door.

I took a step back. "See you around, little devil."

Her nostrils flared slightly. "Let's hope not. And stop calling me that."

I stopped at the bathroom and grabbed a spare toothpaste before heading back to my room. Maybe I should start sleeping in the basement. It was as far as I could get from Ainsley Fisher.

* * *

Only a few bars in town served minors. I had another year before I could legally drink, but age was just a number. It never stopped us from getting our hands on booze. Ever since Josie started working at Lazy Ray's part-time against Brock's wishes, the dive had become our meeting place. And because we knew the owners, getting drinks wasn't a problem.

The cops rarely stopped by the joint with its sticky floors, shabby exterior, and the permanent smell of beer and cheese. Lazy Ray's might be a biker bar, and the crowd tended to be tougher than other places in Elmwood, but they handled their own business. We liked that. No one butted in. No one paid attention to us. No one cared about the group of rich college guys in the back corner. We had our own table.

Josie wasn't working tonight, which was why we were.

It was just over a year ago that Mads had been used in a scheme to hurt Micah, a case of his past coming back to haunt him, and unfortunately, my cousin suffered. The bastard should be six feet under, but none of us were confident Sterling Weston was dead.

That would have been too easy. And until we had hard evidence, we weren't putting our guard down.

Mads would never feel peace until that day came.

Sterling's body had never been recovered from the burning warehouse, and I'd seen enough crime shows and horror movies to know that no body meant the bastard was still out there, licking his wounds, plotting, watching, waiting.

When he made a move, we'd be ready for him. This time, I'd make sure the job got done. Sterling Weston wouldn't hurt another person I cared about.

"How's Mads?" I asked Micah, nursing my second beer of the night. I considered getting hammered, and the notion was still on the table. I hadn't decided yet.

"A trooper," he said with a small grin, but it didn't last long. His fingers circled his pint, a shadow creeping into his light-blue eyes. "She puts on a brave front, but the nightmares still happen. Still whimpers in her sleep whether she knows it or not."

A hard knot of fury pitted in my gut for the suffering my cousin went through. "How long is he going to torment us with his silence?"

"He'll show his face again," Brock said confidently. "A guy like Sterling will want to finish the job. He won't stop until he has destroyed Micah, and at this point, his hatred has extended to the four of us. We were there that night. We stood with Micah. We had his back. He'll see that as a personal grudge."

"Good," Fynn stated, his hands curling into fists on the table.

"I don't have the patience you have," I replied to Brock. Or that Sterling had apparently.

Brock dug his fingers into a bowl of peanuts. "He isn't giving us much of a choice."

"Fynn? Anything?" I prompted. Fynn Dupree was a damn whiz with computers. The shit he could uncover online blew my mind. It also came in handy when we needed to gather dirt on someone—our specialty.

Fynn shook his head. "He's a ghost in the cyber world as well. Not a trace."

"Fuck," I hissed, slamming my hand on the table, rattling the pints gathered on top and spilling nuts from the bowl.

An aggravated silence fell between us, each stewing in their personal degree of vengeance. I tossed back what was left of my beer and reclined in my chair. The TV at the bar broadcasted a recap of tonight's football game. Other than two other patrons, we were the only stragglers left. The hour grew late, yet I wasn't drunk enough to go home.

"Are we getting drunk or what?" Micah asked, reading my mind.

I could count on Micah to lighten the mood.

"I'm up for another round," I agreed.

Brock nodded.

The three of us looked to Fynn. "Someone's got to drive you fuckers home. I'll switch to decaf." Fynn, the responsible one.

We finished our last round. I got up to get some air while Brock paid the tab. Fynn helped Micah stand up, and I left them staggering behind. I gave Zeke, one of the owners behind the bar, a wave, my long legs taking me toward the exit. The door opened before I got the chance to reach for the handle, and in walked another goddamn problem I wanted to avoid.

What the hell is Kate McGuire doing at Lazy Ray's?

The way her gold eyes brightened when they landed on me gave me an idea I didn't like.

I swear this chick was stalking me.

During our sophomore year of high school, Brock made Kate a standby girl, a mistake he regretted almost instantly, but he gave little thought to girls back then. Using girls was something we did in high school, but it wasn't exactly using since they all wanted the title. I still didn't understand many things about girls, even with having sisters.

None of us had any interest in girlfriends then or being tied to one girl. So, we had a list that we would call for hookups. Our standby girls.

And Kate had been one until Brock stripped the title from her for being too clingy. That stated it mildly. She'd obsessed over him and me, but Brock got the majority of her unwanted attention, and when she became too much, he cut her out.

That only made her attempts more devious. She seriously had problems. I didn't need her drama in my life.

Things had changed since high school. Brock no longer had any use for girls like Kate, and Josie would kick her ass.

Kate attended KU with the others, and I made sure when I visited to steer clear of her. I managed to avoid her whenever I visited KU, but running into her at home during my break from Dalton somehow didn't quite feel like a coincidence. Sure, we both grew up in the same town and went to the Academy, yet of all the places to bump into her, it just happened to be a place that the Elite frequented regularly—a place a girl like Kate would never be caught dead in.

I would have chalked it up to chance if it had been anyone else besides Kate.

But this bitch was up to something.

The door swung shut behind her as a slow smile curled on peachy lips. "Imagine running into you here of all places."

Bullshit, I wanted to cough. Everyone at the Academy knew we came here. Time to find a new hangout. This place was compromised.

"What do you want, Kate?" I didn't see the point in pretending with pleasantries. Not with this girl. I was so not interested. And not drunk enough, thank God.

Her eyes raked over me, and I got that feeling she undressed me with her gaze. "You're not leaving already. I just got here."

"Exactly why I'm leaving."

Her lips pouted. "You don't have to be such a dick all the time. We haven't seen each other in ages. It's only polite to catch up. Have a drink with me?"

This girl took crazy to new levels, and I wanted none of her drama mixed up with mine. I'd stayed clear of her in high school for a reason. As an adult, I still had no desire to tangle with her.

Not even for a quick fuck. Nothing about Kate came without strings, and I wasn't looking for anyone to try and tie knots around me. I liked my freedom. I liked not worrying about someone else.

"Not going to happen. And you know damn well I don't have a nice bone in my body. Don't pretend otherwise," I said, disgust dripping in my tone.

"Oh, shit. Is that Crazy Kate?" Micah hooted, leaning heavily on Fynn for support.

"I'm not crazy," Kate hissed, reminding me of a feral cat. Once she got her claws in, she would never retract them.

Micah lifted a finger to his temple, making small circular motions.

I rolled my eyes as Fynn urged Micah to keep walking. Fynn spared Kate nothing but a fleeting glance and a frown. He was not a fan. "Make it quick. I need to get this fool home before he does something we'll all regret," Fynn said to me and dragged Micah outside, a gust of wintry air blowing in.

"Let's not make this habit," I said to a miffed Kate, getting ready to leave. The door opened again. Two other girls came in giggling with rosy cheeks and bundled up in scarves. I let them pass and paused as I caught the door before it closed. I forced my expression to remain neutral despite the wince climbing within me. "Oh, don't think about talking to Brock," I added in case she had any designs to do so.

Kate's sarcastic laugh sounded like nails on a chalkboard, piercing my ears. "Why would I talk to him when I'd rather have you."

I walked out with a horrible feeling this wouldn't be the last time I saw her.

6

AINSLEY

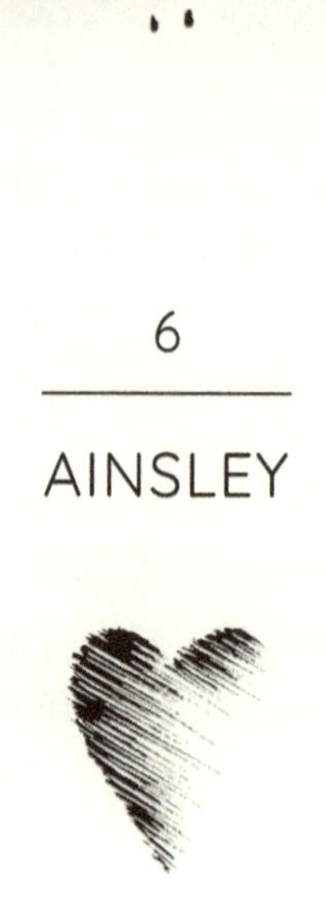

I woke up after my first night in the Edwardses's guest room rested. It had been days since I slept so hard, but unfortunately waking up meant all my problems waited for me, like the shiner that bloomed overnight.

Staring at myself in the bathroom mirror, I gently prodded the purplish mark and hissed. "Fucker," I grumbled, scowling at my reflection.

My first order of business would be covering this thing up. I couldn't go into Pa's Place looking like my boyfriend slapped me around and expect decent tips. Maybe I would get the sympathy tip and earn a little more. Regardless, my pride wouldn't allow me to exploit my injury for gain no matter how much I could use the money.

I hadn't seen Bea and Ralph, aka Pa, since the summer. I'd worked at the diner off and on all through high school since I was fifteen, and the older couple were like grandparents to me. I didn't want our first encounter to be tainted by the bruise or all the questions that would follow. Like many in our town, they knew of my father's reputation.

Before I headed into the diner for a long-ass shift, I had to see Mom. Another reason for the thick coat of concealer and foundation I dabbed on. She already had a mountain of guilt and responsibilities. I didn't want her to see the damage.

Besides, it looked worse than it was. Although, it did occur to me that, maybe if she saw what my father had done to me, perhaps it would give her the fire and courage to finally leave his ass.

Doubtful.

For reasons that escaped me, she never expressed any desire to leave, which left me feeling so damn hopeless. Her safety and happiness were important to me. She shouldn't spend her days tiptoeing through life and being afraid, but I couldn't force her to leave despite wanting to do just that.

It took me longer to get ready than usual, but I had the time. Because I still felt weird moving around freely in the Edwardses's house, I didn't grab anything to eat, ignoring my rumbling belly. Instead, I walked straight out to my car, managing to avoid running into anyone on my way. I hadn't noticed yesterday, but the property was decorated for Christmas. Lights framed the house, which I imagined would look magical at night. The trees had strands of lights wrapped around the trunks and baubles hanging from the barren branches. Green garland draped over the windows and doorways with red ribbons tied at the hanging points. Wreaths dangled from each window.

With the thick coat clutched tight against me, I started my car and cranked the heat. While I waited for the inside to warm up past god-awful freezing, I pulled out my phone and sent Josie a text to let her know I left and wouldn't be back until late. The diner was open twenty-four-seven, but I only had to stay until midnight.

The drive to the textile factory where my mother had been working for over fifteen years took longer than it would have from my house, but at least this time of day, the traffic leaned on the lighter side. Since I had the time and had skipped both breakfast and lunch,

I stopped for coffee and a cinnamon bagel toasted and slathered in butter. Just the way I liked it.

I waited in the parking lot outside the factory, munching on my bagel, until the clock ticked one o'clock and then rushed inside the back door to the cafeteria.

Tears pooled in her eyes when she saw me. I was immediately folded into a hug. Her dark hair had more streaks of gray than from the last time I'd seen her, but still, my mother was beautiful and young for her age. She didn't look a day over thirty despite being well into her fifties. Little freckles sprinkled the bridge of her nose.

She finally pulled back to get a good look at me. "Ainsley," she sobbed. Her hands framed my face gently. She only said my name, but her eyes said everything else.

Forcing a bright smile on my face, I shook my head. Seeing her visibly unharmed, smiling, and looking happy loosened a knot of tension curled since yesterday in my belly. "I'm okay, Mom. Truly."

We both knew physically I would heal. It was the mental damage and scars no one could see that were the real problem. I should see a therapist and might have if I could have afforded it.

I couldn't.

So, Josie subbed as my shrink. We'd been listening to and counseling each other for years.

The cafeteria crowd paid little attention to Mom and me. Most of the other women I knew, and they'd seen me pop in from time to time since I was little. We sat down at the end of one of the long tables. Mom was supposed to be eating her lunch, but she spent the whole time holding my hands and chatting about school. We avoided the real problem, and although the plea for her to leave with me sat on the tip of my tongue, she would have turned me down if I asked. It was reflected in her eyes.

We hugged again when her lunch hour ended. She didn't ask me to come home. Wouldn't. In fact, she was more than likely relieved I stayed with Josie. It meant I was safe.

I collected my bag of clothes and personal items I'd packed from college and prepared for my shift at Pa's Place.

Saying goodbye to Mom grew harder each time. My morbid mind couldn't help but think maybe this might be the last time I'd see her. We both knew someday he might go too far. I didn't know what I would do if that day ever came.

* * *

It was too easy to get back into the groove of serving, and seeing Bea and Ralph gave me the homecoming I'd wanted. Big bear hugs. Happy tears. And food shoved in front of me before they would let me start my shift. I had to be well nourished according to Bea. She wouldn't let me faint on her watch.

If they noticed the mark under layers of makeup, neither of them gave any indication.

A little after midnight, I dragged my tired ass back to the Edwardses's. I turned off the engine, killing my headlights, and was about to open the car door when I noticed a shadow at the side of the house. At first, I thought someone might be breaking in, but the figure moved toward the cars. *Do they intend to steal one?*

The motion sensor lights clicked on, illuminating his face.

Grayson?

Why is he being so cagey and weird? Is he sneaking out?

It was nearly one in the morning, but for the Elite, these were the hours they came alive. His parents were used to him staying out, or I assumed they were. He had no reason to be sneaky. So where was he going? And why did I care? It was none of my business who Grayson snuck off to see. And yet...

A flash of something glinted in the motion spotlight as he shoved an item into his coat pocket.

What the fuck? Why is Grayson packing?

Although I couldn't be a hundred percent sure it was a gun, but if it was...

He got into one of the cars, the engine purring to life a moment later. I should wait until he left and then go inside and forget about what I thought I saw. Then again, I'd never done what I should do. I certainly wasn't going to start now.

Screw it. I have nothing else to do tonight.

I knew for a fact he wasn't meeting up with the Elite because Brock and Micah were with Josie and Mads for quality girlfriend time. They couldn't go more than twenty-four hours without fondling each other.

Yes, I was jealous.

It had been months since someone fondled me. Someone I wanted at least. Drunk creeps at parties didn't count.

I sighed, my weary body groaning, but someone had to provide backup, I reasoned. I wasn't sure what I would do if he got himself in trouble. Phone a friend?

One of the good things about having an older car was it didn't have an automatic headlight feature, making tailing someone slightly easier. I kept my headlights off while I waited for Grayson to cruise down the driveway. Once he started on the road, I backed out after him, and I didn't turn my lights on until we hit the main road. Very illegal, but the Elite wasn't above breaking the law sometimes, and it wouldn't be the last time I did either. Goody Two-shoes was not a nickname anyone would ever associate with me.

This time of night it wasn't too hard to keep track of the yellow Lamborghini, not just because the car was flashy as hell but because only a handful of other cars were on the road. Like the saying went, nothing good happens after dark; precisely why midnight was my favorite hour of the day.

Tendrils of wariness gathered inside me when I noticed he seemed to be headed into my side of town, the lower east side of Elmwood. I had no need to stress until he turned onto King Street.

"Is he kidding me?" I muttered. I had the radio turned low because, obviously, a spy didn't jam out to BTS or Stray Kids when they were on an undercover pursuit.

This territory belonged to the Wolves, a known gang.

What the hell is he doing here?

The gun made sense, but that was all that added up.

Regret gnawed at my gut, and I wished I'd gone to bed.

Grayson turned into a parking lot filled with other cars and slid the Lambo into park at an angle. People lingered on the street in front of the lot, and I wondered if a local block party was in full swing. As I pulled off on the side of the road and flicked off my lights, I caught the blazing glow of a standing firepit in the middle of the street. A few guys huddled around it for warmth.

Getting out of the car and following Grayson was an absolutely stupid idea. On the other hand, sitting in my car alone seemed equally as dumb. I had to make a quick decision about which one was less likely to get me assaulted. All I knew was I didn't want to lose sight of Grayson. Having him in my vision made me feel safer somehow, regardless of how irrational the thought process might be.

Why can't these damn guys do normal shit? Why are they always searching out trouble?

I grabbed my mace and switchblade from the glove compartment just in case. My door clicked quietly open, and I shut it as softly as I could. The lamplight on this side of the road was broken, shielding me in a dark that made my skin prickle with unease.

My footsteps clapped on the blacktop as I snuck off toward the parking lot.

Shit. I'm so not dressed for this.

I glanced down at the black hoodie and leggings I'd thrown on, having changed out of my work uniform before leaving Pa's Place. Despite them not being practical for sleuthing, they blended nicely with the shadows. Flipping the hood up over my head, I searched the lot for the yellow Lambo, the bright color making it easy to spot, but I ran into a problem.

No Grayson.

Where the hell did the bastard go so quickly?

An acorn of nervousness sprouted in my belly. I trotted to the end of the lot, scanning the street and the faces for Grayson. He wore dark clothes and a beanie covering his head. So were half the people here.

Fuck!

I couldn't believe I'd come this far only to lose him, but I had no intention of giving up. For once, I didn't stand out. It shouldn't be hard to keep a low profile and go unnoticed while I looked for Grayson.

I hopped off the curb. Barricades blocked off each side of the road. It indeed looked like a party but not a block party. This was a gang get-together. A place drugs were sold. Illegal bets were made. And gun transactions took place. These just scratched the surface of what the Wolves were notoriously known for.

Strutting down the street, I did my best to avoid gazes. My plan seemed to be going without a hitch until a flurry of wind knocked my hood off, sending my hair flying around my face.

Are you freaking kidding me, I mentally griped, trying to shove the hair out of my face, and smacked into something solid. A hard body.

I glanced through streaks of blowing hair, staring at a leather jacket. My eyes shifted upward, neck craning until I reached the face, and I wished I hadn't looked at all. It wasn't the tattoos on his face that alarmed me. I liked tats. A lot. It was the look in his eyes that sent a chill down my spine like I was a mouse about to be eaten by a wolf. "Shit, sorry," I exclaimed, backing up and intending to move past.

The guy had a paw print inked below his left temple. His huge hand darted out, circling my arm. "Where are you running off to so fast, little mouse?"

Mouse? No one has ever referred to me as a mouse. I'd never been a fan of random nicknames and endearments from strangers. To hear this guy refer to me as *little* prickled my skin. "Last I checked, where I go isn't your business," I replied tartly.

Someone next to him whistled. It was then I noticed he wasn't alone. A string of curses went through my head. *Why couldn't I just keep my mouth shut?* How had I forgotten even for a second where I was?

The guy who whistled stood significantly shorter than the one who still held my arm captive. His hair was shaved, the tips of his ears pink from the cold. "What do we have here?" Beady eyes glanced over me in a way that left me feeling gross like I'd just been visually raped by this asshole's eyes.

"She's too pretty to be a Wolf," a third added, his lips twisting into a sneer.

"Let me go." I gritted my teeth, keeping my voice firm.

"You lost, little mouse?" Big Hands asked, towering over me. The three of them crowded around me, my window to run disappearing. *Brilliant, Ains. Just fucking brilliant.*

My free hand slipped into my pocket, fingering the cold blade. "I'm looking for my *boyfriend*," I replied, trying to play it cool when in fact I shook in my boots. It seemed like a good idea to make up a fictional boyfriend.

"He should know better than to leave you alone on the streets," Baldy said, running the backs of his knuckles along the cheek my father had smacked. "Perhaps he needs a lesson."

Adrenaline pumped in my veins as I jerked away from his hand. Somehow, I got the impression hurting me would be involved in this so-called lesson for a guy who didn't exist. Fear sank into my bones, but my voice came out forceful. "Don't fucking touch me."

He chuckled, eyes darkening. "She's feisty, boys, like a cute, cornered kitten."

"This kitten has claws." I flicked out the switchblade. "Back off."

Big Hands tsked, releasing the strong hold on my arm. "Little girls shouldn't play with sharp toys. They might get hurt."

"The only person bleeding tonight will be you if you don't step the hell out of my way." I lunged the blade forward, and Baldy took a step back, hands raising up in the air, but I saw the second he planned to go for my weapon. I ducked under the arms of Big Hands and bolted, but I didn't get far.

A pair of strong arms came around my waist, preventing me from running any farther. Ready to fight, I started to struggle until my captor spoke. "There you are, babe. I wondered where you went off to."

That voice.

It couldn't be.

Warm fingers slipped under my chin, lifting my face.

I stopped breathing.

Grayson.

Turbulent eyes clashed with mine, and it didn't matter they were a warm brown; the ice blistering from them stung. His jaw muscles pulsed.

There was anger.

There was pissed off.

And there was whatever Grayson felt right now.

If I was a smart girl, I would have been more scared of him than the three guys behind me.

Before I could utter any rational thought, Grayson's head dipped as he tugged me farther into his embrace and sealed his lips over mine.

7

———

AINSLEY

My body froze, and it had nothing to do with the icy weather.

Holy shit.

When my mouth finally caught up to what was happening, my lips parted in a breathy gasp. Grayson didn't keep the kiss light or friendly. His tongue slipped between my lips, brushing against mine.

He tasted like spearmint.

The gum he had in his mouth rolled around my tongue as I automatically responded to his kiss.

I knew we had sparks. They'd always crackled and popped between us, but those little flares ignited into something explosive at the touch of his lips. I melded against him, my fingers bunching into the warm fabric of his hoodie.

I probably smelled like greasy burgers and sweat after a ten-hour shift, but Grayson kissed me as if he couldn't get enough. Skillfully. Thoroughly. Delectably.

At that instant, I realized how dangerous he could be.

Grayson ended the kiss, staring long into my eyes before lifting them to my unwanted companions. Like a flip of a switch, hardness radiated not just in the depths of his dark eyes but lined his body. His tight muscles pressed against me. He turned me around in his arms, stepping up close, and drew me back against him so my spine touched his chest. His arms secured me at my waist, keeping me from going anywhere.

I understood what game he played, and I did my best to keep up the charade all while my heart thudded like a goddamn rabbit thumping its leg.

Holy shit. Holy shit. Holy shit.

Grayson just kissed me. Like really kissed me. Tongue and all. I could still taste the freshness of spearmint. My tongue swirled in my mouth, connecting with something clenched between my teeth. Grayson's gum. I'd taken it from him. I vaguely remembered our tongues toying with the gum as if it had been a game of keep-away. So much had been going on inside me. I hadn't been prepared. Not for the feelings. Not for the feel of him. Not for Grayson.

"Reno." His deep voice rumbled against my back. He nodded in the direction of Big Hands. "I see you met my girl." The warning came out clear. If anyone messed with me, they would have to deal with him.

Reno narrowed his gaze at me suspiciously before moving his focus to Grayson. "Do you mean girl or *girl?*"

I'd forgotten about the switchblade and realized I'd dropped it when Grayson kissed me. It sat on the ground near my feet. I didn't attempt to retrieve it. The Elite's arms weren't budging.

Grayson's hot breath stirred strands of my hair as he growled, "I'm not sharing this one."

Gross. The idea that these guys passed around girls struck me sick. I felt my face pale.

Another tense moment passed between us, and then Reno's shoulder's relaxed, his head shaking. "I wouldn't have believed it unless I'd seen it with my own eyes. Gray with a girl."

Grayson slipped one of his hands into the front pocket of my jeans, his fingers splaying too damn close to my kitty. *Is he trying to torment me on purpose? Is he warming his hand? Or is it another way to keep me from running?*

"Don't bust a nut. I need a minute," he told Reno.

"Step into my office," Reno said, a puff of cold air expelling with his words.

The other two jerks stayed back, moving to the fire to warm their hands. An instant pressure at my hip urged me forward to follow Reno despite my feet being reluctant. I scowled, but since Grayson stayed behind me, my displeasure had zero effect on him.

Reno glanced over his shoulder when he halted at the laundromat door. An interesting place to set up an *office*. With his hand on the door handle, he turned to Grayson. "Not the chica," he snarled, towering over me like a beefy skyscraper.

Grayson's rigid body tightened. "She stays with me," he stated, allowing no room for argument.

I swallowed, waiting to see what Reno would do or say. "Must be serious if you're letting her in on Elite business."

"Or I don't trust your guys." Disdain underscored Grayson's tone.

Reno's eyes glanced over my head to the street cluttered with mostly men. Their muffled voices and deep laughter drifted to where we stood. "Good point." With the same huge hand that had captured my arm only minutes ago, he flung open the glass door, a little rusty bell jingling from the sudden thrust.

We walked through the rows of commercial washers and dryers to the back of the room where a little office was tucked into the corner. Reno plunked down in the chair behind a metal desk, the chunky rings on his fat fingers clattering on the top.

At least it was warm inside. What I wouldn't kill for a hot chocolate right now, but I doubted Reno had any lying around.

Two very uncomfortable chairs were placed in front of the desk. Grayson pulled me into his lap before I could sit in the other chair. My knee-jerk reaction was to bolt upright and yell at him. I caught myself, remembering my part. *Girlfriend. I'm supposed to be his girlfriend. Someone who enjoys sitting on his lap.*

Reno watched me, and I made my muscles loosen, leaning back against Grayson's chest. Only a single light hung over the desk, flickering and swaying a fraction in the air, the slight movement causing shadows to dance over Reno's tattooed python arms. "What brings an Elite to the Wolves? It's been a while."

"I need the whereabouts of a missing person," Grayson stated as his thumb started to draw lazy swipes over the side of my hip in a possessive yet comforting motion. I tried not to be distracted by his touch.

The gang member took out a pack of smokes, offering Grayson one. The cranky Elite declined. Reno tapped out a slim stick for himself, and a moment later, the flame from his lighter flickered close to his face. "Consider me intrigued," he retorted, a cloud of smoke exhaling from his mouth.

Missing person? Who? I tried to keep my face from changing, but my brows scrunched in thought as my mind searched for answers.

"If you decide to look into the matter, I'll send you everything I have, undetectable, of course," Grayson added.

Reno's fingers rapped over the desk's metal top, drawing my gaze to the numerous rings adorning his hand. One of them had a wolf's head on it. "You know our rate?"

Grayson nodded. "It won't be a problem."

Taking a long drag from his cigarette, he flicked the ash onto the floor. "Never is for the four of you."

The stiffness in my joints from being on my feet all day eventually eased, and with each passing minute, I sunk further into Grayson's body, the long day catching up to me. My head rested in the crook of his shoulder and neck, fitting snuggly. Grayson turned out to be like a human pillow. Cozy. Soft yet firm. And warm.

"Someone has to keep the Wolves in business," he retorted dryly.

Reno grinned. "Thank Jesus for rich pricks and the people who cross them."

"And this is why our partnership works."

Sharp eyes shifted to me. "What about the girl? How can I be sure that she won't go blabbing about our arrangement?" The atmosphere in the small office frosted.

A spike of alarm went through me, and I jerked in Grayson's arms. The hand resting at my side tightened, urging not so subtly for me to chill out. "She won't. You have my word. I'll make sure of it," he assured, but would his word be enough to convince Reno to let me walk out of here?

"You see that she does, or we'll come looking for her," Reno warned. "A pretty little thing like her would catch me a fair price."

A new level of fear and revulsion churned in my stomach. The desire to bolt rose swiftly within me, my flight response kicking in.

"She's under Elite protection, in case any of your guys get ideas," Grayson stated gruffly.

"Pity," Reno tsked, his cunny eyes shifting to me. "If you ever get bored of this one, come find me, chica." Another puff of smoke drifted out of his lips.

Highly unlikely that day would ever come, but for once in my life, I didn't say the words that were in my head. My safety depended on me being able to control my mouth.

"Let's go," Grayson whispered in my ear. The command was hard and edged with anger.

Grayson's hand firmly clasped mine, and we left the laundromat, leaving Reno in his office. My gaze lifted upward into the cloudy night sky, the crescent moon hailing a soft glow as flakes of white powder fell. "It's snowing," I murmured, lifting my free palm up to catch tiny unique specks. They melted as soon as they hit my skin.

He yanked my hand, dragging me down the street. I took it he wasn't a fan of the snow. Or me for that matter.

I guess the ruse of being his girlfriend was up.

As we rounded the corner into the parking lot, I contemplated if I would be able to run to my car without him catching me. I wanted to get as far away from here as possible and immediately before something else happened. The chances were slim, and even if he didn't seize me before I got into the car, he would still demand answers when we got home.

What was the point in delaying the inevitable?

He spun me to face him. "Why the fuck are you here?" His voice blistered with rage.

Cranky as usual, but I shouldn't have been surprised. I'd just shown up, and since I managed to get caught, I had to go through the embarrassment of admitting the truth. My hand yanked out from his. "I followed you."

"Why?" he demanded, raising a dark brow from its scrunched position.

Pulling the sleeves of my hoodie down over my hands to combat the wind, I wished I would have grabbed my coat. "I was curious why you were sneaking off in the middle of the night. I thought maybe you were dealing drugs or something."

"And if I was? What were you going to do about it?"

"I don't know, not get caught and harassed by a bunch of thugs who think every time a girl says no or stop it means yes." The fact tonight could have had a different outcome wasn't lost on me. Grayson saved me, but I could also argue I wouldn't have been in the situation if *he* hadn't been acting weird *and* had a gun, which I had completely forgotten about until now. "You brought a gun," I hissed.

He leveled me a hard stare before glancing over his shoulder to see if anyone was in listening distance. "Keep your voice down unless you want Reno to make good on his threats. You heard nothing tonight. You weren't here. Is that clear? Or next time you decide to play vigilante, I won't save your ass from the Wolves."

"You moved awfully comfortable among them. Are you sure you're not a member?" I shot back.

A harsh expression crossed his features. "I'm an Elite." He stopped at the yellow Lamborghini and angled his head to the side, inspecting the car. "Shit," he cursed, forking a hand through his hair and pulling off the beanie in the process.

What can possibly be wrong now?

My gaze followed his glowering eyes, inspecting the car. Something was definitely off. What was it? And then I noticed the tires. Flatter than a damn crepe. One flat tire I could rationalize as shit luck, but all four tires... Clearly, someone had slashed them.

"Looks like you pissed off the wrong dude or asked the wrong questions." Traces of smugness leaked into my voice.

He shoved his hands into his front pockets, blowing out a long steamy breath. "Where did you park? I'm assuming you followed me in your car." The condescending tone wasn't lost on me.

This banter was normal. The kiss and all the touching from before were strange. I liked that things between us snapped right back to our usual snarky behavior. It made the world seem right again, and I could almost pretend as if the entire night hadn't happened.

Well, maybe if his damn gum wasn't still in my mouth.

I should spit it out. Hell, I should hurl it back at him for putting me in danger. The leader of the Wolves knew my face.

Despite the flavor having gone bland, I kept the wad of gum between my teeth.

Crossing my arms, I glared up at Grayson. "I sure as shit didn't run after you on foot in this cold," I responded.

Even in the dark, I caught his eye roll. "Give me the keys."

"What for?" I barked back, wondering why I was arguing out in the cold when all I wanted to do was get in my car and go to his house. Not together though because that would look suspicious.

"Because I'm driving." He held out his hand.

I wanted to snap fuck no, but I could see the frustration and strain in his eyes. He needed a release. Like K-pop and anime for me, driving was Grayson's stress reliever.

Fishing the keys out of my pocket, I dropped them into his waiting hand. "Are you always so pleasant?"

"You should see my bad side."

I headed toward the end of the parking lot where I left my car on the side of the road. "No, fucking thank you."

Grayson opened the passenger door for me before he got behind the wheel. As he guided the car onto the road, he pulled out his phone and made a call, arranging for his Lambo to be picked up and brought to the garage.

Now we were out of Wolves' territory and my heart stopped threatening to leap out of my chest, I had time to reflect, and I had a lot of fucking questions. "Who are you looking for?" I asked when he hung up.

He drove one-handed, his right arm resting on the center console. The lines around his mouth went taunt. "The less you know, the better."

"That shit might work on Kenna and Josie but not me. My mind doesn't work like that. It's like an ingrown hair. I can't stop thinking about it until I dig the bastard out." Some called it relentless.

He glanced over and blinked at me before his gaze turned back to the dark road stretching out in front of my car. "Wow. You're *one of those* girls."

If he was trying to offend me, it didn't work. I'd been called way worse. "And you're *one of those* assholes."

The tires sloshed over the dampening roads as the snow slowly starting to stick to the grassy parts of the ground. "At least we understand each other."

"Hardly," I snort-laughed. "I won't stop asking or looking for the answers if you don't tell me."

Despite the snow coming down thicker and faster, Grayson handled my car skillfully. I hated driving in the snow. "Anyone ever tell you how annoying you are?" he asked.

"Just Josie," I admitted. "I can only think of one person who you might give a shit about his location. Are you guys still convinced Sterling is alive?"

His jaw flexed.

"You do," I muttered, studying his expression in the dimly lit car. His silence was confirmation, and I let the idea someone like Sterling could still be out in the world, lurking about, simmer within me. "Wow. I don't know how to feel about that."

Lips pressed together, he turned the heat down a notch, the car finally warm. "You should feel nothing. It doesn't concern you."

"So, I take it that means the other girls don't know?"

"And you aren't going to tell them."

I bristled, tilting my head slightly to the side. "What do you plan on giving me to keep my mouth shut?"

His head whipped in my direction, his scowl intensifying. "Are you serious right now?"

My arms crossed as my lips lifted in a slight curve. "Nothing in this world is free."

He shook his head. "I saved your ass tonight. That's your payment."

"Fine," I conceded regrettably. "But I don't like lying to my best friend. And since when do you carry a gun?"

He groaned. "You're being a real pain in my ass, little devil. Do you have any idea how much danger you put yourself into tonight? What would you have done if I hadn't been there?"

"I find that it's better for my sanity if I don't think about the what-if scenarios." Because the truth was, things could have been so much worse than Grayson kissing me. "And for your information, I didn't show up empty-handed. I brought protection." *Shit.* Had protection. I had to buy a new blade. My knife was probably in the possession of a Wolf or covered in snow where I'd dropped it on the street.

"It wouldn't have been enough. Maybe you will finally understand that my world is not for you."

Harsh. I recoiled at the sharpness in his statement. "I've been hearing that my whole life. To me, there's only one world, and all of it's my playground."

We hit a stretch of open road, and Grayson pushed my car, picking up speed. "I don't have time to babysit you."

"I didn't ask you to," I snapped.

"And yet you constantly seem to find yourself in need of my help."

"I did just fine before you," I quickly pointed out.

"A fact that boggles my mind."

We weren't far from the house, and I still had one more question nagging on my mind. "Why did you kiss me?"

His foot lifted off the gas, and the car slowed. "Would you rather I had fought? We were in *their* territory, surrounded by people who would have no problem jumping in to kick some rich prick's ass, as they like to refer to us. I could have pretended not to know you at all."

"You also could have claimed to be my boyfriend without locking lips," I pointed out.

"He needed to see that you were important to the Elite. It's the only way to keep you off his radar. He and his guys had to believe that you belonged to me—to us."

Why did my heart skip at the sheer possessiveness of his words? "Should I be worried?"

He steered my car up his long driveway, parking it off to the side. "As long as you stop following me, you won't need to worry."

"Trust me, after tonight, I came to the realization that you're just not that important to me."

I swore his lips twisted, but the interior lights flashed off just then. He dropped my keys into my hand and opened the car door, unfolding his long legs.

He didn't wait to see if I got out, and after a second of watching his shadow move, I hopped out of the car, jogging to catch up. When I did, he had the back door open, waiting for me to walk inside the utterly dark and silent house. Everyone was asleep.

Tiptoeing through the unlit mudroom, I only had two thoughts on my mind. Don't trip and wake up the entire house. And the comfy bed waiting for me upstairs.

"Ainsley?"

I halted in the hallway at the sound of my name. Turning around, I stared at Grayson's shadow.

He stepped over to me and leaned down, whispering in my ear, "We don't talk about this. Ever. The kiss didn't happen."

My head shifted toward him, our lips aligning, and I caught the flash of fire in his eyes. Good. "What kiss?" I retorted tartly. I hoped saying it out loud would make it true.

* * *

My back pressed to the closed bedroom door as I dropped my bag on the ground, the crown of my head hitting the wood. *What is wrong with me? Why am I taunting him?* Sure, I wanted to make him miserable because he was so damn frustrating.

Here I was feeling a million different emotions and confused about nearly everything in my life. The most emotion Grayson had shown tonight was seeing his tires slashed.

He was a damn robot.

Perhaps I should be asking myself why I was so worked up over a kiss. It meant nothing. A tool used to get me out of a sticky situation. He'd done me a favor.

Then why did it feel as if Grayson had cursed me?

Kissing him should have been like kissing Josie. Their DNA was essentially carbon copies of each other.

Was it twisted I found Grayson attractive? Not just pleasant to look at, which he was, but good-looking in the sense my body instantly reacted around him. He could be brooding in the corner, and I'd feel the stirrings of an ache between my legs. The worst was the sound of his voice and what it could do to me.

And tonight, I got my first taste of his lips.

How am I supposed to forget that?

My body warmed at just the thought. I wouldn't sleep at all tonight, at least not comfortably. I needed to stop having impure thoughts of Grayson Edwards and go back to hating the bastard. That was the only way my heart would be safe.

Or the alternative was to fuck him and get this curiosity out of my damn system. Then maybe I wouldn't be so tense around him all the time. Then maybe we could actually be friends instead of constantly growling and scowling at each other.

No.

I shook my head.

He was off-limits. No ifs, ands, or buts about it.

I had no business looking at or thinking about him. Let alone pondering sex with Grayson!

I was obviously tired and needed to go to bed. Tomorrow, everything would be clearer. Tomorrow, I could go back to hating Grayson and forget the intoxication of his kiss.

With a sigh, I slipped off my shoes, wiggling my toes and stretching the arches of my aching feet. How easily the body could forget hard work after only a few months. My clothes came off next, and I tossed them to the side of my bag before pulling out what I hoped was a clean T-shirt. I hadn't had time to do laundry.

Inside the en suite bathroom, I splashed cold water on my face and gently scrubbed off my makeup. I slapped some toothpaste onto my toothbrush when a noise jolted my attention, the hairs raising on my arms.

It sounded like the door handle turned in the bedroom.

My heart gave a yank of alarm in my chest, and I poked my head around the corner, half afraid someone was breaking in. Had a Wolf followed us home?

In my neighborhood, break-ins were a common occurrence, but on the upper side of Elmwood, most of the houses had insane security, including this one. Surely, an alarm would have been set off by now if someone was in the house.

Just as I told myself how silly I was acting, the bedroom door opened and closed softly followed by the click of a lock. My eyes remained on the figure as they crossed the room toward me in the dark, the light from the bathroom spilling into the room.

I didn't need to see his face. The way he moved, and the outline of his body made it clear who slipped into my room. Not to mention the impudence. This was his house, and I was just a guest, but boundaries didn't seem to matter to Grayson.

He didn't say a single word as he crossed the room. His eyes stayed on mine, and the heat I spotted in the center of his irises warmed my blood. But there was also an underlying spark of another emotion. A darker, edgier gleam.

The loaded look caused my stomach to somersault. *Why him? Why did it have to be him that made me crazy inside?*

Would this be a mistake I regretted?

Probably.

But fuck it.

8

———

GRAYSON

Ainsley didn't say a word when I reached her. Didn't tell me to get out, and that was all the encouragement I needed.

Was this wrong?

Would I hate myself afterward?

Was I going to walk away?

Yes. Yes. And God no.

I had no reason for being in her room, and yet I couldn't stop myself. Barely even tried to talk my hard dick into settling for something else—someone else.

I'd been on edge for too long. Something had to give.

Her hip pressed into the bathroom counter as I searched her face, waiting for that flare of annoyance or an inkling of disgust, but her mossy-green eyes glinted with interest. The toothbrush in her grasp clattered into the bottom of the sink. I didn't immediately kiss her like my body screamed to do. Instead, I traced the pad of my thumb along her bottom lip, the tiny diamond stud winking under the bathroom light. Her chest rose and fell through the thin material of her shirt.

Again, with only a shirt, her tan legs exposed. The top of her head barely reached my shoulders, and yet despite her shorter frame, the girl had a body of a goddess.

Her eyes didn't shy away from mine. If anything, they challenged me, taunting us both to see how far I would go.

I never backed down from a challenge. And she damn well knew that.

Parting her lips, I inserted the tip of my thumb, her breath hot on my skin as her tongue brushed up against the pad of my thumb. Those magical eyes darkened. They stayed on mine as she took my thumb deeper into her sweet-ass mouth, tongue darting, licking, sucking, and tasting me.

The visual was too damn much, a correlation to what her mouth could do to other parts of me.

Fuck me, I want her.

My cock swelled, hardening further. I'd already been swollen before I crossed the hall. I'd been fucking hard since I kissed her. For two years, I'd stayed clear of this girl. Two. Damn. Years.

And all it took was one kiss meant to save her ass, and that wall of steel I erected where she was concerned blew apart.

I didn't know how I felt about it.

Pissed off.

I was angry at her for putting me in a position that forced me to jeopardize my internal defense. Whenever we were together, I worked to ignore her, convincing myself it wasn't attraction but contempt that snapped and crackled between us.

It was that *anger* that propelled me across the hall instead of falling into my bed. A part of me wanted to punish her. The other part wanted to punish myself.

One of us should stop this before it went too far. The problem lay in that we were both reckless.

Withdrawing my thumb, I grabbed her waist and hoisted her up onto the bathroom counter. My fingers trailed down to either side of her thighs, spreading them open as I closed the distance. Her palms landed on my chest, and I wondered if she would push me away. She didn't. Fingers curled against my shirt, tugging me closer, a fire of green burning in her eyes.

Her legs wrapped around me, the soft center of her core rubbing against my hard ridge. "You look good natural," I murmured, noticing how much softer her eyes appeared. I'd only seen her fully made up or the next day with mascara flecking under her eyes and smeared. Something about her barefaced did funny things to my stomach.

She angled her head to the side. "That might be the nicest thing you've ever said to me."

My gaze moved to her cheek, and my eyes narrowed. The skin was still red, but shades of purple were starting to show. A bolt of fury lanced through me, knowing someone had put their hands on her. She hadn't come out and told me it was her father, but we all knew. If I ever saw the bastard...

"Don't," she whispered, reading my expression and guessing where my thoughts had gone.

Both of us needed a distraction. I swept in and took possession of her lips, not giving either of us a second to think.

Her lips were everything I didn't want them to be and yet needed them to be. Wild. Hungry. Soft. Greedy. Her tongue dove between my lips, and I moaned at having my second taste of her tonight. The second bite was fucking sweeter.

God, can she kiss.

The tension that had held my muscles rigid all night slowly unraveled as I deepened the kiss. Heat filled my veins, spreading and soothing every inch of me. Her fingers went into my hair, fisting the strands as she held on.

As quickly as I took her lips, I ripped mine away, staring down at the girl in my arms. With my breathing ragged, a voice in my head told me I should stop this before things got out of my control. I was good at control. It was my strong suit. I took in a breath, a last-ditch effort for one of us to come to our senses, except my hands had other ideas. One of them moved to the under slope of her breast.

She shivered from my touch, and beneath the soft material, her nipples pebbled. Desired pulsed in my sweats.

I could still stop this. Walk out, and leave us both aching, wanting, and pissed off. As if she could see the struggle behind my eyes, her legs tightened around me. "For once in your life, don't think," she whispered and kissed me, harder than before, making it very clear she wanted this.

Screw it. Control is underrated.

My hands slid up the sides of her thighs, skimming the edge of her panty lines. I wanted to rip them off and thrust into her without a thought of tomorrow. I enjoyed foreplay, enjoyed drawing out the pleasure but it had been too long. Impatience and greed spurred me, however, I had to make sure she understood the ground rules before this went any further.

Tearing my lips from hers, I kissed the piercing above her lip. "I don't want you to mistake this for anything more than what it is," I clarified, my fingers moving to the hem of her shirt and inching the fabric up her stomach. I wanted it off. I wanted us both naked, skin to skin. I wanted to feel her against me, her warmth and softness.

Her eyes took on a lustful gleam. She must want the same thing because she squirmed in my arms, wiggling against the bulge in my sweatpants. "Basic need. I got it, sunshine." Then her fingers moved to my waistband, shoving my sweats down so she could get a handful of my bare ass. "Now get naked. I want to see what we're working with."

My brows lifted, but the momentary surprise lasted only a second. I tugged the tee over her head, tossing it out of the bathroom. "Fair is fair," I replied, keeping my gaze on her face before I let myself look at her.

I took my fill of her. Full, beautiful, perfect breasts. A slim waist that curved into shapely hips. Her height might be small, but she had a body most girls would kill for, and my control slipped notches. My body begged me to teach Ainsley how to scream my name.

Only my name.

A thought I shouldn't have.

Her lips curled. "I couldn't agree more," she muttered, slipping her fingers under my Dalton T-shirt. Using her nails, she explored the planes of my chest. She watched me, her eyes never leaving mine. Satisfaction pulled at the corner of her mouth as my body instantly reacted to her touch. And then the barrier was gone, lifted over my head.

She gasped as I put my lips on her nipple, taking the bud into my mouth. Her body melted further into me, the hands on my chest falling to grip the edge of the counter. Her breathing quickened.

Leaving her in just her panties, I lifted her off the counter, those creamy legs securing tight around me, and I walked us into the shower. The sweatpants hanging half off my ass slid to the floor. I stepped out of them, kicking the bundle into the corner.

I turned the water on, cranking it to a warm but not too hot temperature. My skin was already on fire.

"The shower?" Ainsley said, lifting her brows. Her fingers threaded into my hair.

"I figured we could both use one. Plus, it will drown out your cries." Testing the temperature, I walked us under the waterfall, watching beads of water roll over her skin, down her neck, and over her breasts.

"What makes you think I'm a screamer?" she countered as I pressed her back into the tiled wall. She unfolded her legs, sliding her feet to the floor.

"This." I pushed aside her wet black panties and slipped a finger inside her. She moaned. My mouth returned to hers, catching the tail end of her audio pleasure. Her breathing grew hard, relishing in the feel of my tongue and the strokes of my fingers inside her.

She rolled her hips, moving and urging me to go deeper, faster, but I wouldn't let her come. Not yet. Not when the fun just began. I wanted to feel her come undone the first time when I was inside.

A soft protest left her lips as I pulled out my fingers to get rid of the black lace hindering my access. Water continued to pelt my back and shoulders. Eventually, we would get to cleaning our bodies but not until I had my fill of her.

I was about to reach for my discarded sweatpants but cursed instead.

"What is it?" Ainsley asked, looking at me with a half-lidded gaze.

"I don't have a condom," I said, remembering I'd come into her room with nothing but my clothes, and I doubted my mom kept spare condoms in the nightstand drawer for guests. At least I hoped she didn't.

Her gaze widened. "You came in here without protection?"

"Honestly, I wasn't thinking." I hadn't anticipated things would escalate this far this fast. Yes, I'd burst inside with sex in mind, but I'd also expected her to shove me back out the door. The fact she was as crazed for the release as I was had taken me by surprise. "Tell me you're on the pill."

"Of course, I am. And I'll grab a morning-after to be extra safe. Happy?"

This goes against every sex code I had. Not once in twenty years had I broken the no-condom rule. *What the hell is wrong with me?* I don't trust girls, not with something like this. I'd met too many that would love to trap me in something I wasn't ready for.

I could always run across the hall dripping wet and grab one from my room. It was unlikely anyone would see, but the risk was there. Ainsley could see the contemplation in my eyes and made the decision for me when she took my dick in hand, applying just the right pressure as her fingers glided down the length.

My hands braced on the wall, boxing her in with my arms. I pressed my forehead against hers, those slim fingers continuing to torment me. My pulse throbbed. She was too good, and if she kept up this pace, I'd come.

Grabbing her hands, I lifted them up to my chest. Little electric currents trailed after her touch as she explored my body, tracing the lines of my tattoos.

Our gazes connected, and I wasn't sure I liked what went on inside me. *Treat her like any other girl. She isn't special. This is just sex. It means nothing.*

"Are you sure?" I growled against her wet lips.

"I know who you are, and I get it. This is just sex. Nothing more. We're both in agreement and consenting, so shut up and fuck me, Grayson," she said.

I don't know if I ever heard more beautiful words than hearing her tell me to fuck her or the way my name sounded coming from lips swollen from my kisses. Capturing her hips, I spun her around, her hands falling against the shower wall. I slipped inside her at the same time she pressed into me. Our height difference made this the easiest position.

Jesus Christ.

She was so damn tight.

I slid out and back in, going a little deeper with each thrust. My fingers gripped her hips, guiding her body to the rhythm of mine. She matched my pace harmoniously. Our bodies seemed to be in tune with each other, and every little breathy whimper drove me crazy.

I'd never done the deed without a condom, but fuck me, this might have been a horrible decision. It was an incredible feeling having her wrapped around me without any barrier. Every movement, every sensation, was so intense.

"Ohmygod," Ainsley moaned. "I'm going to scream if you don't—" Her orgasm ripped out of her, tightening and spasming against my dick.

There was no better feeling than those quaking pulses right as I came a moment later, riding the after waves still pulsing through her. I continued to move until the quivering of her core ceased.

I tried to catch my breath and pulled out, letting the shower wipe the remnants of sex. Great sex.

She turned and I rested my brow against hers, my thudding heart slowing. I met her languid eyes. A pink flush tainted her cheeks. "Why haven't we done this sooner?"

We both knew why. "It can't happen again," I rasped, but the statement sounded weak even to me. And I knew it was a lie.

Her lips twitched. Strands of her wet hair fell over her shoulders as she looped her arms around my neck and said, "Don't worry, sunshine. I have no interest in being one of your standby girls. Now, carry me to bed. I'm too damn tired to move."

She was already more or less in my arms. Not to mention, she weighed nothing. Forgoing an actual shower, I shut off the water and tucked my hands under her ass, picking her up. I walked us out of the shower, grabbed a towel off the hook, and went into the dark bedroom dripping wet. After a quick towel off with her in my arms, I intended to deposit her on the bed and leave. What was the point in stretching out the awkwardness about to ensue?

Ainsley had other plans. Her arms stayed linked around my neck, and she tugged me into the bed with her. "You're better at this than I thought."

I rolled off her, lying on my side with my head propped up. "You were curious about how I'd be in bed?"

She reached to pull the rumpled sheets over us, not in modesty, because I wasn't sure Ainsley had such a trait, but in comfort. "Isn't every girl?" she asked, snuggling her head against the pillow.

"True. I figured you were...different. You don't seem to give a shit about who I am."

Her eyes batted slowly, and I could see the struggle it was to keep them open. "I don't. You're not as special as you think you are, sunshine."

My lips twisted. "I think I proved just how *special* I am."

She rolled her sleepy eyes. "I'm not talking about your dick. Every guy on the planet has one of those."

I smirked. "This might be the weirdest pillow talk I've ever had."

"Why, because you don't stick around long to talk?" It was an offhanded question that hit too damn close to the truth.

Bull's-eye. But I wasn't about to admit she had pegged me on the nose. My expression grew serious, the teasing completely wiping away. "For Josie's sake and yours, you need to stay away from me."

Her fingers tucked under her pillow as she curled onto her stomach, face turning toward me. "Shouldn't that come before you sleep with a girl, not after? And need I remind you I'm not the one who came into your bedroom."

I shrugged. "I never followed the rules."

She yawned, looking on the verge of sleep. Tendrils of wet hair fanned out on the white sheets. "Something we have in common." Her voice grew drowsier with each word. "Don't worry, sunshine. I still think you're an asshole. This doesn't change anything."

If only that were true.

The pit in my stomach forewarned me I'd taken a step of no return. I thought I only wanted to get it out of my system, and don't get me wrong, I felt better afterward. The problem lay in I wasn't sure once would be enough. Ainsley wasn't a standby girl, and yet, that was exactly how I was treating her.

Quietly going back to my room, I left her spread out naked on her stomach, eyes closed.

* * *

The sleep that refused to come over the last week finally dragged me under, and when I woke up, the clock chimed past noon. Only after I was on my second cup of coffee did my mind start to function again, and with it came all the shit from last night.

And the regret.

But thinking about what an idiot I was wouldn't change anything. I had bigger issues. I reached for my phone on the counter. While I was in the middle of sending Brock a text, Kenna walked in.

She went to the fridge and pulled out a bottle of water. Her dark hair sat in a high ponytail, damp pieces sticking to the side of her face. Since she was dressed in a sports bra and leggings, I assumed she just finished working out at our home gym, but it wasn't always simple to tell, considering she wore the same style of outfits to run errands or lounge around in.

Unscrewing the top of the bottle, she glanced at me. "You look like shit. Rough night?"

The double entendre wasn't lost on me and had me frowning. "I don't get laid every night, Kenna." I did just happen to have sex last night, but she didn't need to know that. My private life was just that. Private, regardless of how much my two sisters might like to meddle and stick their noses in my business.

"Maybe you should," she retorted.

"Where's Josie?" I deflected. Changing the subject. Something I'm good at.

Kenna was easy to rile if you knew what buttons to push. "How the hell should I know? I'm not her keeper."

Kenna and I were close until the year Carter Patterson decided to take something from her. She changed. And I didn't know how to fix what was broken in her. Didn't know how to let go of the guilt that still, to this day, gnawed inside me. I should have been there that night. I should have stopped that asshole from slipping Rohypnol, a common date rape drug, into her drink. After the incident, it took Kenna months to piece together what happened that night, the drug also messing with her memory. She left Elmwood, needing to get away from all the reminders, to get away from her attacker. We drifted apart from the distance, and I spent those two years she was gone vowing to get revenge on the bastard who hurt her.

In the process, I found out my other sister, the one we thought had died as a baby, was in fact very much alive and living only miles away from us. That was a kind of shock that either brought families together or tore them apart. We were lucky it was the first. The new girl who was my enemy's stepsister turned out to be my dead triplet sister. I didn't immediately welcome Josie James with open arms. Trust had never come easy for me, and at that time, she'd been on enemy territory.

"I forgot how pleasant you're to live with," I grumbled, staring into my black coffee. I didn't fuss with sugar and cream.

Kenna grinned before chugging some water. She pulled out a chair beside me and sat down. "So, what's really bothering you?"

This was one of those triplet things people always wondered about. We'd always been able to feel or sense when something troubled the other. It went beyond just worrisome problems. It could be happiness, anger, or sadness, the emotion didn't matter.

The difficult thing about my lifestyle was opening up to those close to me. Protecting them sometimes meant I lied or kept shit bottled up. A slew of crap nagged at my mind, most of which I couldn't reveal to Kenna, but I plucked the one problem I figured was safe. "Someone slashed my tires last night." Like I needed another problem. I'd actually forgotten about the Lamborghini until this morning after seeing a voicemail from the garage saying the new tires had been installed.

Her feet dangled above the floor as she twisted back and forth on the stool. "Which car?"

I shot her a dull look, my thumb drumming over the side of my mug. "Does it matter?"

She wrinkled her nose. "I guess not. Who did you piss off? Or would it be easier to list who you haven't pissed off lately? Because I've been in your presence for like five minutes and I'm already well on my way to being pissed."

"You're the one who asked," I reminded her, my first dose of amusement for the day nagging at the corners of my lips.

"And this is my reminder to learn to shut my mouth. How did you get home?" she asked. "Were you with one of the guys?"

This was a trick question, seeing as we both knew everyone had been busy last night.

Shit.

I flicked her forehead. "Focus, Kenna. That's not important."

Her lips turned into a pout as she rubbed the spot on her head. "You'll pay for that, dear brother." Kenna had been threatening me since she learned to talk, which unfortunately had been early. "Seriously, though. Do you think it could have been a prank?" she asked, finally offering a reasonable question.

"It's possible, but I'm not so sure." My hunch urged it was a personal attack.

She toyed with the water bottle top on the counter, and her brows drew together in thought. "Do you have any suspects? Was there someone with you? Or did you run into anyone?"

I didn't know when either of my sisters turned into little detectives, but both were getting eerily good at uncovering clues and getting in trouble in the process.

A name popped into my head. *Ainsley.*

She'd been there last night. She'd followed me to the Wolves' territory. I had no reason why she would deflate my tires, but also the girls in our group did shit that didn't make sense.

Speak of the little devil.

Movement from the kitchen doorway pulled our gazes over our shoulders to see Ainsley walk in. Her eyes clashed with mine before she came to a dead stop, and she immediately looked away, a bit of color creeping up the side of her neck. "Sorry. I was looking for Josie."

Sorry?

Ainsley never apologized, not even offhandedly. She was flustered.

I scowled.

"I don't think she came home last night," Kenna said, spinning in her chair to face Ainsley.

"Oh," she replied, her gaze lifting.

I stared at her. She stared at me. And an awkwardness descended in the room.

Neither of us had thought much about the day after or how either of us would navigate the fact we were living under the same roof.

A sudden splash of cold hit my face, wet droplets running down my neck. I glared at Kenna and at the water bottle she'd squeezed at me, soaking not just my face but my shirt as well. "Payback," she grinned, barely suppressing the laughter bubbling out of her.

Whoever said having a sister was fun had to be delusional in my book, or they didn't have a sister like Kenna.

"What the hell, Kenna," I growled, shooting to my feet and wiping at the water dripping down my face.

"Okay, what did I miss? Why are you both acting weird? Did you guys have a fight?" Kenna inquired, picking up on the stranger-than-strange vibe straining the air between Ainsley and me.

I needed to shut this down before it turned into a full-blown investigation. "Nothing happened, Kenna. Mind your own damn business." I shoved the stool out of my way, dumped my coffee cup into the sink, and left.

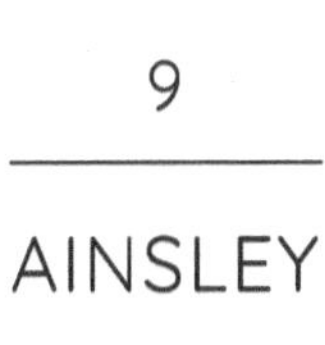

AINSLEY

I blew out a breath the second Grayson left, the tension in the air deflating like a balloon. Last night, the whole sex thing didn't seem like a big deal. We were two consenting adults who'd been curious. This wasn't a new concept to either of us. I thought we had an understanding, and yet this morning, seeing him made what had been so clear in the middle of the night senseless now.

Kenna twisted in her chair to follow my steps as I walked farther into the kitchen. "And the look on your face makes me think you had a fight. Spill it, Fisher."

The bastard left me to deal with the vulture. I wouldn't forgive him.

I went straight for the coffee, pouring myself a cup before taking the seat Grayson had vacated. For a split second, I thought about telling her what happened because a part of me wanted someone to talk to, someone to tell me I wasn't crazy or that last night wasn't a big deal and I should brush it off. Kenna wasn't that person. Not to mention, I'd slept with her brother. "I don't know what you're talking about."

Her lips pressed together. "Uh-huh."

I gave her the side-eye. It was all the energy I could muster. "Where's Josie?"

"Why the fuck does everyone think I know where she is? I'm not her damn assistant. I don't keep a calendar of every day she's off screwing Brock."

"Got it." I sipped my coffee, debating if I should take it to my room.

"Your bruise looks worse," she commented. If there was one thing about Kenna I admired, it was she also had no filter where her mouth was concerned. We had that in common.

She wasn't wrong. I gasped this morning after getting a glimpse of myself in the mirror. By the end of the week, I'd be sporting one nasty-looking reminder of an event I wanted to forget. At least it would be cleared up by the time I returned to school, assuming I didn't get in any more fights. "I don't remember asking."

"If you need something to cover it up before work, I've got some really good concealer. It will last all day." This was Kenna's way of being nice. Her delivery could use some work, but I appreciated the effort.

My lips twitched. "Thanks. I might take you up on it. I have another ten-hour shift today."

Kenna's nose bunched up. "Do you plan on working the entire break?"

A concept that was completely foreign to the rebel princess. "Unfortunately," I admitted, staring into my cup.

She unraveled the rubber band from her ponytail, shaking her dark hair free. "You're going to kill yourself."

"I'll keep that in mind." It was either that or starve to death. "I'm sure you're not thrilled about me crashing your winter break."

"I don't mind. I'd rather have you here than..." Her voice trailed off, and she clamped her mouth shut before finishing her thought, but I could fill in the blanks.

...than at your house.

...than getting the snot beat out of you.

...than living in fear of your father.

I could take my pick because they boiled down to the same problem. "You don't have to tiptoe around my feelings, Kenna. It's okay."

"Are you really okay though?" she asked after a moment of studying me. Her eyes probed mine as if she could see through all the layers of my defense, straight into my heart where I had locked away any feelings I didn't want to deal with. At this point, it was crowded in there.

I blinked away my surprise. Kenna and I didn't have the kind of relationship where we shared feelings. We tended to keep things light and minimal. She understood pain, so I took her question seriously. "I'm not sure. Right now, I'm not giving myself the time to assess what happened. I can't." Saying the words out loud made me wish Josie was here. I swallowed the lump in my throat, no longer craving the coffee in front of me.

She nodded, her features softening in a way that reminded me too much of my best friend. I couldn't always see the similarities between the two. They seemed so different to me, but then Kenna would smile or laugh in a way that showed genuine joy, and that was when it would hit me. "I get that. We might not always agree on everything, but if you want someone to talk to, I can be a good listener despite what people think."

My lips turned up. "And to think people thought we'd never get along."

"Fuck 'em."

"Fuck 'em," I echoed.

* * *

Time had a funny way of passing by without you really realizing it. At least, that was how it felt to me the first week at the Edwardses's. In that time, I only had one day off from the diner, utterly my choice. Working kept me from thinking about other shit. Mainly my family and Grayson, who I hadn't spoken to since that awkward morning after the run-in.

The last thing I wanted was for things to become weird between us. I thought we'd both been under the notion we wouldn't make a big deal about us sleeping together. One of us had to set things back the way they were before the others grew suspicious and avoiding him wouldn't accomplish that.

I had to talk to him. Clear the air.

With Christmas less than a week away, it hit me I wouldn't be home or spending the day with my mom. I'd be a Pa's Place, which honestly was where I wanted to be. The diner was safe, warm, inviting, and full of cheer. It would be a relatively slow night, and Bea and Ralph would sneak me a gift like they had done every year—a check.

Maybe I could get Mom to come by and have dinner. We could exchange gifts, and she wouldn't have to spend the night watching my father get drunk in front of our small Christmas tree.

That's what I wanted this year.

Jogging down the stairs with my phone in hand, my thumbs flew over the keys, shooting off a text to Mom, asking if she could sneak away on Christmas Day and come to the diner. If not, I had off Christmas Eve, although I did have plans with Josie and the crew, I could squeeze in time to see her.

I turned the corner, striding toward the back of the house where the side door to the cars was. My shift at the diner started in an hour, and I had an errand to run beforehand. Just as I clicked my phone screen to lock a hand grabbed my arm. My head snapped up, and I looked into Grayson's scowling eyes.

I glanced over my shoulder to make sure no one lingered downstairs who might see us. "What are you—?"

"We need to talk," he cut me off sharply and proceeded to drag me into the closest room. The door clicked shut behind me, immersing us in darkness except for the wee little bit of light coming from underneath the door.

Before I had a chance to catch my breath, he backed me into the wall and had my arm pinned over my head. "This better not be some kinky fantasy you're trying to act out," I huffed, waiting as his hands fumbled with the wall, looking for the light switch.

"Not everything is about sex," he sneered.

"Is that why you locked us in the laundry room?" Both the washer and dryer were running, creating a gentle hum throughout the space.

"Yes. No," he corrected with a growl. "You're twisting it around." At last, the light flipped on, bathing the room in a soft glow.

"Let me go," I hissed, jostling my wrist under his grip.

He didn't budge. In fact, he nabbed my other hand and secured it above my head with the first.

"Really," I said sharply, my eyes lifting to my trapped arms over my head.

Like a boulder blocking my path, his body remained firm and intrusive in my personal space. "Stop fighting," he hissed.

My chin lifted, teeth gritting. "I would if you released my hands."

"I rather like you at my mercy."

"Mercy?" I scoffed, an absurd laugh bubbling out. "Let me show you mercy." My knee came promptly up, fitting between his legs.

His groan became music to my ears. The hands at my wrists unfurled as more important parts of his body needed attention. "God-damn it, Ainsley," he seethed, bending over slightly as he rode out the sudden pain of having his nuts crushed.

I had no sympathy for his pain. He had asked for it. "Is that what you wanted to tell me? Why you hauled me off into the laundry room? I'm not going to be your dirty little secret, sunshine."

Stretching to his full height, he raked a hand through his hair, giving me a hard stare that made me believe he could be capable of murder. "Did you slash my tires that night?"

My body went still while I processed the sudden change in conversation. "Wait, you think I was the one who went crazy ex-girl-friend on your car? You mean before I nearly got assaulted by the Wolves?"

"You had a knife," he pointed out.

True, I had. A knife that I had lost and had yet to replace.

My lips hardened. I didn't have time for this, not that Grayson gave me much choice in the matter. "Yeah, because I had loads of time to slam my five-dollar switchblade into four tires. And why would I do that?"

"I don't know. You're the one who followed me," he said.

"Do I need to remind you that you had a gun? Last time I worry about you. I won't make that mistake again." I moved for the door, but he stepped in my path again. Anger stirred like the wind inside me.

He pinned me with dark eyes. "See that you don't."

I tried to go around him, and he put himself in my way. Feeling past irritated, I pierced him with a dry glare. "Prick. Like I care enough about you or your stupid car to waste my time slashing them to death. Find another girl to blame because it's not me."

His finger hooked under my chin, forcing my eyes to stay on his. "Who then?" he demanded like I had all the answers.

I gave a dramatic shrug, my jaw tight. "Perhaps you have a stalker."

His expression turned thoughtful and suspicious as if he ran through any other possible names. "Son of a bitch," he muttered under his breath.

I shot him an amused look. "So, you do have a stalker. Fucking classic. Who's the bitch? I'd like to meet the psychopath who thinks your obsessed-worthy."

The muscles in his jaw tensed. "I need to go."

This time it was me who stopped him. My hand went to his chest, not that I could have actually prevented him from leaving, and the gesture had him looking down at me. "Wait. We're not done here."

His brows went up. "Don't tell me you actually want to..." He crowded me, my back hitting the wall.

I swallowed, getting lost in the sudden heat thawing his eyes. "No, not that," I said, shaking my head. "I thought you wanted to talk about what happened the other night. I don't want things to be weird between us because we hooked up."

"It never should have happened," he stated flatly.

Why were the words I wanted to hear like a stab to the heart? I didn't care about Grayson. Not like that. Maybe it was wounded pride, but I refused to let it show. "Right," I agreed, the word like sandpaper. "It was a mistake."

"One I won't make again."

Did he have to be such a dick about it? Like I was beneath him, and he couldn't believe he had stooped to sleep with the poor girl. "What's wrong with me, sunshine?" I asked, poking him hard in the chest with my finger and ending up hurting my index instead of doing anything to his hard pecs.

"I never said there was anything wrong with you."

"Am I not rich enough? Not pretty enough? Not classy enough? Do I not have the right kind of clothes? Or fit your little mold for the ideal girl to bang the infamous Grayson Edwards?" I punctuated each question with a poke to his chest until he snatched my finger.

"You made your point. And it's nice to know what you think of me. You really want to know. You were there. It could have been any girl."

"I was just a convenient lay. Glad we cleared this up. I'm going to be late for work." This time, he didn't stop as I went for the door, swinging it open with a thrust.

10

GRAYSON

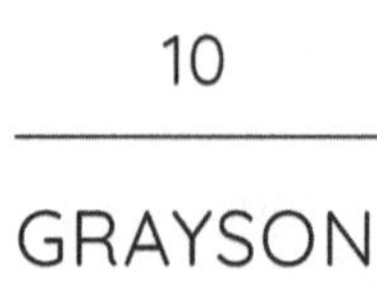

I leaned back against the dryer and exhaled, scrubbing a hand over my face. *Fuck, I handled that brilliantly.* But I didn't know how else to draw a line between us and put things back on neutral ground. I never should have gone to her room, and I'd been kicking myself for doing exactly what I told myself not to do.

Rule #5: Never get mixed up with my sisters' friends.

I had a list of rules, most of which I followed. They were there for a reason. To prevent complicating my already complicated life. I disliked family messes. Josie had just come back into our lives. The last thing I wanted to do was create problems, and fooling around with her best friend seemed like a loose thread that could quickly turn into a tangle of knots.

There were times in my life when I had to be the asshole, and in most of those moments, it rarely bothered me. This was one of those scarce occasions when being the jerk sucked.

It had never been my intention to hurt Ainsley, and although she did a good job of pretending otherwise, I'd seen that quick flash of pain.

The truth was, I was no good for her, not the other way around as she assumed. Was it better to let her think I was *that guy*, someone who gave a damn about prestige and wealth?

If it meant keeping her away from me, then yes.

Besides, I had other shit to worry about. When Ainsley mentioned stalker, Kate McGuire's name immediately popped into my head. If I thought about it now, she made perfect sense.

Cursing under my breath, I left the laundry room, slamming the door closed behind me. Like I needed to deal with this bitch's crazy ass. *Why do I always attract the psychotic ones?*

"What were you doing in there?"

I flinched at the sound of Josie's voice. She would happen to be walking by as I stepped out. "Laundry."

"Ha." She snorted. "Is that your idea of a joke? Elise is here."

"And?" I retorted, continuing to walk down the hall. I didn't have time for sibling shenanigans. I had a stalker to track down.

She skipped behind me. For someone who had grown up as an only child, she fell into the role of an annoying, prying sister with ease. One would never know we'd been separated at birth. "And in two years, I've never seen you once do laundry. I was convinced you didn't even know where the washer and dryer were in this house."

I grabbed my coat off the mudroom hook, slipping my arms into the sleeves. "I didn't. Stumbled in there by accident." Sarcasm dripped from my tone.

She crossed her arms and leaned on the corner of the wall. It was hard to take her seriously in fuzzy socks, sweats, and an old T-shirt that was probably Brock's. "Where are you going?"

"Out," I replied sharply, hoping she wouldn't question me further. Josie never blinked at my moods. Never had. She often gave me the attitude right back. Something Josie, Kenna, and I seemed to have in common in our older years. Kenna hadn't always been so jaded. It was only after she had come back from her two-year hiatus in high school that she found courage and self-confidence. Gone was the meek girl who only wanted to please everyone. She was tougher now, and when Josie and Kenna teamed up, they kind of scared me sometimes.

Josie rolled her eyes. "Good chat."

"I'll see you later." I brushed past her.

"I could come with you," she offered, trailing after me.

"Is something wrong? Did you and Brock have a fight?" I asked, leveling her a sidelong look.

"Nooo," she said, elongating the word. "You and I haven't hung out at all since we've been home. Forgive me for wanting to spend time with my only brother. Our break will be over before you know it, and we'll both be back at school."

Our schools were only two hours away, and we did see each other at least once a month for a weekend, but I got what she meant. Time flew. "I've got someone I need to see, but afterward, I'm free. We can go out to eat, watch a movie, you pick."

"Can we make popcorn and hot cocoa?" she asked hopefully, the expression on her face changing.

"I'll be disappointed if we don't."

Josie smiled. "I'll tell Kenna."

God, when was the last time just the three of us hung out? I couldn't remember. We were unusual triplets who were still navigating our relationship. Had I felt an instant connection to Josie when I saw her for the first time? No. Not really. Even after I discovered who she was, it didn't seem real even though she looked so much like Kenna. But now, a few years later, that link between us blossomed. Same with her and Kenna. Perhaps more so with them since the night they got their vengeance on Carter. That seemed to be the shift in their relationship, an understanding between two sisters who'd been hurt by the same guy. It was something they would always share, and I couldn't fully understand.

My part had always been the guilt of not being able to protect them fully.

* * *

The McGuires's house was only a five-minute drive from mine. Too close if you asked me. We lived in the same gated community, so I didn't have to deal with the security gate. Our parents ran in the same social circle. Our mothers went to the same clubs, but that was true for most of the students who had attended Elmwood Academy.

Perhaps I shouldn't have just shown up at her house. I didn't want to involve her family, but her parents worked. She had an older brother the same age as Sawyer, the brother I lost, but I knew little about him. The last thing I needed was him on my ass for harassing his little sister, because if Kate was behind slashing my tires, our *talk* wasn't going to end well.

One thing everyone knew about me was to not mess with my cars. Especially the ones that my brother drove, like the Lambo. It was a surefire way to get on my bad side.

There was always the chance she wouldn't be home, and if that turned out to be the case, I'd shoot her a text.

Only one car sat in the driveway as I pulled in, Kate's little red Corvette with a light dusting of snow on the windows. The car hadn't moved since last night. Even the vehicle she drove screamed prissy little bitch. How very cliché, and somehow that little nugget of her personality irked me. Kate was literally a carbon copy of every girl at Elmwood Academy. Nothing about her differentiated her from all the others. They were all Janes, every one of them interchangeable like a pair of socks. Boring. Fake. Selfish.

Her house leaned more on the modest side compared to the others in the gated neighborhood. A two-story redbrick colonial with black shutters. The pathway to the house had been shoveled, and I walked up to the door and pressed the bell. I'd never been to Kate's house. Never had a reason to, and while I stood waiting for someone to answer the door, I thought this was a mistake. Something about Kate had always made me leery.

Before I could change my mind, the door swung open, Kate's blonde head turning in my direction, loose beachy waves framing an oval face. To the naked eye, she looked like a sweet Georgia peach, but if you looked deeper into her coppery eyes, you would see the glint of a calculating viper patiently waiting to strike.

With sun-kissed glossy lips, she grinned, standing in the doorway dressed in black tights, a flared skirt of the same color, and a red sweater. She looked like she was on her way to a Christmas party and impractical for the current weather. "I wondered if you would call me, but this is better. I must admit, it took longer than I would have hoped," she greeted.

I scowled, my default expression whenever I was in her presence, and shoved my hands into my pockets. "I was busy last night. Sorry to say you were the last thing on my mind," I replied harshly.

Her composure rattled slightly, and if I hadn't been closely watching her, I might not have noticed it all. "You're here now," she purred, a hand running down the zipper of my coat. "Come inside. It's cold."

My hand attached to her wrist, yanking her arm back. "I'm not here to flirt, Kate." I flung her hand away from me. "Put on a coat and come outside unless you want to freeze to death. I couldn't care less either way, but we need to talk." I didn't know who was home, if anyone, and didn't want to risk anyone overhearing what I had to say.

The smug glimmer in her eyes dimmed a fraction. "Suit yourself." She leaned into the foyer, grabbed a coat from the closet off to the side of the door, and slipped her arms inside before stepping onto the porch. The door clicked closed behind her. Her sugary smile was back in place on her lips; those few seconds of putting on her coat had given her time to recompose herself.

Kate was good at wearing masks. She wanted to be seen as a good girl, and that was the image she portrayed, but I didn't buy it. Too many times in high school she'd let the mask slip for a few seconds during her ardent pursuit of Brock. And when he didn't give her the attention she craved, Kate turned her fixation to me.

I have no idea why. She would have had better luck with Fynn or Micah if she was that damn determined to snag an Elite. Never once had I given her any inkling I might be interested in her. Just the opposite, but I had to believe Kate liked the challenge—the chase.

She really was clueless. How could she not see this was the last place I wanted to be? It wasn't the place. We could have met at the Eiffel Tower in France, and I still wouldn't have wanted to be anywhere she was. "Let's get one thing straight. This isn't a social visit. I need to ask you something, and then I don't want to see you again. Don't call me. Don't text. Don't show up at the places I hang out. And don't fucking come to my house. Ever. My dorm at school is also on the list of places I don't want to see you at."

Her delicate features schooled into an expression of confusion, her bottom lip pouting slightly. She should have been an actress. "I don't understand. What did I do?"

I could have asked Kate straight up if she was the one who had slashed my tires, but I chose to go with a different approach and cut the bullshit. "I think you know exactly what you did last night. If you wanted my attention, you fucked up messing with my brother's car."

Long, thick lashes fluttered, the puzzlement still on her face. "What are you talking about, Grayson? What happened last night?"

She'd been expecting me, had said so herself, so this charade of innocence didn't fool me. "You know damn well that your games don't work on me. They never have. Why did you do it, Kate?"

A moment passed, the wind blowing, shaking the branches of a tree that towered over the porch and sending flakes of snow twirling in the air. Her guise dropped, a glint of fire sparking in her golden cat-like eyes. "I saw you kiss her."

"Who?" I recounted the events of that night. "You mean Ainsley?"

"I don't give a shit what that slut's name is. She's not good enough for you." There she was. The real Kate McGuire, spurred by jealousy and hatred of other girls.

Hearing the malice in her voice and the way she spat her words when calling Ainsley a slut struck a cold fire in my veins. My hand darted through the air, wrapping around her throat. Shock widened her coppery eyes as I shoved her back against the brick house. "She's not your concern. Stay away from her."

Most girls would have pleaded, or their eyes would have trembled. Not Kate. The bitch grinned. "Why is she staying at your house?"

I didn't want to know how she knew Ainsley was staying with us. The answer would only fuel the icy flames licking within me. My fingers remained firm on her neck with enough pressure to make a point but not harm her. I might leave a mark, but it was the least of my concerns. "Again, not your business. Find some other sap to obsess over. You and I will never happen."

Her fingers went to my wrist, but not to push me away. She would have stepped closer if I allowed it. I didn't. "We're the same. She isn't on your level. Never will be."

Disgust descended over my features. "Stay the fuck away from me."

"You don't scare me, Grayson."

"I should."

"You're not the only one who harbors secrets, and I think you'll eventually change your mind about me."

This bitch was straight-up mental. Not only could she not take no for an answer, but she was also delusional. Hell could freeze over, and I wouldn't give her a second chance. We could be the only two people left in the world, and I'd go celibate for the rest of my life. Humanity would die off before I touched her. "Is that a threat?"

She lifted a slim brow. "This year's been a little dull, don't you think? Perhaps it's time for some Christmas fireworks."

My fingers gave one last squeeze before I shoved away from her. She sunk against the house, and where I should have seen fright in her eyes, there was only intrigue. And specks of desire. "Try me, Kate. We'll see who loses." I left her there in the cold and stalked back to my car. Revving the engine, I glared at Kate through the windshield. The bitch grinned, slim fingers touching her neck. I reversed the car out of her driveway, my tires squealing when I took off down the road.

11

AINSLEY

I sat behind the diner counter, staring at the clock above the door and willing the little hands to move faster. This night dragged ass. We hadn't had a single customer in over an hour. I didn't know what everyone was doing tonight. Not even the regulars were stopping in, and having two waitresses on staff didn't make sense. We'd both go home with crappy tips.

Ten minutes later, Bea gave me the boot, ordering me to go home and take the rest of the night off, insisting I'd been working too hard the last week.

She wasn't wrong, but it was exactly how I wanted it—needed it; otherwise, my mind went off to places I didn't want to deal with.

At first, it had been my father.

And now, my mind was filled with nothing but thoughts of Grayson. Particularly the moments in my bedroom.

Why couldn't he have been mediocre in bed? Average even? Why did he have to be goddamn spectacular? And when would I stop dreaming about the jerk? It seemed like every quiet minute my mind got it drifted directly to Grayson. And it wasn't just my mind, but my body betrayed me too, remembering what it felt like having his weight against me. How he filled me. The way he moved in and out, rolling his hips. The way he tasted. The way he smelled. The feel of his hands.

But that wasn't all my brain mulled over. I was good at self-sabotage. Really good. Despite being confident in myself, I had days when I let the words and voices of others get to me. If I wasn't daydreaming about Grayson's firm ass or his brooding lips, my mind went to dark places I'd fought hard to stay out of.

Sometimes it sucked me in like a polar vortex.

Why would a guy like Grayson be into me? I knew his reputation, knew he didn't date. I wasn't a stranger to hooking up, yet somehow this felt different. Probably because of who he was. I couldn't run away from Grayson. He was a part of my life. That's where the problem lay, complicating matters.

I hated I let a guy make me doubt myself. I liked who I was, and I had no plans to change because of a guy.

It wasn't like I sought a relationship. I didn't have time for a boyfriend. Not while I was still in school. I had a ten-year plan, and nowhere in the plan was there a bullet point for a boyfriend. School. Career. Those were the things that mattered most. Getting the hell out of the lower east side of Elmwood and making something of myself. I was tired of being poor. I had aspirations. I wanted to be proud of what I accomplished, of who I'd become, and of the career I'd make.

To do all those things, to feel them, I had to stay away from Grayson Edwards. I also needed money. Just not tonight it seemed.

I untied my apron and cashed out for the night. The digital clock on my car dash rolled just past eight p.m. when I drove into the Edwardses's driveway. I nearly missed my turn tonight, thanks to those wandering thoughts of Grayson, and almost ended up going home instead of here. I wasn't sure what I planned on doing about my father. If I would talk to him before going back to school. If I even wanted to. We didn't have a super close relationship, not like I did with Mom. Not once had he called me while I'd been at college to check on me or chat. It was hard to care about someone else when you couldn't take care of yourself or stay sober long enough to remember you had a daughter.

Enough with my sob story. I refused to think about either man. No Dad. No Grayson.

I let myself into the side entrance, keying in the code to unlock the door and thinking about that deep soaking tub in my bathroom. Mrs. Edwards knew how to pamper a guest. She even kept little travel-size products for every beauty care item one could think of including a basket full of bath bombs, bubbles, oils, and other shit I didn't know the name of but was eager to try.

Lavish baths weren't a thing in my house.

I could download a new manga on my phone and soak until my skin turned into a wrinkly prune. Blissful. Maybe I'd sneak into the kitchen and grab a snack and a bottle of wine. Eating cheese and crackers while taking a bubble bath seemed like something rich people did, and tonight I would pretend that Ainsley Fisher did this on the regular.

I didn't, but I could.

When I got out of college and had my own place, no matter how small my apartment might be, my one request was it needed to have a bathtub.

Warmth cascaded over me when I walked inside the house, slipping off my damp shoes in the mudroom. I hung up my coat and padded into the hallway. The smell of buttered popcorn tickled my nose. A rumble vibrated the floor under my socks, followed by a muffled boom, the kind you heard when you darted outside the movie theatre to pee and missed an important scene. It sounded like someone was having a movie night. I passed down the hallway, noticing the basement door was open. Voices carried up from the stairs during a lull in the film.

I stood in the doorway, chewing on my lip, wondering if I should sneak upstairs for that bath or go downstairs. Maybe I would just pop my head in and see who all was here.

The lights were all off as I crept down the carpeted stairs, only the glow of the massive TV that took up an entire wall to guide me. I stayed at the bottom landing, peering over the U-shaped couch to identify the shadowy figures. There were three, and it was easy to guess from their outlines.

The triplets. Grayson, Kenna, and Josie.

Grayson noticed me first, his head lifting and turning in my direction before I could sneak back upstairs. The TV screen flicked at that moment to a brighter frame, allowing me to see his deep eyes, a hint of amusement teasing his lips. That rare smirk hung me up, and I couldn't look away.

My pulse raced, and I cursed him in my head, my mouth pulling into a straight line.

Josie's attention shifted to Grayson, and then she turned to see what had his focus. "Ainsley! You're home," she sang, smiling at me brightly.

I moved to the back of the couch, in between Josie and Kenna. "I didn't mean to intrude."

"Intrude my ass. Get your butt on the couch." Josie and Kenna shared a look of pure mischief. The next thing I knew, they each grabbed a hold of an arm and hauled me over the back of the couch. I flipped, landing with my face smashed into a cushion and my feet sticking awkwardly in the air.

Their giggles were infectious, and I couldn't help but smile even with my nose pressed into the couch. I twisted and turned, sliding down the deep cushions as I righted myself into a seated position. My hair came undone and tumbled in a complete mess around my face, but I didn't care.

I snuck a glance at Grayson who still stared at me. Thank God, the darkness hid the flushing of my cheeks. Only hours ago, we'd been in the laundry room having a spat. I adverted my eyes, turning them to the TV screen. "What are we watching?" I asked.

Kenna scrunched her nose. "Only the worst Christmas movie ever."

"Grayson's pick," Josie explained, stretching out her feet onto an ottoman that turned the couch into a chaise lounge. It was one of those couches that could be configured into a dozen different layouts, piecing together like Tetris.

"*Die Hard* is goddamn classic," he argued, tossing a few kernels of popcorn at the three of us. "I had to sit through *The Polar Express*," he complained.

Kenna climbed onto the other L-shaped couch, allowing Josie and me to stretch out on the center section, but that also meant nothing but a few pillows sat between Grayson and me. "It was either that or *Frozen*," Kenna explained.

Grayson groaned, neither movie appealing.

I shifted on the couch, snuggling a pillow, and weaving my legs around Josie's. "I like *Die Hard*," I said, keeping my eyes on the screen.

"I rescind your invitation to join. You've got to go now," Kenna grumbled. I could barely see her face, but I sensed the disapproval of my taste in movies through her voice.

I leaned on my hand, my head not too far from Grayson's. We were close. Too close. Over the buttered popcorn, my nose picked up traces of his cologne. "Bruce Willis is not Keanu Reeves, but there's something hot about his smirk for an old dude," I reasoned.

"Right," Josie agreed, her foot bumping my leg.

"Want a drink?" Grayson asked as he stood up to refill his.

I craned my neck back to look at him. "Sure. Why not."

He poured me a glass of wine, and our fingers brushed slightly when he handed me the drink. I wanted to pretend like I didn't feel the electric current surging through my body at only a measly accidental touch. Or had it been an accident?

It didn't matter. What mattered was gaining control of my traitorous body. I was not the girl who swooned over a guy or got all gaga.

I watched Grayson refill the other glasses, looking to see if he had any reaction. He didn't.

Snuggling back onto the couch, I curled up with one of the softest blankets I'd ever felt, sipped my wine, and got sucked into the movie.

Josie and I had watched a million films over the years, usually at her house, and as an Elite group, we binge-watched several shows together but sitting in the dark with the triplets somehow felt different. Or perhaps it was that my body was hyperaware of the only guy in the room.

My eyes drifted to Grayson repeatedly, and I wondered what the hell was going on with me. Why couldn't I get him out of my head? Grayson was a prick. I shouldn't be thinking about how close our hands were or that I only had to move a few inches to interlace our fingers. What distracted me the most was a stupid strand of hair that fell over the side of his face. It beckoned my fingers to brush it aside.

Resisting the urge was like denying myself the last slice of pizza after starving all day.

Knock it off, Ainsley. You're a grown-ass adult now, not some teenager with unpredictable hormones.

God, is it getting hot in here?

I tossed the fuzzy blanket off despite how posh it felt against my skin. Maybe the wine was messing with my system, but I reached for my almost empty glass to drain the rest of it. I was the queen of making bad decisions.

The three of them were so comfortable with each other, and I imagined Christmas movie marathons were a tradition for them, one Josie quickly joined in on over the last few years. She had no idea how lucky she was, and at least for this year, I was glad to be spending the holiday with my best friend.

The Edwardses were big on traditions. The only Christmas Eve tradition in my family was how fast my dad could slam down a six-pack. It was impressive.

Would I actually get to have a normal Christmas this year with a family who cared about spending time together? I wasn't sure my cynical bones could handle all the love and cheer spreading throughout the Edwards's home.

Josie's phone lit up during the final scene on the roof with Bruce Willis spraying bullets into the air. She checked the text message, standing up a moment later.

"Where are you going?" Kenna asked as Josie inched her way around the couch.

"To bed. I'm done for the night," she replied, stretching her arms over her head.

"Seriously?" Kenna protested. "Can't you have phone sex with Taylor another night?"

"Gross," Grayson complained. "Did you really have to say that out loud right before bed? The last thing I want to visualize before I close my eyes tonight is Brock yanking his chain while Josie's doing God knows what."

Kenna flipped Grayson the middle finger. "That sounds like a you problem."

Ah, sibling banter. How much I loved this.

My lips twitched. I could sit here and listen to them for hours.

Grayson's eyes flicked to me for a second, noticing my amusement. My stomach flipped. I'd always been a sucker for dimples, not scowls, and yet it was Grayson's downturned mouth that had me clenching my legs. If only my damn mind would stop undressing him. How was I supposed to know having sex with Grayson would be like crack? One taste and I was hooked—a damn addict who could do nothing but think of wanting more.

Was I doomed to constantly objectify him in my mind? Want what I couldn't have?

"We still have Christmas Eve," Josie reminded as she began to ascend the stairs.

"Christmas Eve is Harry Potter all day. You'll love it," Kenna explained. "Even Scrooge over there loves a little Hermione magic."

Grayson rolled his eyes, turning off the TV and signaling the end of movie night.

"Mads will be here with the rest of the guys," Kenna said. "Did you get your gift for the exchange?" she asked Grayson, grabbing the almost empty popcorn bowl to carry upstairs.

Sitting up, Grayson shoved a hand through his hair. "Fuck, we're doing that this year?"

He wasn't the only one who'd forgotten. I still had to get Josie her gift as well, and I had only three days left.

"We've been doing it every year," Kenna replied.

"You coming?" Grayson asked me when I hadn't moved.

"Yeah." Taking off my makeup and crawling into that cozy bed upstairs sounded divine. I just had to make my body move. "Any chance you can carry me?" I meant it as a joke, but the darkening of Grayson's eyes started my heart racing, and before he took the question literally and scooped me off my feet, I jumped up, skirting past him after Kenna.

Upstairs, Josie had already locked herself into her bedroom, and Kenna slipped into hers, leaving me alone with Grayson. I felt him behind me as I shuffled to the end of the hall. I pretended the air hadn't suddenly gotten stifling being alone with him, that every nerve ending in my body didn't come alive.

Without looking over my shoulder, I reached for the doorknob. Grayson grabbed my wrist, whirling me away from my room and into his. The door shut with a click, submerging us in darkness before I fathomed what happened. Grayson backed me against the wall, trapping me with his body. His hands pressed into the paint on either side of my head.

I lifted my eyes, my heart hammering against my ribs. "What are you doing?" I hiss-whispered, keeping my voice low enough to not alert Kenna or Josie.

He dipped his head, his scent and lips only inches from mine. "I don't know."

"Grayson," I groaned, searching for a semblance of self-control. This morning, he was telling me what a mistake I'd been, and yet, in the dark, he looked eager to go down the rabbit hole again with me. I refused to be his dirty little secret. "What do you want from me? I thought we agreed nothing can happen between us."

"That was this morning."

"Pray tell, what happened between then and now that suddenly changed your mind. Other than your dick getting hard." I didn't want to think how hard he was, yet I could feel the length of him, giving me little choice.

"You need to leave." His hot breath cruised along my cheek.

My lungs tightened, and I physically forced myself to breathe. "Like your bedroom or the house?"

"Both," he said against the corner of my mouth.

I had no intention of kissing him, but then his lips touched mine, and I completely forgot why I hated Grayson so much. I pushed at his chest. "We can't keep doing this." My protest came out weak and pathetic, giving *me* mixed signals.

"I know," he murmured, his lips moving to my neck.

"Grayson, I'm serious," I partly groaned, partly moaned. "I don't want to hurt Josie or do anything that might piss her off. You have this huge family. She's all I have. She *is* my family."

His fingers splayed over the side of my throat, curling into my hair. "That's not true. You're one of us. You need to accept it."

"Am I?" I shook my head. "A minute ago, you were ordering me to leave. And if I am one of you, isn't that more of a reason why we can't keep doing this? Why are we doing this? I don't even like you."

"Are you sure about that?" He took my earlobe between his teeth.

My eyes narrowed, and I kept my hands off him. "I used to be sure until you kissed me, but it helps for me to remember when you say cocky shit like that."

He chuckled. "Just doing my part."

Fire spat into my veins. "I'm not here to be your fuck buddy. I'm not one of those stupid standby girls who wait around to bounce on your dick."

"You wouldn't be in my house if you were."

"Let me go," I commanded, staring up into his face.

Our gazes locked, and for a moment, I was sure he wouldn't release me. His jaw clenched, fighting the desire burning in the center of his eyes.

Relief flooded through me when he took just a small step back. A part of me knew Grayson hadn't meant to make me feel used like I was nothing but a quick lay to him, but that was exactly how I felt. Used. Trashy. Unimportant. All those cliché things I promised myself I'd never feel again. It didn't matter that I wanted Grayson the same way he wanted me.

Hypocritical?

Fuck yes.

My phone buzzed in my pocket as I spun to leave, my strides quickening and taking me across the hall into my room. Pressure clamped down on my chest, a mixture of regret, pain, sadness, and heartache. Inside, I was a clusterfuck of messed up. The last thing I needed to do was screw around with Grayson when my life felt like it was suddenly spinning wildly out of control.

Holy shit. I nearly slept with him again!

My mental state had to be questioned.

I needed to focus on school. Paying the bills. And getting the hell out of Elmwood. Those were my priorities.

The parties. The fun. The random hookups. It was time I took life seriously because, when college ended, I didn't have a loving home to run to. I had to figure my shit out.

Flopping down on my bed, I pulled out my phone and read the message flashing across the screen.

What the fuck is this?

It had to be a joke or a wrong number. I read the text again, the phone almost slipping through my fingers.

Stay out of his room. Or I'll make sure you lose more than a place to stay.

My eyes immediately lifted, scanning the dark room as if I might find someone lurking in the shadows. They couldn't possibly mean for me to stay out of Grayson's room. Who could even know I'd been there? Not without having access to the house.

I glanced at the text again, reading the anonymous number from which it had come. Not a number I recognized. I shouldn't engage with this troll, and yet I couldn't stop my thumbs from sending back a quick reply as if I expected them to just hand over the answers.

Who is this?

A moment later, my text came back as undeliverable.

Son of a bitch.

Okay, strange, but not the weirdest thing that had ever happened to me, and I was too damn mentally exhausted to deal with a cyber-bully. Convincing myself I was getting worked up over nothing wasn't hard.

Light spilled from the bedside table as I flipped it on and rummaged through my purse for my nightly birth control pill to take. I skimmed the rows of little white pills and stopped. Today was Thursday. Right? But that couldn't be correct. I was three days behind. How the fuck?

One missed day I could understand. But three? How had I done that and not noticed until today?

And this was another reason why I couldn't be having sex. My mind was too damn scattered to remember the important shit like taking my pill!

Or remember to stop at the pharmacy for a morning-after pill.

I smacked my forehead with the heel of my palm and back-tracked through the last two weeks. I'd gone to a party. Grayson carried me home, and I'd passed out before we got there. Definitely skipped my pill that night. Sunday, I drove home, my dad hit me—good times—and I'd been too distraught and preoccupied that night to have remembered my birth control. That had to be night number two. And on Monday night...I'd had sex with Grayson in the shower and fell into bed sated and exhausted. I hadn't slept that well in days.

Those were my three missing days, and I had apparently just picked up where I left off, not realizing I took the wrong day of the week. Not much I could do about it now. Tomorrow I would stop into the pharmacy. With a sigh, I popped out the next white pill and went to get ready for bed.

* * *

I don't know what woke me, but my eyes flew open. This prickling sensation crawled over my skin, the kind you sensed when you knew you were not alone in the dark. My first thought was I'd had a bad dream, but I couldn't remember anything beyond being jerked awake. My pulse raced.

I stayed still, my arms and legs heavy like stone. Only my eyes moved, looking around the room, searching the shadows. I shivered, a sudden gust of cold air rushing over my skin. I felt like a five-year-old little girl again, afraid of the monster under her bed.

But the creature wasn't hiding beneath the bed frame or in the closet. The bastard stood in the window.

Fear lodged into my throat, gripping my chest. A drop of cold sweat rolled down my neck as the curtain danced around the figure. Their head tilted toward me, and for an unreasonable second, I swore my father's eyes glared at me, but that made no sense. Drunk or not, he had no reason to be creeping around the Edwardses's property, let alone in the windows. I didn't think he even knew where they lived, and the only time he left the house was for a beer run, but my mind wasn't thinking clearly.

I swallowed the scream surging up my throat.

I should scream.

Right?

Alert someone there was an intruder. That was what sane people did when someone broke in. They didn't freeze and do nothing, praying the creep would tiptoe away.

Screw it.

I wasn't waiting for this bastard to realize I was awake. And I definitely wasn't hanging around for him to rape me or whatever his nefarious reasons were for breaking into my room.

Tossing back the blankets, I bolted from the bed, my bare feet pounding into the wood floor as I ran to the door. Too afraid to look over my shoulder, I fumbled with the knob and flung it open, stumbling across the hall with my heart knocking against my ribs.

I burst into the bedroom across from mine.

"Grayson," I said breathlessly, not quite a cry but louder than a whisper.

12

GRAYSON

"Grayson! There's someone in my room." A voice invaded my dreams—a panicky voice, dragging me out of sleep when I was far from ready to wake up.

I didn't want to deal with my sister's bullshit. "Kenna, if this is a joke—" I started to grumble, rolling to my side.

A body hurtled into my bed, shaking me. "Grayson, it's Ainsley. Get up."

Persistence shook the mattress, and I groaned, the voice finally piercing through my clouded mind. "Ainsley?" My brows drew together as I forced my eyes open despite the heaviness weighing them down.

Small fingers attached to my arm, nails digging into my skin as they clung to me. "Yes. Did you hear what I said? Someone's in my room." An air of desperation layered underneath a coat of fear in her tone. The trembling of her lips spiked alarm through my blood. The understanding of what she had said came next.

Someone's in the house? Things cleared quickly, and I sat up in bed, a hand running through my hair. I found her eyes in the dark.

"Who?" The demand came out sharp and edged with anger. *Who would dare break into my house?*

I started to untangle myself from the bedding, Ainsley climbing out of the way. "I don't know. That's why I came to get you."

In only a pair of basketball shorts, I strode out of my room, keeping my steps long but light so as not to scare off the intruder. I wanted to catch the asshole in the act. Ainsley was right behind me. "Stay here," I hissed.

"No fucking way. You're not leaving me alone," she argued, and I didn't bother to dispute it. Perhaps it was better if I could keep an eye on her. I could sense how distraught she was.

Hovering in Ainsley's doorway, I scanned the dark room. My gaze immediately went to the open window. The slightly parted white curtains twirled in December's cold evening air, a gleam of moonlight streaking over the wooden floors. So much for hoping Ainsley had only been having a very real nightmare.

"Son of a bitch," I murmured. Who the hell was dumb enough to climb to a second story?

I dashed across the room, flinging aside the billowing curtains. The only shadows moving below were the swaying of tree branches. A light coat of white snow covered the ground, and a swell of cold rage burned my chest as I looked at the footprints imprinted in the white powder. I listened to the howling of the wind, the warmth of Ainsley's body pressing into my back. Her hand rested on the side of my arm, and I felt a shudder roll through her.

We had cameras and a security system, both of which I would be checking in the morning, but for tonight, whoever had been sneaking around was gone.

I slammed the window shut, securing the locks securely into place on either side. Charging across the room, I flipped on the light and did a quick sweep just in case. The perp had to have had a reason for breaking in. Did they take something? Were they looking for something? Had they known this room was usually vacant? The easiest way in undetected? Had they been surprised to see Ainsley? Or had she been the target?

If only I'd been able to get my hands on them.

Ainsley sat in the middle of the bed as I finished poking behind the doors. She chewed on her nails, watching with large green eyes.

"Did they say anything?" I asked her flatly.

She didn't respond. Her gaze stayed on the window, just staring.

Shit.

Something about seeing her shaking snapped against my chest. I wanted to hit someone.

Exhaling, I sat on the edge of the bed, facing her. She didn't pull her gaze from the window. It was as if she was in a trance, fixed on the memory of a figure I couldn't see. "Ainsley," I whispered. "Hey, you're okay." I hooked a finger under her chin to get her attention on me.

She flinched. Those huge eyes blinked before landing on my face. "I swear I saw someone." Her lip wouldn't stop trembling.

My thumb brushed over her lower lip. "I believe you, but they're gone now. You don't need to worry." Not entirely true, but that was the kind of shit you said when someone was on the brink of freaking out. I didn't know how else to calm the churning fear in her eyes.

"The window was open, but it was closed before I went to bed. I'm sure of it," she rambled. I could see the confusion in her eyes as she tried to make sense of what happened like it could have somehow been her fault.

People can do irrational things. "You're not the one to blame here. Did he do or say anything to you?"

She shook her head. "How do you know it was a man?"

This was a good sign. Her mind was working again, sharpening. "I don't. Did the figure look like a man?"

"I don't know. I was too scared to pay attention to the stature of their shadow."

"You sure you didn't leave the window unlocked?"

"Positive. I haven't touched the window since I got here. It's too damn cold."

I nodded. "Valid point."

Ainsley wrapped her arms around herself, suddenly looking so small in the bed. She might be a short girl, but her snarky personality made her seem taller than she was. "Is there anywhere safe?" she muttered. The words were spoken so softly, they were said more to herself than a question she was looking for an answer to.

For once, I didn't know if it was my past or hers rearing its ugly head.

If we were weighing the number of skeletons in our closets, then the scale tipped pretty heavily in my favor. Other than her father and where she came from, I wasn't sure Ainsley had any dirty secrets worth exploiting. Not like the Elite did.

"A padded room," I joked.

She blinked at me before the corner of her lips curved up. "You got one of those somewhere in this mansion?"

I shrugged. "It's best you don't know."

A bit of color had come back into her cheeks, which on Ainsley's vampire porcelain skin really showed. "What time is it?" she asked, drawing her knees up to her chest and including them into her self-hug.

I crossed my arms to keep from touching her. "Just past three." I was fucking ramped up now. The itch to climb into one of my cars and take off stirred like a wild wind within me, picking up speed with each passing second. The mattress shifted under my weight as I pushed to stand up, not trusting myself to keep my hands to myself. I had to leave now while I still had the willpower to go.

A hand darted across the bed, clamping on to my arm. "Don't leave."

My gaze sought hers, and I realized I'd broken my only rule not once today but twice. Well, technically, it was a new day and so not off to a good start.

DON'T BE ALONE WITH HER.

It seemed like such a simple rule, and I was damn good at self-discipline except when it came to this girl.

Walk out.

Tell her you can't stay.

Tell her to go sleep with Josie.

That was a solution we could both live with.

Fuck. Why can't I say no?

It was her eyes. They drew me in and did something no girl had done before. Touched the shield I kept around my heart.

Scooting to the head of the bed, I stretched out my legs and opened an arm. "Come here." It came out as a command, firm and raspy.

She angled her head to the side at my tone, eyes narrowing, and that spark of fire was precisely what I hoped for. "Anyone ever tell you that you kind of suck at being the knight in shining armor?" Yet she eased into the crook of my arm, snuggling her head against my chest.

"I'm more likely to be the dragon than the knight," I replied, staring at the ceiling. My mind was in a million places, but I knew she needed me to be here, present with her.

"Thank you for staying. I promise I'll keep my hands to myself."

I glanced down at her and said, "I won't."

She pinched me in the side.

"Hey," I protested. "No touching."

The effort to lighten her worry hadn't worked. A haunting expression clung to her face. "Will he be back?"

I could lie to her, but I didn't see the point. "Not tonight," I said with conviction.

She swallowed. "But tomorrow?"

My fingers went to her hair, slowly toying with the strands. "Depends on if they got what they were looking for, but my guess is they didn't. For now, it doesn't matter. Get some sleep." God knew she'd probably be working herself to death tomorrow. And the day after.

A yawn pulled from her lips as she settled farther against my side, her head sliding onto the pillow. "I've never had a stalker before."

"Fun, right?"

The hand on my chest started to move. light movements, tracing the lines of my tattoos. Her skin was cold. "You guys really know how to live on the edge. I can't wait to go back to school. Everything is normal there. Plus, I won't have to stare at your abs all night."

I chuckled. "Is my chest bothering you?"

Her lips turned down slightly. "You could say that."

"Close your eyes and go to bed, little devil," I ordered. "Problem solved."

"You're so methodical. It's boring."

And she was anything but boring. Vibrant. Tempting. Determined. Alive.

Ainsley had always been one of those girls who could drop off into sleep with little effort. It wasn't long before gentle snores rose and fell from her chest, her body still curled around me. I only planned on staying until she fell asleep. The last thing I needed was to be caught in Ainsley's room by one of my sisters, even with a reasonable explanation.

I dozed off before I could escape, but it seemed as if neither Ainsley nor I would be getting any sleep tonight.

Her soft moans woke me, and I hadn't fully grasped I wasn't in my bed when a small fist hit my chest. Before it could whack me a second time, I grabbed Ainsley's hand. Another moan tumbled from her lips, her head thrashing from side to side. The mumbling turned into protests. Whimpered nos. They grew louder, more forceful, her head twisting back and forth. I wondered what nightmare she was living inside the world of dreams.

"Ainsley," I murmured, my hand moving to her shoulder, jostling her.

She smacked at my hand. "Don't touch me," she cried.

Grabbing her wrists, I pinned her arms over her head, covering her body with mine to quiet the thrashing before she hurt herself.

Or me.

But it didn't seem to be helping. "Ainsley, wake the fuck up," I growled lowly, hoping my voice would penetrate through the haze of fear gripping her.

Her knee hit between my legs, and I groaned, my entire body flinching, and yet I managed to keep a hold of her wrists.

I had two choices. Slap her or kiss her.

I chose the less violent approach, seeing as she'd grown up with violence and it wouldn't have the same impact. I needed to jar her out of the dream.

My lips crushed down over hers.

Her body froze.

Encouraged by her stillness, my lips moved over hers, demanding a response in return. It didn't come immediately, not until every muscle pressed against me relaxed. Then she kissed me.

Her warm lips parted, an invitation I couldn't ignore. My tongue swooped in, and the moment her tongue touched mine, lust slammed into me. Her taste was one I hadn't been able to forget and had taunted me for days; I had wondered why her sweetness differed from other girls and how she drove me nearly as mad from wanting to lick her again.

"Grayson," she whispered against my mouth, the nightmare no longer constraining her.

I gazed down into her face, my fingers holding her wrists loosening. Ainsley stared at me for a long few seconds as if she couldn't figure out if I was real. And then she lifted, closing the distance between our lips again. Her mouth was intoxicating, plump and soft as if designed solely for me, and I kept going back to take more.

A shudder went through her.

I'd only meant to pull her out of the dream, but now I found myself presented with a new problem.

I didn't want to stop what I'd started.

Releasing her arms, I slid the strap of her tank down her shoulder, kissing and nipping flesh as I went. Her head fell back on the pillow.

I nuzzled my leg in between hers, pressing the upper part of my thigh into her core. Her hips ground into me as she bit down on her lip. My dick throbbed at the friction, swelling and hardening more with need.

She arched her back off the bed, and I wrapped my teeth around a nipple straining through the thin fabric of her tank. The material bunched together, hindering what I wanted. It had to go. I needed to see all of her.

With greed and impatience, I rolled onto my back, taking her with me so her legs straddled either side of me. My fingers glided up her spine, shoving the tank up and over her head, and discarded it somewhere on the floor.

She was poised above me, her creamy skin highlighted by the moon's glow, dark hair tumbling over her shoulders and back. It might have been cliché, but my breath caught. She was fucking gorgeous, and a flare of irritation kindled with the fire. Not enough to override the desire I felt, but of all the girls in this world, why did it have to be her?

Why couldn't one of the million other girls out there have the same fluttering impact Ainsley did?

I had to have her.

I had to touch her.

Consequences be damned.

My fingers closed around her hips, holding her on top of me. She placed her fingers on my chest as she gave me a "fuck me" look.

Not yet, my expression replied.

Sitting up, I took her nipple between my lips, sucking and teasing the bud until it was hard. She shoved her fingers into my hair, holding my head against her breast. No matter how much I took, how much of her I tasted, it wasn't enough.

Inside, my control was a thin piece of thread about to snap.

Shoving aside her last piece of clothing, I slid a finger inside her and then a second. Her muscles clenched around me as she rocked her hips against my fingers, sinking down into my hand. "God, you are so wet."

"Grayson," she panted, her head falling back as she rode the fingers I moved in and out.

"Tell me what you want."

A delicious shiver trembled through her as my breath caressed her nipple. "More," she rasped out. "I want more. I want you."

I didn't expect the impact hearing those words would have on me. Desire took over. With steady fingers, she grazed the hem of my waistband. I lost the damn basketball shorts and boxers, shimmying them down far enough for the important part to break free.

Her fingers wrapped around me, the pad of her thumb stroking over the tip. She lifted slightly, guiding me to the opening between her legs. Then she sunk down, and I slipped inside her. I groaned, my eyes closing as her heat surrounded me in a tight cocoon of pleasure.

She urged me to move faster and harder. I was powerless to decline. My body took over, giving Ainsley whatever she asked for.

We moved together seamlessly as if our bodies were well acquainted and needed little guidance on what pleased the other. I might not be able to stop the nightmares when she closed her eyes, but for now, the only thing she thought about was me.

* * *

Spent, we lay sprawled on top of the bed, the sheets a tangled mess at the footboard. "I didn't mean for this to happen again."

Her head turned to the side, facing me. "God, Grayson. Just shut up before you ruin the only good moment between us. You don't have to tell me everything that's on your mind. I can figure it out on my own tomorrow when you go back to scowling at me."

I frowned in the dark, my side of the bed succumbed in shadows. "I don't want there to be any misunderstandings."

Her skin glistened, highlighted by a streak of moonlight cutting across her body. "We had sex. I don't think you're suddenly my boyfriend. I needed you. You were there. It's that simple. Or it can be if you don't complicate it with overthinking it."

In my experience, girls often said one thing but meant the complete opposite. Not Ainsley. She didn't BS and was as straightforward as they come. "Are you always this casual about sex?"

She gave a one-shoulder shrug. "Yes, and no. Depends on the guy, but I meant it when I said I won't be a standby girl. This can't happen again."

"Agreed."

We both knew it was a lie.

Once hadn't been enough. I doubted twice would either, not after I knew what it felt like to be deep inside her, the way she whimpered or sunk her nails into my skin right before she went over the edge.

I was already thinking about how soon I could stick my dick inside her. Was now too soon?

13

AINSLEY

My first thought when I woke up wasn't *oh, my God, I could have been murdered last night.*

No.

It was *holy fuck, I slept with my best friend's brother. Again.*

As much as I'd loved to pretend last night had been a dream, waking tangled up in Grayson popped that blissful bubble quickly.

I broke my one cardinal rule.

I was a shitty friend who couldn't control her impulses. I was self-ish. And only cared about the sins of the flesh. Pleasure could be an addiction, particularly the kind of pleasure Grayson Edwards dished out.

Who knew sunshine could be so mind-blowingly insatiable between the sheets?

I was in trouble.

Big trouble.

If I didn't tread carefully, I might find myself catching feelings for the jerk, and that would be a catastrophe on so many levels. I didn't have time for feelings.

Friends. Period. Just friends.

Grayson and I needed to maintain our friendship. No more fucking. No more kissing. No more knee-weakening orgasms.

An insufferable sigh left my lips as I glanced at the empty spot on the bed beside me. I was partly glad I didn't have to deal with any morning awkwardness and partly sad I couldn't snuggle into his arms. I had no right to feel anything. One way or the other.

Swinging my legs over the bed, I found my tank top from last night on the floor and slipped it over my head. I adjusted the material, my eyes drawn to the window.

Holy crap. How could I have forgotten?

Rooted in place, I stared at a smudge on the window that looked like a handprint. Freaky. It made the horror of last night very real. Then I remembered the text message I'd gotten before going to bed, warning me to stay out of Grayson's room. I looked back at the tangled sheets.

Well, I hadn't ignored the warning.

Grayson had come to my room. I doubted the person behind the message cared much for semantics. Of course, I couldn't leave out the small detail of me running into his room first. What really bothered me was the possibility this person knew details no one should.

How?

Were the texter and the window stalker the same person?

It seemed likely. The idea of having more than one person threatening me bordered absurd. Unless Grayson and I each had our own unhinged fan.

Since staying with the Edwardses, I'd never been more eager to get out of this room.

Good thing I had a lot to do today. Starting with a shower and some clothes.

I stared at the bathroom door, hesitation dancing inside me. I'd never been scared to take a shower before, but now, the idea of locking myself in the bathroom felt like a cage—a trap. What if he came back? What if he waited for me in the bedroom? What if he picked the bathroom lock? It wasn't like these house locks were fail-proof. Any idiot could get in with as something as simple as a butter knife.

Or a sharp as hell knife. The kind you murdered people with.

My overactive brain was so not helping.

I glared at the little lock on the door, unable to decide if I should keep it open or closed. These had never been thoughts or problems I had before. How could one incident in the middle of the night suddenly change my thought pattern on literally everything?

I felt more like a victim last night than I had when my father hit me. Talk about screwed up.

In the end, I left the bathroom door open; that way I could hear any usual sounds and at least have a chance at escape.

The shower turned out to be uneventful and quick, my anxiety making me rush through the motions, taking the pleasure out of something I enjoyed. I took a few extra minutes drying my hair and doing my makeup, hoping the routine would calm my frazzled nerves. The bruise on my cheek lingered but was nearly gone.

Feeling almost like myself, I ran around town, picking up my last few Christmas presents. Not that I had a lot to buy.

The Elmwood Commons bustled with people. Specks of holiday cheer were sprinkled all over the shopping center. Wreaths with a red bow hung on each lamppost. All the storefronts glowed with warmth from lights stringed in the windows. Mechanical Santas waved as reindeer bowed their heads to shoppers passing by. Stands of hot cocoa and roasted nuts were parked at the corners with lines of patrons chatting on the sidewalks as they braced the cold for a treat. Festive classics sang from the speakers, and the light dusting of snow we'd gotten overnight added to the magic of Christmas.

The shopping plaza could have been featured in one of those Hallmark movies. It gave me a sense of nostalgia and loneliness, seeing all the couples holding hands, laughing, and snuggling together while they checked off items on their shopping list. It was a painful reminder I was alone for the holidays.

It wasn't just that I didn't have a boyfriend to share peppermint mochas with. It was also me missing my family, regardless of how damaged we were.

With my bags in tow, I wound through the sidewalks, heading toward the Pizza Shack to meet up with the girls before work. No shocker, I was the last to arrive.

Kenna, Josie, and Mads sat in the back booth, closest to the roaring fireplace in the middle of the dining area. I let the hostess know I found my friends and headed to the table, dropping my bags on the floor as I took the empty seat.

"Holy shit, it's about time," Kenna greeted, her brown eyes flashing over to me with a mixture of playfulness and annoyance that perfectly described her. She was always a bit of both.

"Kenna's stomach is eating itself," Josie informed, rolling her eyes. She had her pink hair in two braids that peeked out from under a dark-gray beanie.

"I skipped breakfast this morning," Kenna explained. Her knitted cream sweater had threads of gold woven into it, complimenting her complexion.

Josie toyed with her straw, swirling the ice in her Coke so it clinked against the glass as she glanced at me. "How is it that you've been living in our house and yet I see less of you than I do in college?"

"Seriously," Mads agreed as she toyed with her gold dangling earrings. "We never go this long without hanging out."

Guilt stabbed me. I'd never had this many friends before, and I struggled to balance work, school, *and* maintain my friendships. "Sorry, as you all know, my life has kind of taken a dive into the dumpster."

"That's not true," Josie argued.

My brows lifted. "Really? How do you figure?"

"You still have us," she retorted with a smug grin.

It's weird to think the first time we'd come here had been when Josie transferred schools, and Mads and I came up with this scheme for her to snag an Elite as protection. Little did any of us know how well that plan would be executed. Now here we were, years later, still friends and me lusting after her brother.

Fuck. My. Life.

Just the mere thought of what Grayson and I had done last night made my cheeks burn.

Our server stopped by to grab my drink order and drop off silverware on the white-and-red-checkered cloth-covered tables. Once he left to get my Coke, Kenna looked at me and asked, "Are you coming to the race tonight?"

This was news to me. "What race?"

Josie beside me shook her head. "This is what happens when you work all the time, and we don't get to hang out. You're out of the loop. Grayson's racing tonight."

"Again? Didn't he just have a race? You know the one that ended in a gun show," I reminded as if any of us could forget. After everything that happened, I wasn't sure I was up for any more *excitement*, but the chances of another shooting were probably slim. Right?

Mads tucked her hair behind her ears, leaning forward in her seat. "There are more meetups during break when everyone is home."

"And I'm sure the shooting was a fluke," Josie added, echoing my thoughts, but it didn't pacify the apprehensiveness floating inside me.

I sunk against the back of my seat. "Is that supposed to make me feel better? Especially after last night?"

Josie's brows drew together. "Last night?"

As I glanced around the table, my friends gazed at me with expectancy and confusion. *Did I just put my foot in my mouth?* "Grayson didn't tell you?"

Our server appeared with my Coke, setting it down in front of me as my three friends shook their heads. He picked up on the sudden tension. "I'll give you a few more minutes to look over the menu," he said, trotting off.

"Oh," I stated when we were alone again.

"Ains," Josie rumbled in her scary voice.

My bracelets clanged together as I reached for my drink, my throat suddenly dry. "I'm sure it was nothing. Besides, Grayson said he would investigate, check out the security today."

Josie's eyes narrowed. "None of this is reassuring me. What happened?"

"Someone broke into my room last night." There. I'd said it.

Kenna blinked from across the table. "What did you just say?"

"Broke in?" Mads echoed. "How?"

I relayed the events of last night, leaving out the less important parts like sleeping with Grayson. The point was the break-in. Not what Grayson and I'd been doing under the sheets.

"Shit," Kenna muttered, running a hand through her soft curls.

Mads looked like she needed a cigarette, a habit she hadn't been able to break yet continued to try.

"I want to believe you're joking. That this is a twisted prank, but it isn't, is it?" Josie asked.

My foot tapped the slightly sticky floor under the table. "If it's a prank, it's not me behind the joke."

"Fuck," Mads swore as she picked up her discarded straw wrapper and started twisting it. "Are you okay?"

I nodded, brushing my hair off my shoulder and out of the way. "Yeah. Nothing happened other than him scaring the shit out of me."

"And you didn't see his face?" Kenna inquired, going into detective mode.

"No. He wore a mask. I think." The details were getting fuzzier as time passed.

Mads gaze panned over the three of us. "What are we going to do?"

I had so many problems on my plate. Did I really need to tackle this one as well? "Grayson said—"

Kenna cut me off before I could finish. "The Elite aren't the only ones who can get shit done." A spark flamed in her eyes.

"We can't sit by and be prey from some asshole with a vendetta," Mads agreed, touching the side of her face. Whether it was a conscious move or not, it was clear she still harbored deep resentment toward the guy who left her scarred.

Josie squeezed Mads's hand across the table. "Never again."

They were right. We weren't helpless. And we'd taken on worse.

Josie leaned over the table, lowering her voice but still loud enough to be heard over the restaurant noise. "The guys are up to something, and if they aren't sharing information, then we need to take matters into our own hands."

"We're just as capable of getting answers," Kenna affirmed.

Mads untucked the side of hair she'd tucked behind her ear only a few minutes ago, shielding her cheek. "Like who this bastard is. And what does he want."

"Maybe it has something to do with the Wolves," I said.

Once again everyone at the table looked perplexed. "The gang?" Kenna asked, brows pinched together.

I shot myself in the foot again, but this time, I didn't care. I'd been keeping too many secrets from my friends. Some had to give. "Yeah. Grayson met with Reno."

Josie studied me like she didn't recognize her best friend. "I guess I know why you haven't been hanging around lately. You've been off gallivanting with my brother."

She had it wrong. So wrong. "It wasn't planned. Trust me."

Our server approached the table, a bubbly smile on his lips. He looked about a year or two younger than us. A senior in high school if I had to guess. We put in an order for three pizzas to split. Once we were alone again, Mads asked, "What was he doing there?"

"I promised I wouldn't say anything," I replied although I had every intention of telling them. I had to at least make it look like I tried to resist, regardless of how weak that effort might be.

Josie's eyes pierced mine. "Ains."

"Fine," I conceded as if she'd twisted my arm. "But you guys didn't hear shit from me. They hired the Wolves to search into Sterling's disappearance. They don't think he's dead."

"Son of a bitch," Kenna hissed.

Mads paled at the mention of Sterling's name, and I regretted bringing him up. The last thing I wanted to do was cause her any pain, including those difficult memories she wanted to forget.

Josie's phone vibrated on the table. She gave it a quick glance before ignoring the text. "I'd like to say I'm surprised. But I'm not. I knew something was going on. I just hadn't expected this."

"Brock hasn't said anything to you?" Kenna asked her.

My best friend shook her head. "No."

I wasn't sure any of us actually believed Sterling was gone for good, but the more time that went by without a stitch of proof he was still alive, the easier it became to believe the bastard burned in that building.

Kenna tipped back in her chair. "How did you end up tagging along to this meeting with Reno?"

"Funny story," I said, making light of the situation. "And trust me, your brother was pissed I was there."

"When isn't he pissed?" Kenna grumbled.

True. "I came home after my shift, and Grayson was leaving. Didn't think anything of it until I saw that he had a gun. So, I followed him."

Mads rolled her eyes. "Totally makes sense. Exactly what I would do if I noticed someone had a gun on them. Follow them."

My lips formed a straight line. "I never said I acted rational."

Josie leaned forward on the table. "It doesn't matter. If she hadn't, we wouldn't have this information."

"And what do we plan to *do* with this information?" Mads queried.

Josie tapped her thumb on the table as she contemplated our options for a moment. "Nothing, right now. But if Sterling isn't dead, we all need to be careful. He could be the one who tried to break in last night."

If there was any chance Sterling was involved, we deserved to know. Especially Mads.

"The guys will kill him this time. They'll make sure he stays dead," Kenna stated.

An ominous cloud hung in the air over the table. Our server, having a knack for showing up at the tensest moments, arrived with our pizzas. Shifting aside drinks and condiments, he set down the round pans, filling the table with scents of tangy herb tomato sauce and freshly baked dough. I hadn't been hungry before, but when I saw the cheesy temptation in front of me, my stomach started to growl. Other than coffee, I hadn't had any real sustenance, and my body let me know.

Kenna dug into the Margherita, taking a slice onto her plate, cheese oozing off to the side. "So, you're coming tonight, right?"

Ugh. The race. After the conversation about Sterling and the break-in, I'd completely forgotten about Grayson's race tonight. I scooped up a slice of veggie. "I'm supposed to work."

Mads jumped in after taking a bite of her pizza. "It's one night. Don't you deserve a night off? Especially after everything that's happened."

"I don't know if I'm up for a race," I admitted, wiping a drop of sauce from the corner of my mouth.

"There will be hot guys." Kenna dangled the idea like I was starved and staring outside the window of a bakery with no money.

The last thing I was thinking about was a hookup. I'd had plenty of that already during break. Not that any of them knew that.

"It's best if we stick together. Protect each other. Plus, there's a party afterward," Josie said.

Coming home after work to a house without Kenna, Josie, and Grayson suddenly sounded very unappealing. Who knew how long they would be out tonight; I definitely didn't want to be alone. "Okay. I'll see if I can get out of the diner early."

Somehow between the four of us, we managed to polish off all three pizzas. I overate and left the restaurant feeling like a balloon about to burst, but I did feel less burdened after unloading on my friends and knowing we had each other's back.

Was I still freaked about last night?

Yes.

But at least I felt slightly more prepared. The asshole wouldn't blindside me again. I knew he was out there. I'd be expecting him to strike again.

I just hadn't expected it to be so damn soon.

Two steps from the diner, my phone buzzed. A sinking dread took hold of my heart and pissed me off. My phone used to be a thing of joy. Now the notification of a text sent a ribbon of panic unfurling within me. I should ignore the message, but what if it was my mom? Or Josie?

I couldn't avoid my phone. Not indefinitely.

Pulling out the slim device from my bag, I read the preview without unlocking the screen.

Stay home or die.

Creative as fuck.

In one text they were threatening me if I didn't leave, and in the next message, I had to stay home. *Make up your mind, motherfucker.*

Not that I would listen.

Unless my stalker planned to pay for my bills and food for the next semester, I had to work. Or perhaps it was the race tonight they were warning me away from.

I shoved my phone deep inside my back pocket and walked into the diner.

14

AINSLEY

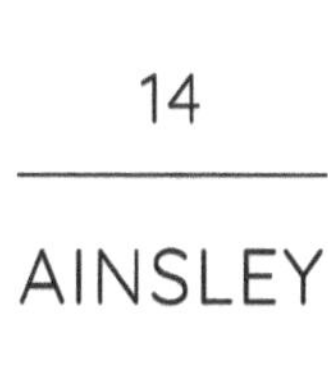

Three hours into my shift, the little bell hanging over the diner door jingled. The thing had been going off every few minutes for the last hour—our dinner rush. Compared to the more popular chain restaurants, this wasn't considered much of a rush, but for the diner, the place was packed. I didn't look up to see who wandered in from out of the cold. My order was up for table thirteen. Besides, Bea would greet them and take care of the seating.

After I set down the plates for the couple at thirteen, I headed back to the kitchen and noticed table eight in my section had new occupants. I went to take their drink orders on my way to the kitchen.

Three heads gathered, engaging in what looked like gossip, friends who hadn't seen each other for a while catching up. They were slow to glance up when I stopped at their table as if I interrupted something. Perhaps I had.

"Can I get you guys a drink?" I offered in a voice as pleasant as I could muster.

"Ainsley?"

I glanced at the blonde with coppery eyes, a nagging familiarity tugging at my memory. I wasn't wearing my name tag tonight, yet she knew my name. Had we met before? But where?

Regardless, girls like these didn't come all the way from upper Elmwood to dine at Pa's Place.

I wracked my memory, trying to place who this girl was. Just based on her friends and the way she held herself, the connection had to be the Elite.

Kate. I'm pretty sure that was her name. The girl who had a thing for Brock in high school. I remembered Josie talking about her and how she had run into her at KU. It was so long ago, but at the time, Josie had been worried this girl might try to start trouble between Brock and her. As far as I knew, that hadn't happened. We'd all been too busy dealing with Sterling and worrying about Mads.

Was it a coincidence she showed up with her friends at the place I worked?

I didn't think so.

"What do you want?" I asked, cutting the bullshit. I didn't want to play games. Petty girls could be dangerous. The put-together polished look and the perfectly made-up face didn't fool me. Someone didn't need a gun or a knife to be a threat. I'd gone to school with my fair share of bullies and mean girls. This little clique screamed all the makings of bullies.

Kate's glossy lips curled. "I haven't looked at the menu yet."

"You know that's not what I meant. Why are you here? If you're looking for Brock or any of the other guys, they aren't here."

"I should hope not," she sneered, leaning her chin onto the heel of her palm. "This isn't the kind of establishment the Elite chooses to hang out." Her clueless friends giggled.

I shifted my weight to one foot. "Which still poses the question as to why the three of you are?"

"Curiosity," Kate said smugly.

I crossed my arms. "About?"

Her eyes glanced over me, doing nothing to hide the judgment from her expression as her lips soured. "I've seen all I needed to.

Come on, girls, I'm suddenly not hungry anymore." She scooted out of the booth, her minions following her lead.

I didn't have time for this, not with tables full and people waiting for their food, but it didn't stop me from stepping in front of Kate. She had at least two inches on me, yet I somehow managed to get us nose to nose. "I better not see you in here again." Girls like Kate didn't scare me, not like the guy who had hovered in my window last night.

Her lips twitched. "You don't have to worry. This place is as special as you." It was meant as an insult.

A flashback of seeing my best friend after she'd been beaten by a trio of Academy bitches flickered through my head. It hadn't been Kate who hurt Josie, but it might as well have been, and from the day I saw Josie battered, I'd been waiting for an opportunity to put my hands on one of them. Didn't matter which bitch. "I'm not above kicking your ass."

"You should try learning to fight without getting your hands dirty." She flipped her hair over her shoulder and left.

My fingers itched to reach out and grab her by those golden locks. Something about Kate got under my skin and rubbed me the wrong way. It had been less than a five-minute interaction. I couldn't imagine what I might have done if it had been longer.

By the time I got back to the Edwardses's, showered off the stain of grease from my hair, and reapplied my makeup, I'd completely forgotten about my encounter with Kate. I looked forward to a night of fun. A night to leave behind my problems.

Kenna, Fynn, Josie, and I rode in Brock's SUV to the Devil's Drop, a local stretch of road full of sudden twists and turns, but what made the Devil's Drop the highest accident spot in Elmwood was the bridge connecting the cliffs, Burnout Bridge. If a driver lost control of his car and hit the guardrails, depending on conditions and speed, there was a good chance he would go over the edge, the car tumbling into the icy river below. It was likely the fall killed the passengers, but if they managed to survive, the river took them.

Like what happened to Sawyer, Grayson's brother. He had lost control of his car on Burnout Bridge, spun into the railing, and gone over. I remembered reading about his death in the paper, but then it had little impact on my life, other than thinking he was too young to die.

It still bewildered me how much Grayson enjoyed the thrill of racing, a high he seemed to constantly chase.

"Is this a good idea?" I asked as we pulled into a parking lot stuffed with cars. I couldn't be the only one worried about Grayson driving tonight.

Fynn sat on one side of me in the back seat and Kenna on my other. His long legs touched the back of the seat in front of him, knees creeping into my personal space, but I didn't mind. Fynn Dupree had a comforting presence about him, a less scary persona than Brock, but that wasn't to say Fynn wasn't dangerous. He gave off big brother vibes. Fynn glanced out the window, looking up at the night sky. Only a sliver of moonlight cast through the darkness. "The roads are clear. If there's ever a night to race, tonight's an optimal night."

The parking lot was like a damn car show when we pulled in, boasting some of the most expensive rides in the country, but it wasn't just the make and models that gave them a hefty price tag. It was also what was under the hood, the aftermarket parts, the flashy paint jobs, the booming stereos, and the tires and rims for starters. Some of these cars cost more than my college tuition, and my brain couldn't fathom why anyone would spend so much money on a hobby.

One of the reasons Grayson and I would never work.

I didn't understand him. The need for escape I could relate to but not the frivolous spending.

Brock rolled his SUV next to Micah's parked Hummer. The cars were all sporadically arranged around the lot. Some on an angle. Some bumper to bumper. Others in a row. It was chaos but in the best possible party way. People were already drinking, sitting on lawn chairs or on the trunk of cars. Others stood, laughing and talking, in numerous groups.

Josie's other dad, Ethan, would geek out at an event like this. He was a mechanic who had a love for all things cars. Basically, everything I learned about maintaining my Honda had been from what Ethan taught me.

I might have had a little girl crush on him when I was thirteen.

I stepped out of Brock's Range Rover. Music from a variety of genres blasted from one end of the lot to the other. My hoodie and fitted leather jacket cut away a chunk of the bitter wind, but when the air was still, it was a rather lovely December evening. Huddled between the SUV and the Hummer helped protect against the breeze, creating a barrier. A few cars down, someone had brought a tin portable campfire. Grayson was here somewhere, but among the sea of people, I couldn't find him.

Brock pulled Josie into his arms, offering the warmth of his body.

Athletic fields and nature trails surrounded the parking lot. They were maintained by the Elmwood Park District, but no one minded the closed-after-dusk signs placed throughout the park.

While we waited for the race to begin, coolers of booze rolled out from the trunks, and for the next hour, we sat around drinking and laughing. I paced my alcohol consumption, keeping it to two drinks per hour, and yet my bladder couldn't be controlled.

"I need to pee," I announced, setting my beer on the ground.

"Me too," Kenna said and pushed off the Hummer.

I shot her a grateful smile. The idea of going alone made me leery, thanks to the recent threats. During work, I'd been too busy to dwell on the text I received prior to work, but now that I was here, the warning came back to me.

"You okay?" Kenna asked, noticing my silence. "You've been... quiet all night."

It wasn't like me to have nothing to say, and I'd only had two beers. Again, out of the ordinary. "Yeah. Just working through some shit."

"Is it about what happened the other night?"

"Partially. My life suddenly feels like it's spinning out of my control." Why was I unloading my problems onto Kenna of all people? Perhaps because she was here and inquired as if she truly cared. She listened. And most of all, because she'd been through shit herself and came out on the other side not completely fucked up. "The path I'd been on and been so sure of has derailed."

"I know you have a lot going on, but I've never seen anyone work as hard as you do for what you want. And there is no way anyone will stand in your way."

We weaved between the cars, making our way to the edge of the parking lot. "You have no idea how much I needed to hear that."

Her shoulder bumped mine. "It's why I'm here. To set you straight."

I rolled my eyes. "More like to be a pain in my ass."

Kenna grinned. "That too." Some idiot whistled as we walked by. "So, what's up with you and my brother?" she asked.

I coughed, the night's air in my lungs suddenly colder than it had been a second ago. "What do you mean?"

"Okay," she said, shaking her head. "We can keep pretending nothing is going on."

"Nothing *is* going on," I insisted. Nothing worth repeating, that was.

"Uh-huh," she said, pursing her lips. "She'll figure it out eventually."

She meant Josie. The thing was, I still hadn't figured it out.

We reached the bathroom, and I was relieved to see there wasn't a line wrapping around the building. Girls' bathrooms were notorious for being busy. Now that I thought about it, there weren't a ton of females here. Most were girlfriends tagging along to spend time with their guys. A few were here for genuine interest in the sport. A least one had paid the entrance fee to race.

The overhead light at the girl's side of the bathroom was out. My boots crunched on fragments of broken glass scattered on the ground near the lamppost's base. Kenna followed me into the bathroom where three other girls were cramped around the small mirror hanging on the wall.

As far as public bathrooms went, this wasn't the worst, but it didn't matter how much perfume, body spray, or hair products were misted in this room. It couldn't cover up the stench of piss and dampness clinging to the air.

"Kenna?" one of the girls said, surprise lacing her tone.

"Oh my God. It is you," another girl added.

The hugs happened next. They were old cheer friends from the Academy back when Kenna had been on the squad. I went to a free stall, leaving Kenna to catch up with old friends. When I came out, they were still talking and laughing. Not wanting to interrupt the reunion, I washed my hands quickly and stepped outside to wait for her. I wasn't much in the mood to fake pleasantries with girls I didn't know. Nor cared to know really.

I inhaled a breath of crisp air, cleaning the musty stench and smorgasbord of perfume from my nostrils. Headlights and neon under glow lit up the parking lot in a rainbow of colors. Engines revved in the distance as six cars got into position, the wind carrying traces of exhaust and oil, smelling a hell of a lot better than the bathroom. The race was about to begin.

I glanced over the vehicles, looking for Grayson. It was hard to tell from where I stood. Their windows were all tinted, blocking the drivers from view, but when I spotted the yellow Lamborghini, I knew who was behind the wheel.

My eyes stuck to the car, an acorn of worry winding into my stomach. I'd never cared what Grayson did before, never worried about him, but suddenly, I didn't want him to race. What if something happened? What if he went off the road? What if he was injured? Or fucking worse?

I took a step forward, about to do something utterly insane like get in the car with him, until someone called my name.

"Ainsley."

I whipped my head over my shoulder toward where I thought the voice came from. "Hello," I called out, walking toward the side of the building. Alarm bells should be blaring off in my head, but as I peeked around the corner into the dark, there was no one there. No one I could see.

Fuck this.

I turned to face forward again, and something hit me.

Correction. Someone.

Before I could catch my breath or comprehend what the hell happened, I slammed into the brick building. My face smashed into the rough surface, scratching my cheeks. A groan of protest and pain expelled from my lips on impact, jarring my senses. For a few harrowing seconds, I was too stunned to do anything. My brain stopped functioning until a voice whispered in my ear.

"You should have stayed home, but then I wouldn't be able to have any fun. Perhaps I should thank you." His arm dug into the back of my neck, keeping my face pressed into the wall. His other one grabbed my wrist, twisting and securing it around my back.

I bucked, trying pathetically to dislodge him. It was pointless. The asshole was too damn strong. With my free hand, I attempted to scratch him and failed, looking like a fish flopping on the ground. "Let me go!" I screamed before his arm pushed harder against the back of my neck. My discomfort kicked up several notches causing my fear to spike.

"Shut up, you little slut," he whispered in my ear, his breath hot on my skin, yet I shuddered, revulsion churning my stomach.

Despite being on the side of the building, only steps away from dozens of cars and people filling the parking lot, I felt alone, isolated, and in deep shit.

Would Kenna come out of the bathroom and look for me? Did I want her to? We might both be in trouble. I didn't know what this asshole was capable of or how far he was willing to go to scare me. Hopefully, Kenna would assume I'd gone back to our crew; at least then when she found I wasn't there, she wouldn't be alone in her search.

From the corner of my eye, I got a glimpse of him, but it wasn't much as his face was concealed under a black ski mask, and it was dark as shit. I remembered the broken light and wondered if he had smashed it on purpose.

"What do you want?" I rasped, my lips hardly able to move against the bricks.

"I was hired to send a message, but I'm thinking a girl like you might need a little more encouragement to keep from spreading your legs for guys above your station." His knuckles ran down the side of my cheek as he pressed the hard length of his body into me.

I gagged in the back of my throat at the implications of his methods. I'd obviously pissed someone off by sleeping with the wrong guy, but the only person I'd slept with in months was Grayson.

Was this about him?

It's not like he had a crazy ex-girlfriend. He didn't do relationships. Had he spurned a vindictive bitch at college? If so, why take it out on me? Why not hurt Grayson?

Or was I a means to hurt him?

The joke was on the mastermind behind this plot. Grayson didn't care about me like that. Not as fervently as Brock or Micah loved Josie and Mads. They would have killed anyone for looking at them the wrong way.

Grayson and I were friends who had stumbled their way into friends with benefits.

That was all.

I wasn't a threat.

"You're wrong. Hurting me won't hurt Grayson," I said hoarsely, taking a stab that this was about him. If my assailant didn't let up soon on the pressure against my neck, my air passage would dwindle. Already my panic made it difficult for me to stay calm.

If his goal was to kill me, he had a good start. The fear clutching my chest was almost enough to stop my heart.

He must have sensed my struggle and eased up slightly, but he still didn't give me enough room to break free. "Perhaps not. But we've come this far. What's the harm in seeing the job through? I'm being paid after all."

Should I scream?

How much worse could it get?

Much worse it turned out.

I screamed, but it was cut off quickly as my attacker spun me around, slapping his hand over my mouth. We were face-to-face, my lungs gasping for gulps of air behind his hand.

Wildness shone in his eyes the only part of his face I could see other than his lips. "Scream again and I'll do more than scare you." He waited for a beat to make sure his threat registered.

Of course, I did the most stupid thing possible when he removed his hand. I spit in his face.

The bastard hit me. Not a slap like my father had done. This was a full-on punch to the gut. Air became impossible to take in. Every last ounce of it was sucked right out of me from the force of his fist planting into my stomach.

I swear I blacked out from the pain for a few seconds. Maybe longer.

Wheezing, I doubled over, dying to fall to the ground, but he grabbed my arm, shoving me against the wall. "Feisty little bitch." A cruel grin curled on his lips. His fingers dove into my hair, yanking my head back with a control and force he seemed to enjoy. I would bet my safety this asshole craved dominance, but when the mask was off, he was just another pussy who couldn't get a girl to look twice at him. "Be a bad girl, and make this exciting for me." His tongue licked down my cheek.

Another shiver went through me, cold and brimming with despair. This couldn't be my life. How had I gotten here? Alone. Threatened. Scared shitless. And...angry. Really angry.

"Who hired you?" I asked, my voice shaking. I didn't expect him to give me the truth. Their identity wouldn't be easy to uncover, but I had to try. If only to stall for as long as possible.

His chuckle was like a blade being dragged across my chest. "If you want a name, you're going to need to leave Elmwood. My client wants you gone. Not just from *his* house, from his life."

It was good to want things.

I wanted this asshole to burn in hell. Only time would tell whose wish was granted.

Engines revved from the parking lot, and the noise from the crowd grew. The race was about to start.

"I'll make this quick," he murmured near my ear, teeth scraping against my lobe. Wedging his knee between my legs, he trapped me with his hard, muscular body as his fingers went under my sweater.

It was one thing to scare me or even hurt me. Quite another to rape me. He wouldn't, would he?

That doubt bloomed when he slammed his lips down on mine in a bruising kiss I fought against with all that I had. My hands beat against his chest, but the only good it did was waste my energy.

I had to fight. The alternative wasn't an option. As long as I still had a pulse, I would fight.

The fucker bit my lip. Hard. Pain sliced through my bottom lip right before the tangy taste of blood hit my tongue. What was this freak? A wannabe vampire?

Fire blazed in his eyes, but through the violence was something frightening. Enjoyment. The more I fought, the more it got him hard. Merciless hands pawed at me, squeezing and pinching. If I survived this, if he left me alive, my body would be battered and bruised. "If you can spread your legs for him, surely my dick is just as good."

I turned my head from side to side, avoiding his mouth again. His fingers went for the button on my jeans and then the zipper.

No. No. No.

This can't be happening.

Everything inside me went dark. My body went numb.

Being poor hadn't broken me.

My father hadn't broken me.

But this prick, he might just destroy me. If he succeeded, if I didn't find the strength to fight back and escape, he might do what many had tried and truly break me.

A bright light flashed through the darkness, blinding me for a few seconds as it bounced over the field. *Fuck, am I about to pass out? Is that what the light is?* I had to hold on. I couldn't let go now. The idea of what he might do to my body while I was unconscious made me want to throw up the beer I'd drunk.

Spots danced in front of my eyes, the world becoming nothing but a buzz in my ears. The back of my head hit the building, and then all hell broke loose.

Suddenly my attacker was gone, his violent and rough hands no longer on my body, bruising and tormenting me. I slumped against the cold bricks, my legs barely holding me up. A part of me wanted to crumble to the ground.

The unmistakable crunch of fists meeting flesh and bone resounded through the darkness. Shadows moved in quick succession. I tried to follow their movements and distinguish their faces, but my vision had gone blurry.

I should be running. This was my chance to get away, to scream for help, yet I didn't move. Perhaps I already knew help had arrived and sensed the danger was over.

Thud.

Jerking, I was pretty sure that was the sound of a body hitting the ground. But whose body? My worst fear was it wasn't my assailant's and the attack would start all over again. How much would I regret not running then? An icy sweat broke out over my skin.

A head turned toward me, and I caught a glimpse of a familiar face. His expression was terrifyingly full of cold rage.

Grayson.

15

GRAYSON

I caught her before Ainsley fell to the ground. Her lip bled. Her clothes and hair were a mess. And the wild fear in her eyes broke something inside me. Ainsley had always been a force to be reckoned with, but right now, she looked more fragile than I had ever seen before.

The sight of her made me want to put my hands around the asshole's neck and squeeze until not an ounce of life remained. Being knocked out unconscious wasn't enough. Not for someone like him. Not for what he'd planned.

If I'd been a minute later...

The overwhelming urge to kill the bastard barreled into me.

"Grayson," Ainsley whispered my name and blinked as if she didn't believe I was real.

"You're safe now," I assured her, but her expression showed she didn't trust me. I tried to soften my tone and warm the ice in my eyes, but it was hard when the fire for violence hadn't been extinguished. "Come on, let's get you out of here." I kept my arm around her, guiding her to my car, but we had to bypass the body lying on the ground.

Leaning into me, her small fingers clutched tightly to the front of my hoodie. She halted and stared down at her attacker. The headlights from my car provided a little light off to the side. My gaze followed hers. I'd ripped the mask off his head, and blood oozed from his mangled face. He was damn lucky all I had done was beat the living shit out of him.

I had no idea what was going on inside her head as she glared at him, but I imagined her thoughts ran as dark as mine. Surprising us both, she straightened and kicked him in the gut. His lifeless body gave a little jerk from the force.

Blinking at her, I rubbed at the back of my neck, the muscles in my body still coiled tight. "Feel better?"

She shook her head. "No." Her response came out feeble and shaky. Ainsley's hands balled into fists at her side, her expression an emotional storm. A soft cry of pain and frustration left her lips as she hauled her leg back and kicked him again and again and again. The chest. The shoulder. The groin. A pathetic moan escaped the prick after the fourth kick.

I grabbed her from behind, picking her up off her feet before she hurt herself more. "You done?" I whispered.

A shudder rolled through her, strands of dark honey hair falling over her face. "No. Not by a long shot." A long breath expelled from her chest.

I understood her fury and the desire to inflict pain on the person who hurt her. Those same feelings vibrated within me, and it took every cell of self-control I possessed to think about Ainsley instead of killing the bastard. "He won't get away with this. You have my word."

She nodded.

"Good. Now get in the car," I ordered, keeping an eye on the body. I needed him to stay out cold for at least another few minutes.

As she turned away, I noticed something on the side of his neck. A tattoo. A distinctive tattoo. It was a wolf's paw print.

Son of a bitch. He's a Wolf.

Why would Reno want anything to do with Ainsley? Was it

because she was with me at our last sit-down? It didn't feel right. Reno did many shady things, but roughing up a girl under our protection... He wouldn't have crossed that line unless he wanted a fight.

With long strides, I went to the passenger side of the Lambo. Ainsley had the door open and carefully climbed in just when I reached her. I waited until she was seated before closing the door and walking to the other side. My door was still open from when I had rammed the car into a dead stop, the engine idling in a deep purr.

I got behind the wheel and hit the gas, the tires spitting up frosted grass and dirt. The car fishtailed, and I hit the pedal harder, steering into the curve that pulled at the wheels until the tires caught on the pavement and lurched forward.

My knuckles covered in *his* blood gripped the steering wheel. He'd managed to get in one solid punch, but after that, I'd let loose. I might not have stopped if it hadn't been for the small gasp from Ainsley. Such a scant sound, yet it had penetrated through the haze of fury just enough for me to grapple for control.

I had a million questions running rampant through my head, but I sensed now wasn't the time to press her. When I gave her a sidelong glance, she had her arms wrapped around herself, tucked against the seat in a ball. I grabbed my phone sitting in the cupholder and dialed Brock. He picked up on the second ring, and I wondered if he'd been waiting for my call.

"We have a problem," I stated the second he answered.

His voice came through the speaker. "Other than you forfeiting the race?"

I steered the car with one hand, speeding down the twisty road. Perhaps too fast. Easing my foot off the gas slightly, I wanted to get her far away from that place, but it was equally as important I get Ainsley home safely. "I didn't have a choice," I groused.

"I was about to call you. Have you seen Ainsley? Kenna lost—"

"She's with me," I cut in before he could finish and snuck a glance at her. She continued to stare out the side window, eyes unfocused, no doubt lost in fresh memories that would haunt her for a lifetime.

"What's going on, Gray?" Brock picked up on the tension and that it had something to do with his girlfriend's best friend.

"I'll explain later. Tell Josie I'm taking her home. Right now, I need help cleaning up a mess," I explained, my jaw taut.

"Where?" No questions. No hesitation. That was what it meant to be an Elite and have friends who always had your back. The questions would come later after the deed was dealt with.

"I left him unconscious on the side of the girls' bathroom."

"Micah and Fynn will take care of it," Brock assured. From the other side of the phone, I could hear movement and knew Micah and Fynn were already on their way.

"I'll see you back at my place." I ended the call.

Not even a mile down the road, her body started to shake, the aftershock of what happened finally catching up to her. Her fingers fidgeted with her rings, and I could see how hard she tried to keep her shit together.

I didn't know what to do or say, so I remained silent, leaving the choice in her hands. For once in my life, the silence killed me. Normally, I preferred solitude, the quiet. I loved the rumble of a car engine drowning out all other noise including the crap that lived in my head.

Not Ainsley.

She was a talker.

Sometimes when we were together as a group, I wondered if she ever shut up.

Tonight was the first time since we'd known each other I'd ever heard her be so subdued. It worried me.

Her nails were pressing into her thighs as I pulled up the driveway and slid the Lambo into park. I was out of the car before Ainsley could undo her seat belt. When I opened her door, she turned in my direction and blinked, a glimmer of disorientation clouding the centers of her eyes. I held out a hand. She stared at my fingers and sucked on her bottom lip, deciding whether it was safe to touch me or not.

I took a step back, not wanting to crowd her, and as I did, her hand reached for mine. Our fingers touched. Her lips quivered.

"I got you," I whispered. I had many things I wanted to say, the top being how sorry I was. I didn't know the details of what happened yet, but I couldn't shake the feeling this was somehow *my* fault. Ainsley had been attacked to send *me* a message.

But what exactly was the message here?

Tears pooled in her green eyes. Unable to stop myself, I pulled her into my arms and gently held her. I didn't want to be forceful but someone for her to lean on. I wanted to be solid and dependable. If she fell. I would catch her.

Ainsley's head buried into my chest while uncontrollable sobs shook her body. Every bone in her shivered against me. The pain went so deep, beyond what happened tonight, her breathing came out choppy. And the unchecked tears finally fell. She'd held it in, held it together the entire drive home, but it had taken one small gesture from me to unleash the dam.

I had sisters. You'd think I would be used to tears. But somehow, seeing Ainsley like this, nearly on the verge of brokenness, hit me differently.

She was so damn small in my arms. Smaller than usual.

My fingers brushed over her hair as she soaked my hoodie with gut-wrenching tears. Her fingers fisted into the material of my sweatshirt. I could do nothing but stand outside, shielding her from the bristling wind, and let her purge herself.

"Don't let go," she whispered, her throat sounding gravelly and raw, muffled against my chest.

My arms tightened around her in response.

I don't know how long we stayed like that. I just knew it was for as long as she needed. When the shudders slowly subsided, she sniffled and lifted her head. "Thank you," she said, eyes bright and shining from the moisture starting to dry. Her fingers continued to cling to my clothes.

Her cheeks were damp and pale. I brushed at the streaks on her face carefully with the pad of my thumb. "You don't need to thank me." The truth was, I hadn't done enough. Ainsley coming to stay with us had been for safety, and yet since she'd been under our roof, she'd been in more danger than at home.

"You saved me. I don't know what..." Her voice hitched as she shook her head, denying what could have possibly happened.

I wanted to stop those terrible thoughts. I could beat the fuck out of her attacker, but the one thing I couldn't do was control her mind. "Are you hurt? Do you want me to carry you?" She needed to get inside, warm up, and change her clothes.

Ainsley stared into my eyes. They shone under the starlight, still glittering with tears, but underneath the pain and sadness, I caught a flicker of fortitude. He'd tried to destroy her, but he'd failed.

Her chin lifted, and she shook her head. "I can walk."

Something in my chest swelled. Pride? Admiration? Respect? This girl had been attacked and very nearly violated. For many girls, this would have shattered them, and when I had found Ainsley, I'd seen defeat in her. But now...a grain of anger and all her other emotions burned. That fire, no matter how small, would save her.

Silence greeted us as we slipped into the house through the kitchen. The light above the sink Elise always left on glowed like a beacon. My parents were asleep in their room.

Once we were upstairs, I sat her on my bed and turned on the lamp, chasing the darkness from the room. The dim light was soft enough to be comforting and still allowed me to see her. Ainsley might insist she was fine, but I needed to check for myself.

I held her chin in my grasp, scowling at the cut on her lip. It wasn't deep, but it made no difference to me. She'd been hurt.

The bastard shouldn't be breathing.

My face tightened, the frown on my lips carving deeper.

"Is he dead?" she asked, eyes cast downward at her hands.

I shook my head and released her chin. "No." Did she want me to kill him? Because I could do that. I could go back and finish what I didn't get to finish. Nothing would please me more. By now, Micah and Fynn would have found him, and the interrogation would begin. I sent Brock a quick text.

He attacked Ainsley.

That was all Brock needed to know to handle the rest. The details would come later when we were all together, and hopefully, some of the pieces would start to fit.

I set my phone on the nightstand and pulled my hoodie over my head, tossing it on the chair nestled into the corner.

A heavy sigh lifted Ainsley's chest before deflating it in a long exhale. "How did you know?"

Fucking sheer luck. But I didn't think that's what she wanted to hear, that one simple change and things could have ended very differently for her tonight. "It doesn't matter." The truth was, I'd caught a flash of something from the corner of my headlights as the race began. Instinct had me taking a second, longer look. I hadn't known at first when I whipped my car off the road that it was Ainsley, not until I got closer and a beam of my headlights hit her face.

That was a sight branded in my memory.

"I want to kill him," she whispered.

I sat on the bed beside her, but she still didn't look at me. "Get in line."

She finally glanced up. "I haven't thanked you yet."

"I don't want your gratitude," I said, my teeth gritted together to hold back the fury still churning within me. I didn't want to direct it at her, but it was difficult to contain.

"Thank you," she said, holding my gaze.

I couldn't look away. My hand lifted to touch her, and she flinched. I hated the guy who put fear into basic gestures. I'd never had a girl afraid of me without cause. "What do you need?" I asked gruffly, uncertain what I could do for her.

"A shower," she replied plainly. "And could you burn these clothes? I never want to see them again."

"Consider it done."

She stood and immediately groaned, clutching her stomach. "Son of a bitch," she hissed.

"Take your shirt off," I demanded, not thinking about how that might sound. It had nothing to do with sex. She was in pain, and I had to know how serious it was.

"I'm fine," she insisted.

I got to my feet, straightening to my full height, and lifted a brow, daring her to test me. She might hate me if I ripped that sweater off her body, but I wasn't above doing so, even after what she'd been through, if it meant making sure she didn't need to go to the hospital.

With a huff, she grabbed the hem of her sweater and yanked it up over her head with a jerky, annoyed movement. An irritated Ainsley I could handle. It was the tears that flustered me and the defeat that undid me.

Under the faint bedside lamp, my eyes examined her torso. The redness around her belly, just above her belly button might not appear to be severe, but that wasn't the point. "He fucking hit you," I growled, the muscles along my jaw hardening.

Her fingers slid into the back pocket of her black jeans as she shifted most of her weight to one foot. "I said I'm fine." I recognized the firm press of her lips and the infliction that entered her voice. She didn't want to talk about it, and I didn't want to make her cry again, so I didn't press the matter.

Without another word about it, I walked to the bathroom. She followed a moment later.

Moving into the shower, I turned the knob to hot, adjusting the temperature until it was just right. I went under the sink and grabbed a fresh towel, thanks to Elise. "I'll get you some clean clothes. Just leave the others on the floor, and I'll get rid of them for you."

Why did she look so small standing near the door, chewing on her nail?

As I went to leave, her hand reached for mine, lacing our fingers. I knew the minor feat took effort. "Will you stay?" she murmured, her eyes lifting to mine, and took her bottom lip between her teeth, waiting for my response.

I could do better than just staying. It didn't take long for steam to rise and fill the room. I reached for her hand, pulling her slowly into the walk-in shower still dressed.

"What are you doing?"

"Showering," I stated, stepping farther under the water, fully soaking myself.

She didn't resist and stood under the waterfall with me. "I think you missed a step."

Wet clothes didn't matter. "It can wait." The blood on my knuckles washed down the drain.

Ainsley's eyes closed, and she tipped her head back, letting the water rush over her face. I gave her a moment, and when she opened her eyes, I reached for the shampoo.

"You don't have to do this," she said.

I shrugged, my white shirt plastering to my chest. "When do I ever do something I don't want to? Just relax for once in your life, and let someone take care of you."

Black streaks of mascara began to run from her eyes, the water washing away her makeup. "I never thought that person would be you."

Squeezing a glob of shampoo into my hand, I combed my fingers through her hair, lathering her long locks. "Me neither. Not all guys are assholes."

Her fingers took over, and she dipped her head back, rinsing out the foaming suds. "Maybe not. But I still think you're an asshole most days."

My lips twitched.

As I looked down at her, it occurred to me we were having another first. Why did this girl break all my rules? And why did I never realize it until after the fact?

I'd never *just* showered with a girl before. I'd kick them out after I'd gotten what I needed. Ainsley wasn't wrong. I was an asshole.

Her arms came around me, the water raining down on top of us. "Just not today," she muttered.

Now was not the ideal time for my dick to get hard. Sex shouldn't be on my mind at all, but seeing Ainsley's clothes suctioned to her curves was a sight I couldn't ignore. My body responded to her.

I didn't bring my arms around her but kept them at my side. If I touched her now, I wouldn't let her go, and despite how suddenly tired I might be, my night wasn't over.

"You're going to have to cut me out of these jeans," she said, pulling back and glancing down at herself.

My eyes followed. She wanted me to undress her. *God, give me strength.* Really, this shouldn't be a big deal. I'd seen numerous girls naked and not felt a damn thing. Fuck, I'd seen Ainsley naked. Nothing new. I could control my dick.

"I hadn't really thought this through," I admitted.

It took some effort, considering how tight her jeans were. Stripping Ainsley of her wet clothes and leaving on just her undergarments, I lathered up a washcloth. With gentle strokes, I washed her body, taking extra care of her belly, barely letting the cloth touch the skin I knew would be a massive bruise in the morning.

This girl and her poor body had been through so much in a short amount of time. No person should be put through the pain she'd endured—would continue to endure.

I wrapped her in a towel before peeling off my jeans and T-shirt. I gathered the pile of drenched attire and tossed them back into the shower to dry out some. As Ainsley slipped off her bra and underwear, I padded into my room to toss on dry clothes and grab her one of my clean shirts. When I returned, she had dried herself off, damp hair curling slightly and framing her face. I took the shirt and tugged it over her head. She slipped her arms into the sleeves and let the towel fall.

I grabbed two pain relievers from the drawer and handed them to her with a glass of water from the sink. She tossed them back. I could see her mind was still working, relieving detailed moments despite trying hard to pretend she was okay and wouldn't fall apart.

I tucked her into my bed.

"Do you know who he is?" she asked mildly, her damp hair fanning out on the white pillow.

My gaze met hers, and I schooled my face to remain expressionless. "Not yet. But we'll find out. You don't need to worry about him. I won't let him hurt you." *Not again*, I silently added.

Fuck, I needed a drink. Something strong.

She had the blankets pulled up to her chin looking half her age. As I turned to shut off the light, a tender hand wrapped around my wrist. I glanced back at Ainsley.

"Don't leave," she whispered, blinking up at me with tormented eyes.

The sleeping agent I'd given her inside the pain reliever would help a little for tonight, but until then, I'd stay. "Do you want the light off?" I asked.

She shook her head, her delicate fingers still encircled above my hand.

I climbed into the bed alongside her, slipping a hand under the pillow. Ainsley snuggled up against me, resting her head in the crook of my shoulder. She fit so perfectly in my arms as if her head was meant to rest there. The scent of my shampoo and body wash clung to her, producing a possessive streak I didn't want inside me.

This girl wasn't mine.

I didn't want her to be mine.

And yet...

I couldn't stop myself from wondering what it would be like if she were.

Clear danger signs. I was getting too damn attached to this girl.

It had to stop. I wasn't going to be the one who crossed the line. We'd agreed to keep things casual. No strings, which should have been simple for me. No attachments were how I lived my life.

Her hand lay over my heart, and I turned my face toward her, my lips brushing over strands of wet hair.

Perhaps it was time I end this.

It would keep her safe. Keep us both safe.

Ainsley drifted off into sleep maybe fifteen minutes before the commotion downstairs alerted me of my friends' arrival. Untangling myself, I crept out of the room and carefully left the door slightly ajar. I wanted to be able to hear her if she woke up.

Pitch-black darkness greeted me in the hallway, the mumbles and footsteps below growing closer. I caught Josie at the base of the stairs. The worry etched into her features deepened when she saw me.

"Where is she? What happened? Is she hurt? Why didn't she call me?" The questions rapid-fired one after another all in a single breath.

I didn't know which to answer first. "She's in my room sleeping."

Kenna and Mads came around the corner after Josie. "Why is she in your room?" Josie asked as if I'd done something wrong.

My hand rested on the banister. "She didn't want to be alone."

"I'll stay with her," she said. "You can take my room for the night."

I wanted to argue. The refusal surprised me, how quickly it rose within me, but I stopped myself. It wasn't my place. I had no claim. Ainsley and I weren't in a relationship, and if I demanded to sleep in the same bed as her, Josie would ask more questions. Questions I didn't want to answer. "She's shaken up and a little bruised."

Josie nodded, her color paling slightly. She took off up the stairs, Mads following behind her, to check on Ainsley. I was glad they would look after her and she wouldn't be alone.

Kenna hung back for a moment. "Is she okay?"

I studied my sister. "Yeah. I got there before it got worse."

The tightness in her shoulders loosened.

Kenna knew firsthand how worse it could get, and I recognized the shadows in her eyes. "It's not your fault."

A haunting look stirred in her eyes as she moved onto the first step. "Maybe not, but I still feel like shit."

This asshole had attacked one of us, but what he didn't factor in was the trickle-down effect it would have. Not just on Ainsley but all of us. When one of us hurt...we all hurt, especially the girls. They related to each other. The pain. The trauma. The scars. We all had them, and nights like tonight dredged up those old wounds, no matter how healed they might be.

I found the guys in the basement, each with a bottle of beer. Micah handed me one as I dropped down onto the couch next to him. He looked far less relaxed than usual, his deep-blond hair messy and eyes a bit bloodshot. "What did you find out?" I asked, getting straight to business.

Micah's fist opened and closed, tension still vibrating through his body. The knuckles on both his hands were in worse shape than mine. "The bastard's a Wolf," he seethed.

Fynn leaned forward, elbows braced on his knees, and pressed his hand to his temple. "It doesn't make sense. Why would Reno hurt one of our girls?"

Brock frowned, his beer bottle perched on his thigh. "I don't think it was Reno."

My brows furrowed. "He took a side job? Still, Reno would have to approve it."

"Unless he didn't," Brock speculated, doubt shadowing his features.

None of it made sense. If the order didn't come from Reno, then who? "You think he went rogue?" I guessed, following the line of his thought.

"Only one way to find out," Brock said, his voice cold and devoid of emotion.

Fynn swirled the last bit of beer in his bottle. "It's against Wolf law. If he took this job without Reno's knowledge, Reno will be pissed."

"Not as furious as I am at the moment." I put the bottle to my lips and tipped back my head. "Did you get his name?"

"Slade," Micah spat as if the name disgusted him.

I was with him. Fury flurried like a storm in my gut. The masked fucker had a name.

"He refused to give up the identity of who was paying him," Fynn added, only feeding my anger.

Micah shook his head, reaching for another beer from the case on the coffee table. "The bastard laughed."

"He's lucky to be alive," Fynn grumbled.

"If we want to find out who hired him, we need the jackass alive. He'll lead us to them eventually. Fynn made sure of it," Brock added.

I noticed Fynn had blood on his off-white shirt, and since I didn't see any cuts on him, I assumed it was Slade's. "I'm tracking his every move. Digitally and literally," Fynn said.

God, I loved Fynn, that fucking genius. I knew how much his family pushed for him to have a career in football, but I couldn't help feeling as if he was wasting his other talents.

Micah tossed the beer cap back into the cardboard case. "Is anyone else thinking Sterling could be behind this?"

Dread twinged in my chest. The only thing worse than him not being dead was the deranged jackass screwing with our girls. Again.

"We'd be stupid not to consider him. After the holidays, we'll pay Reno a visit. Kill two birds with one stone," Brock said.

Christmas Eve was in a day, and whether Ainsley liked it or not, I wouldn't be leaving her unprotected again. Not until we uncovered the true name behind the threats.

16

AINSLEY

Streaks of sunlight peeked through the curtains the next time I opened my eyes, and for a split second before reality hit me, I snuggled deeper into the bed, Grayson's scent surrounding me like a warm hug.

I rolled over expecting to see him.

It wasn't Grayson lying in the bed beside me.

It was Josie, and when I saw her face, the memories of last night crashed into me, stealing my breath. The aches came next. I winced at the pain lancing through the upper part of my gut, right below the ribs. My fingers lightly prodded the area.

Josie's eyes fluttered open, and her deep-brown gaze found mine. "Hey," she greeted softly.

I'd woken up beside Josie a thousand times before. From sleepovers to drunk nights to escaping my house in the middle of the night. She was home to me, and hearing her voice, even a single word, brought a rush of emotions.

"Hey," I replied, tucking my hands under the side of my face, the one with the almost gone bruise.

She brushed a strand of hair off my cheek. "You okay?"

"I am now." Having my best friend with me installed an instant sense of comfort. For her sake, as well as mine, I made my lips curve.

Josie saw through it, her expression remaining somber. "You scared me."

"Me too."

"I can't lose you, Ains," she said, her brows serious.

I didn't want to admit she nearly had, or how close I'd come to losing myself. "You'll never lose me. You're stuck with me for life. Brock better get used to sharing."

She snorted. "I can handle him."

A moment of silence lapsed between us, neither of us knowing what to say, but it wasn't uncomfortable. It never was with Josie. Being in her presence, I didn't feel as if I had to put on a show. I was often considered a battery sucker as far as personalities go. If that was the case, Josie was my battery recharger. Her energy calmed me.

"If you need to talk, cry, or scream, I'm here," she said softly.

"I know." She was always there for me. Through the good or the bad. I didn't want to imagine my life without her. She brought me into this world of wealth and power, allowing me to have opportunities that seemed so out of reach to me before. "I think I'm going to leave. Go back to school."

Was I running away?"

Yes.

But I didn't care. I had to get away from all of this, whatever it was, and pray to God it didn't follow me to school.

Was I giving in and giving the bastard what they wanted?

Again, yes.

It was clear this had something to do with me staying at Grayson's house. The closer I got to him, the more danger it seemed to put me in. Who's to say those around me wouldn't suffer next?

"Are you sure that's a good idea?" Josie asked, her lips turning down in not quite a frown, but it was enough to know she didn't like the idea.

"Honestly, I'm not sure of anything. I know we said we'd stay together, but I need to go. There's nothing for me here. Except you, of course," I added with an obvious eye roll. At school, I had so much waiting for me. And I missed it.

The classes. The people. The parties. The routine. My dorm.

No one was trying to kill me there.

It felt safer somehow. Whether that was actually true remained to be seen. I didn't want whatever bad juju to follow me back to KU.

"At least stay through the holiday," Josie pleaded. "And if you still want to leave, I'll help you pack."

I could see how much she wanted me to stay, and disappointing her wasn't in me, not when I felt vulnerable and glum. "Fine. But not a day longer. I'm leaving the day after Christmas." I'd stayed too long with the Edwardses as it was.

Despite it being only a little over two weeks, I'd managed to tangle myself up with Grayson. It was time for me to unravel this thing between us before my heart got involved. Already I was too close to falling for him. What I needed was a clean break to find my footing again.

I'd be fine without him.

And I'd be fine after him.

It will still hurt, a voice in my head warned.

I ignored the pesky voice.

"How about I make us some breakfast? Pancakes?" Josie offered, a cheeriness encroaching into her tone.

My smile was genuine. Perhaps not as bright as it would have normally been at the mention of my favorite breakfast, but it was a start. "When have I ever turned down pancakes?"

She sat up, and I realized for the first time that Josie was still in her clothes from last night. She'd slept in them, which told me how worried she'd been about me. "Strawberries and blueberries with whipped cream?"

"Is there any other way to eat pancakes?"

"I'll start the coffee." Scooting off the bed, she padded across the room. She hovered in the doorway a moment, turning back to face me. "They will find out who is responsible," she said, a solemness on her features.

They being the Elite. Perhaps I should have gone to the authorities and reported the incident, but the fact it never occurred to me until now was a telling sign. Much like where I'd grown up, the Elite had the mentality of never involving the police if it could be helped. They took care of shit themselves.

Did the Elite think they were above the law?

Sometimes. Okay, more often than not.

It still wasn't too late for me to report the attack to the authorities, but even as the thought crossed my mind, I knew I wouldn't.

On the off chance the cops did track down the asshole who assaulted me, he could very well drop the names of Brock, Grayson, Fynn, and Micah.

Alone, I sat in the middle of the bed, staring at Grayson's room. There were little reminders of last night strewn everywhere I looked. The hoodie he tossed on the chair. The towels discarded on the bathroom floor. The water glass on the nightstand next to a white bottle of pills.

Panic sprouted in my chest, spreading like a weed about to coil and suffocate me. I fucking hated weeds.

And apparently, I've developed a phobia of being alone. I didn't know if the thoughts in my head scared me more or the idea that, at any moment, a masked man might appear from behind the curtains.

My heart picked up, thumping harder in my chest as I scanned the room, sunlight streaking over the floors. I dug my nails into the mattress. Those shadows I was concerned about—one of them lurked in the doorway.

My hand flew over my mouth, suppressing the scream rising in my throat. Grayson leaned in the doorway, a cup of coffee I desperately hoped was mine in his hand. "You scared the shit out of me."

His lips twitched, but the flash of humor wasn't enough to rid him of the worry in his eyes. "I noticed."

The anxiety spreading within me receded as if Grayson's presence was a flashlight shining light on the dark corners of my mind. "Did Josie send you?"

In a pair of sweatpants and a white tee, he moved into the room, coming toward the bed. "Fuel," he said, offering me the cup of coffee. "A shot of espresso and a shit ton of steamed milk."

"Thank you," I replied, taking the mug. I brought the cup to my lips and blew on the steam. The smell alone was enough to banish the lingering remnants of sleep. "You left," I said after an awkward moment of us staring at each other.

"Josie was worried about you."

I had this feeling Grayson knew I wouldn't want to be alone this morning. The coffee warmed my hands. "Did you find anything out?" I didn't want to ask the hard questions and wasn't sure if I was ready for the answers, but I didn't know what else to say. I suddenly felt so weird around him.

It might have something to do with Grayson seeing me at my lowest, most vulnerable state. I didn't let people see that side of me. Only Josie. And I wasn't sure I liked it.

Grayson would use it against me. If I'd been anyone else but his sister's best friend, he wouldn't have thought twice about locking it up in the Elite's virtual little black book.

Grayson's jaw tightened. "You don't need to worry about him."

Until I got the next text.

Should I tell him I'm leaving? That this has been fun while it lasted?

"Do you want me to stay?" he asked.

Yes! My response screamed inside me.

Swallowing, I shook my head. "I'll be down in a few minutes." If I was going to leave, I had to stop depending on him. I had to stand on my own.

He lingered, and I thought he might stay regardless of what I said, but he left.

I took my coffee and got out of bed. Inside the bathroom, I leaned against the closed door and took a long breath. I turned my head to the side and stared at my reflection. The girl gazing back at me was someone I didn't recognize. Physically, I looked the same. It was inside that had changed, and I could see it in my eyes, feel it in my heart.

This was why I had to go. I had to get away from all the shit stalking me. I needed distance from Grayson. And not just a few steps down the hall. I needed miles put between me and that brooding face, those deep, knowing eyes, and that glorious body.

After washing my face and sipping on my coffee, I contemplated putting on my makeup. In a way, it was like warrior paint, making me feel tough and confident. What I needed to learn was it didn't matter how I looked or dressed. I was fierce, bold, and courageous regardless.

My chin lifted as my phone buzzed on the counter.

It was like being swept away by the tide. The small amount of self-assurance I had restored vanished with a simple text.

Don't look. Don't read the messages. Just turn off your phone, go downstairs, and have breakfast with your friends.

I picked up my phone.

I warned you. You should have stayed home last night.

The expected feelings didn't consume me, at least not prominently. The fear was there, but anger took center stage. I was furious. The cold in my blood from yesterday burned like lava in my veins. I was sick of being afraid—of feeling weak—of losing myself.

I hurled my phone into the sink, hoping it would crack. The device clattered into the ceramic squared bowl. Destroying my phone wouldn't fix my life, but at least I wouldn't have to read any more deranged threats.

I also wouldn't know when something might be coming.

"Fuck," I said under my breath, my fingers gripping the edge of the sink as I stared at myself in the mirror. *I'll be fine.*

* * *

On Christmas Eve, I planned to meet with Mom for brunch since I wouldn't be spending the holiday at home, and she had to work Christmas Day. Then later that evening, the Edwardses were hosting a party.

With my mom's gift in hand, I walked through the house. Every room I swore had a beautifully decorated tree or some kind of Christmas decor. All the banisters were strewn with frosted garland. The house smelled of pine and mulled cider. Despite it being cold and frosty outside with a chance of snow in the forecast, the inside exuded nothing but warmth.

I declined Grayson's offer to come with me. His presence would create questions I didn't want to answer. And what would be the point? I didn't want Mom to be confused by Grayson not being my boyfriend.

It was better all around if I went alone.

This was the start of me gaining back my life and telling my fears to fuck off. I liked people. I liked going out. I liked partying.

Hiding inside or behind the Elite wasn't the life I wanted to live. I had places to go. People to see. And a career to build. No one would stop me from living my dream.

I left as everyone got things ready for the party tonight. It was a small gathering, but small didn't mean simple. I didn't know if Liana knew how to throw anything other than a posh party. Most of the food was catered. The house had been professionally decorated weeks before.

The drive to Lakeside Brunch was hectic and took longer than usual thanks to the last-minute crowd trying to buy the Christmas gifts they procrastinated weeks getting. Not that I had room to complain. I was usually one of those procrastinators.

I got to Lakeside Brunch before Mom. The memories this place held for the two of us put me in a chokehold. Whenever my father had been on a binger when I was little, she would get me out of the house, and we would come here. Afterward, we would go to the toy store or the bookstore, mostly to waste time, but I hadn't realized then what she was doing.

Dodging the thick snowflakes beginning to fall from the sky, I went inside the restaurant to get a table. I was able to secure a booth by the stone hearth in the main dining area. The wood crackled, flames licking over the logs. I stared out the window, watching the snow pepper the ground before melting away and listening to the bustling of the restaurant.

"Ainsley." Mom's soft voice had me turning around, a smile appearing on my lips. I tried to hide the wince as a sliver of pain went through my lip. Smiling was not a good idea; the cut under a layer of dark lipstick was still tender. Hopefully, she didn't notice. The last thing I wanted to do was talk about the attack. Staying with the Edwardses was supposed to have been the safer option. I wasn't sure anymore if that was true.

"Merry Christmas, Mom," I said, scooting out of the booth to give her a hug.

She felt so small in my arms. Our frames were similar, but she had lost weight, and the guilt I could be the cause nipped at my heart.

"I've missed you." She gave me a tight squeeze before pulling back to look at my face. "Are you eating enough? Sleeping?"

"I'm fine," I lied, not wanting to worry her.

She saw through my lie, the light in her eyes dimming a fraction, but she didn't press me. We slid into the booth, getting out of the aisle. Mom cast a glance at the entranceway before facing me with a smile. "Tell me, what have you been up to? I can hardly believe it's already Christmas."

I took the pitcher of water that was on the table and poured us a glass as she slid off her coat. As usual, I hadn't worn one. "I've been working at Pa's Place most of the time." I intentionally failed to mention anything about the texts, the stalker in my window, or the attack at the race. She had enough to deal with at home with my father. It had become a habit to shield Mom from my problems. I hated the stress she already put herself under.

"I'm sorry, honey. I wish there was more I could give you."

"Mom, I'm fine. You don't have to be concerned about my finances. I got a scholarship, remember? Everything's okay."

Fidgeting with her plain gold wedding band, she spun it in circles around her finger.

Why did she seem nervous or like something was bothering her?

I started to worry. "Are you okay?" I asked.

The smile on her lips slowly faded. "You haven't changed your mind? Your father—"

I cut her off right at the mention of my father. "I'm going back to school after the holiday," I informed her, praying she would leave it. No matter how much my mom wished for me to be at home, I wasn't ready to see my father, and I sure as shit didn't want to hear her excuses for him. As if my father really gave a damn about me.

Her hand reached for mine on the table. "Ainsley, if you just—"

I sensed someone behind me, a shadow, and I assumed our server arrived at the table. Glancing up, my entire world fell out from underneath me as I stared into eyes so similar to mine.

All the sounds and chatter in the restaurant faded to nothing but white noise as I continued to gape, a sense of disbelief numbing my body.

I shook my head. "No." The word was a whisper of doubt, but it didn't last long, the stirrings of anger igniting in my gut. They spread through me, a swoop of fire that mimicked the flame in the hearth.

Glaring at my father, I curled my fingers into fists, nails digging into my palms. My gaze whirled across the table. "What's he doing here?"

Mom shrunk back into the booth. "He came to apologize. You have no idea how sorry he has been these last weeks. He wants a chance at forgiveness."

She is fucking kidding, right?

This was a bad dream. A messed-up Christmas prank. Surely, she didn't expect me to sit here over eggs and bacon and forgive the man who'd done nothing but hurt me one way or another most of my life.

"Stop," I said, my hand coming down on the table, rattling forks, spoons, and glasses. "Just stop."

Numerous times she pleaded my father's remorse, assuring me how sorry he was or that he promised it would never happen again.

Lies. They were all lies. The same bullshit song and dance.

I just wanted Mom to see it.

I couldn't believe she sprung this on me. Today was supposed to be about her and me. It was Christmas Eve. A time for cheer and giving. The only thing I wanted to give was my father a black eye.

Betrayal stung like a bitch. It hurt so much more when the disloyalty came from someone you loved. A part of me knew how hard Mom tried to keep this family together, all the sacrifices she made in staying with him, but those had been her choices. Not mine.

All I asked her was to respect my decisions.

It caused me pain to accept that, for reasons beyond what I could fathom, she loved my father. But I did. I gave up trying to convince her happiness existed outside of him.

"Ainsley, if you just—"

Before he could say anything else or had a chance to sit down, I was up and out of the booth. "Fuck this." I didn't need this. Not today. He was the last person I wanted to see.

Screw Christmas Eve.

Dealing with my father when I had so much other shit going on might send me over the edge. I couldn't. I was out of here.

A hand wrapped around my wrist. "Don't talk to your mother like that."

The familiarity of his touch and the pressure sent me into a tailspin. I yanked my arm. "I wasn't. I was talking to you," I said, raising my voice.

I didn't give a flying fuck if I made a scene. Nobody in this restaurant mattered to me. No one but Mom.

Casting a glance at her in the booth, I could see how much she wanted her family together, but what she failed to *see* was I didn't. We both had pain fracturing in our eyes. "I don't want his apology,

Mom. I wanted to spend the day with *you*." Tears stung the backs of my eyes.

Not giving a shit about the people who stared at me or the scene I'd created, I flew out of the restaurant, storming across the parking lot. I took shelter inside my car, fury heating my blood and hurt thumping against my chest. A thin layer of snow covered my windows, making it feel like I was huddled inside an igloo.

The scream ripped from deep in my gut. My hands beat against the steering wheel as the surge of unbridled emotion tore through me. I released it all, letting go.

17

GRAYSON

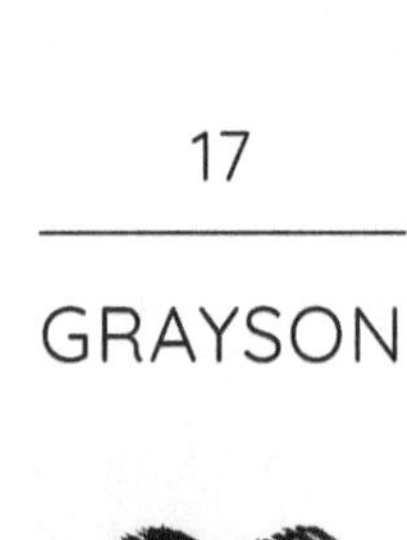

Hauling a box of liquor down into our basement, I started stocking the bar, filling up our fridge with beer, and replenishing the hard liquor bottles.

I had wavering feelings about having a party this year. It might be a welcomed distraction, or it could turn out to be a disastrous opportunity.

Regardless, letting Ainsley leave this morning had been difficult, and my mind wandered in her direction too often over the last hour.

Despite Fynn tailing her, I worried. He was to stay out of sight while keeping an eye on her. It was less complicated if she didn't know.

I checked my phone before grabbing a case of Coke to unload. No news was good news, I told myself.

As I put the last few cans into the fridge, someone trotted down the stairs. Josie appeared a few moments later and walked to the bar. We hadn't talked much since the race. Yesterday after breakfast, I'd left, leaving Josie with Ainsley, and as much as I wanted Ainsley in my bed last night, she'd slept in Josie's room.

I'd realized something in the middle of the night when I couldn't sleep.

Somewhere over the last week, I developed this urge to protect her. If she wasn't with me, wasn't within line of vision, then she wasn't safe. At least, those were the signals my brain was sending.

It had to stop. *I* had to stop stressing over this girl. A girl I had no intention of dating. I hated admitting how turned up inside she made me feel, and for so long, I blamed it on her being Josie's friend. Now I wasn't so certain that was the only reason.

"Hasn't anyone ever told you that if you keep frowning like that it will be permanent?" Josie asked, plopping onto one of the high back stools.

My eyes left the bottle of vodka I'd been staring at and lifted to her face. For a second, I'd been so lost in my thoughts I'd forgotten she was there. "Only you a million times."

She grinned. "And I was right, wasn't I?"

If I wasn't already scowling, I'd scowl. "Funny. Do you need something, or are you just here to annoy me?"

Her hair fell in loose waves over her shoulders. "Both," she replied, leaning her chin on her hand. "I didn't get a chance to thank you for the other night."

I tossed the cardboard box into a pile with the others. "What are you talking about?"

"Saving Ainsley," she stated.

"I don't need you to thank me for giving an asshole what he deserves." I wanted to brush off the incident. For starters, because I didn't feel like talking about it, and secondly, I didn't want Josie to see my stepping in as anything other than helping a friend.

"Still, she's my best friend. And I'm worried about her."

"We'll figure out who hired him."

She leaned on the bar. "I know. And it's not just that. It's every-thing. She's strong, but even the strongest people break."

"Why are you telling me this?" I asked as if I didn't give a shit because that's how I would normally react. The difference now was how confused I felt. I hated feeling mixed up inside. My life needed to be orderly, neat, and tidy.

Nothing about Ainsley was neat and tidy.

She was a damn rainbow of storms and had more or less tornadoed her way into my life.

Josie rolled her eyes. "Just try to not be a dick to her tonight. I want her to have fun."

If she only knew. It was better she didn't, or we'd be having a very different discussion. "I'm not a dick to her."

Josie lifted her brows. "You're a dick to everyone."

"Don't you have something to do other than lecture me about my personality faults?"

She reached across the bar, grabbing a bottle of bourbon. This girl and her Jim Beam. "Of course, I do, but I like your scowling face. It makes me feel better." She unscrewed the top and took a swig.

Now it was my turn to arch a brow. "Pre-loading?" Pre-loading was basically starting the party before it began. Josie wasn't normally one to get wasted before the guests arrived. That was Ainsley's MO. "What's bothering you?"

"My brother."

"Bullshit."

She shrugged, taking another drink before passing me the opened bottle. "It feels like I've gone back two years. All the secrets. The crazy shit."

Drinking before noon. I was game. I took a swig, the room-temperature liquor going down smoothly. I wanted to tell her she knew what she was getting herself into by dating Brock, but I held my tongue knowing that wasn't what she wanted to hear. "You ever think maybe it's better to not know everything?"

She took the bottle and put it to her lips. "As usual, your words of wisdom are unparalleled."

I snorted, snatching the bottle out of her hands before she took it with her. Josie drunk wouldn't help Ainsley. "Go annoy Kenna."

Josie shot me a mischievous smirk. "I already irritated her. She caught me in her closet."

Kenna didn't like people in her space, not even us. "And you're still alive? Impressive."

"She threw a can of spray paint at me."

I laughed. My first smile of the day, I realized. "Wish I would have seen that. What did you toss back?" I knew them so well. Josie wouldn't let that shit fly any more than Kenna would.

Josie grinned, jumping off the stool. "I caught the can and hurled it back at her."

Shaking my head, I watched her leave, heading back upstairs to cause more trouble. Hopefully, Mom would assign her some chores to keep her out of the liquor before the party started.

Shit.

That little brat.

She'd snuck off with the bourbon.

I took out my phone and shot Brock a text. He needed to get his ass over here and take care of his girl.

Josie didn't come right out and say it, but she hurt inside for her friend.

Gathering up the recyclable boxes, I took them upstairs and into the garage to discard. I finished breaking down the last of them when a car came flying up the driveway. Ainsley's Accord. I leaned against the open garage door, waiting for her, but she didn't get out of the car right away.

Through the falling snow that kicked up over the last hour, I watched her drop her head against the steering wheel. I thought about going over and knocking on her window, but I figured perhaps it was better to give her a few moments to collect herself.

It was difficult to tell, but when she did get out of the car, I was pretty damn sure she'd been crying. Her makeup was smeared. Eyes puffy and red. Lips pulled into a tight line.

She went straight for the side door, and I went after her.

I caught the door before it closed, slipping inside. Preoccupied,

Ainsley didn't notice me until I stopped her. I reached out, latching on to the back of her arm. She jumped before whirling to face me.

"Grayson," she hissed, the alarm in her eyes fading. "I'm not in the fucking mood."

"And neither am I. We need to talk." I stepped in front of her, pulling her down the hallway. For reasons I didn't want to unpack, I couldn't let her go off on her own, not until I found out what was wrong.

"Grayson," she growled my name, trying to detach my fingers from her arm.

I wasn't budging. "Move your ass, or I'll move it for you," I tossed over my shoulder, shooting her a warning glare.

She stopped resisting, going from zero to a hundred in a split second, dragging me down the hall. "Is this what you want?"

I yanked her into the first room. As soon as I closed the door, I whirled and pressed her against it, all gentleness gone from me.

She was in a mood. She wanted a fight. Someone she could take out all her frustrations on. Whatever happened with her mom hadn't gone well.

"What's wrong?" I demanded, my fingers gripping her chin and lifting her face.

Her chest heaved as she glared up at me, eyes blazing green like poisonous venom. "None of your damn business, sunshine."

"Did you get a threat? Did someone hurt you?" I snarled, softening my fingers.

Pain sliced in her eyes, a different kind of agony than one caused by fear. This one cut deeper. An old wound perhaps reopened. "Not in the way you think. Now let me go," she spat, shoving at my chest.

I did no such thing. Instead, I took possession of her lips.

It was a quick kiss meant to redirect her frustrations. I wanted her to know she could use me. I offered myself to do as she liked if it helped.

God knows I'd used plenty of girls in my days.

I released her lips as swiftly as I took them and stared into her stormy eyes. "Better?"

Her eyes filled with angry tears. "You can't kiss me and expect everything to be fine. It doesn't work like that."

"Maybe not, but I find that it helps."

She snorted, lifting her chin. "Sex. Your answer is sex."

I dragged my hands down the sides of her body, landing on her hips. "Don't knock it until you try it, little devil."

Her sigh came from deep within her, but the fire in her eyes had shrunk. "I'm having a shit day. Okay? Can we leave it at that?"

"Fine." My voice softened, and I gentled my touch, tracing lazy swipes with the pad of my thumb right above her waistband. "For now." Our bodies flushed, and I was keenly aware of every part of Ainsley.

I should back off, but I didn't move, except for the finger I hooked inside her jeans. My gaze flicked to her lips as my tongue traced over my mouth, tasting the sweetness of her lip gloss. The soft intake of her breath had my eyes returning to hers. The green in her irises was smoky.

"Fuck it," she murmured right before she sealed her lips firmly to mine, kissing me with all her frustration, anger, and fear she'd pent up over the last few weeks.

I didn't hesitate.

I claimed her.

My thumb went under her chin, keeping her mouth angled just the way I wanted. Her tongue brushed against mine, and my pulse went from stirring to a full sprint.

You're mine. I own you.

The words were a vow in my head, and what surprised me more was I actually wanted to say them to her.

Her fingers glided up the back of my neck diving into my hair, and I crushed her body against the door. A soft moan escaped her mouth. I reached behind her and flipped the lock on the door.

She might be feeling a confused swirl of emotions. We all had our issues, but for a few minutes, I could make her forget them. I could make her feel something other than hurt, betrayal, rage, and fear.

"Grayson," she whispered. Raw desire darkened her eyes, and I'd never seen anyone so beautiful.

"Say it again," I demanded, my lips cruising along the side of her jaw, up to her ear. My breath danced over her skin, and she shivered in my arms. The good kind of shudder, brought on by passion and need.

A knowing smile curved over her lips full of female empowerment. Her realizing she had any sort of power over me had not been something I planned to reveal, but it was too late now. "You like it when I say your name?"

I chuckled. "I like a lot of things."

She ground against my cock. "Grayson," she said breathily.

I grabbed her ass, lifting her against me as her legs hitched around me, and I covered my mouth with hers. She provoked a maelstrom of sensations, and she expected intensity from me. Things between us struck like a moth to a flame. Once the spark ignited, it burst into a roaring fire of need. Then it became a frenzy of tongues, hands, teeth, and emotions spurred by lust.

That was one thing neither of us lacked.

We desired each other.

Now might not be the appropriate time to flip the script. She needed stability in her life, and I probably would have stuck to my rules if she hadn't thrown me off balance with that damn wicked smirk. It knocked me on my ass for a second.

I returned the favor.

Despite every inch of me screaming at me to take her now, I softened the kiss, turning it into something tender and meaningful perhaps.

It was only after that I questioned what I'd done.

At the moment, it felt...right.

She felt right.

Red flags all around, but I ignored them.

With Ainsley's legs wrapped around me, I walked us into the room to the couch and sat down, her straddling either side of me. The softness between her legs pressed down onto the hardness throbbing in my pants.

"What was that?" she asked, looking at me with dazzling dazed eyes.

"A kiss," I replied, my fingers moving from the back pocket of her jeans to the hem of her shirt.

Her head angled to the side as she studied my face and toyed with the back of her lip ring. "You've never kissed me like that."

I'd never kissed anyone like that, but she didn't need to know that little tidbit of information. It was safer with me.

My fingers drifted under her shirt, splaying over her spine. "It's just a kiss," I murmured, making light of it and redirecting her focus, my fingers skating up her sides. The knitted material of her sweater bunched with my movements, and I brushed my thumbs over her nipple. On the second swipe back, they pebbled through her lacy bra, and she closed her eyes again, savoring the torment I created.

The teasing touches soon were not enough for either of us. Her chest rose, the fullness of her breasts seeking more. With a quick yank, I had the sweater gone, discarded somewhere on the couch, and leaving her nipples nearly directly in line with my mouth was a temptation I couldn't suppress.

Through the thin fabric of lace, I took her nipple between my teeth, and her head fell back, a husky purr vibrating in her throat. The sound had my dick pulsing.

Fuck me, I want to be inside her.

Ainsley wasn't what I would call a selfish lover. She loved to be on equal ground. Not just in her daily life but in the intimate parts as well. Her hand slipped into my sweatpants, wrapping around my length. With slow strokes, she moved, exploring the smooth texture.

I groaned, my head falling to the back of the couch. Everything swelled, my body warming. Her tongue flicked over the throbbing vein in my neck while her fingers continued to test my control. Another minute or two, and I'd lose myself in her hand.

No other girl made me feel this level of excitement. "My turn," I growled against her ear, nipping at the space just below her lobe.

Urgency taking over, I fumbled with the clasp on her jeans, popping it through the hole before working the zipper down. My fingers dipped inside her underwear. She pressed against my hand, seeking more friction, more pleasure.

My lips curved right before I thrust a finger inside her.

Ainsley gasped. "Please, Grayson," she begged, her hips grinding against my finger.

God, why does the sound of my name leave me so damn breathless?

"Take off your pants," I ordered, shoving at my sweatpants.

She shimmied one leg out of her jeans and panties, not bothering with the other. With my hands on her hips, I guided her slightly up on her knees, not that Ainsley needed much guidance.

She sunk down onto me, more than ready, and our eyes locked. My hands stayed at her hips, guiding her movements. I went deeper the second time, and her eyes drifted shut.

Goddamn it. She was so wet. So tight.

I kissed her, taking my sweet time and tangling our tongues. Her nails raked down my back, her body gleaming as her hips rolled and moved with mine.

"Grayson!" she cried, her core spasming as pleasure rocked through her body. I fell after her, my orgasm pumping into her, and I questioned my sanity.

My lungs emptied, and I collapsed against the couch. "Holy shit," I murmured, my fingers running up her thighs.

Her hands dropped to my chest, a look of pure satisfaction glimmering on her features. She never looked more beautiful than at this moment. "You have a library?" she breathed, her voice wispy and uneven.

Of all the things I expected her to say after screaming my name, this hadn't been it. My lips twitched anyway. "Yeah, but no one comes in here."

"Why? I never want to leave." She untangled herself from me, dropping onto the couch and panning her gaze over the room.

I couldn't remember the last time I spent any time in here. It had been an idea my mother had when we'd been much younger, an encouragement to read more and a cozy space to study, which never happened.

Standing, I glanced at Ainsley still gaping at floor-to-ceiling bookshelves and adjusted my pants. The door squeaked open behind me, and my head snapped around just as I pulled my sweatpants over my ass. Kenna stood in the doorway, surveying the situation. It didn't take long to figure out what Ainsley and I had been doing moments before she burst in. Hell, Ainsley had her jeans only half on and was in a bra.

"Well, isn't this a pleasant surprise. An early Christmas present?" She crossed her arms, smiling like the damn Cheshire Cat from *Alice in Wonderland*.

"Fuck off, Kenna," I growled, tossing Ainsley her shirt.

The twinkle in Kenna's eyes brightened. She enjoyed this too much, and I needed to put an end to it. "It looks like you already got off."

My gaze narrowed at her. "I locked the door. How did you get in?"

"This door?" She indicated to handle with her gaze. "If you ever bothered to come in here, you'd know this lock has been broken for more than a year."

Son of a bitch. My fault for not checking. "What do you want?" I asked, catching Ainsley slipping her leg into her pants from the corner of my gaze.

Kenna's back pressed against the doorframe, looking far too relaxed as if she was in no rush to leave. "Everyone's looking for you."

I wanted her gone, but I also wanted her to keep her mouth shut. "Why?"

"Because Josie noticed your car," she said, gaze shifting to Ainsley.

"Fuck," I hissed under my breath.

"I'll say." Kenna's smugness caused my eyes to roll. "So how long has this been going on?" she asked, making a crude gesture with her fingers.

"None of your business," I shot back, running a hand through my hair.

Kenna toyed with her necklace, not the least bit deterred. "I bet Josie would beg to differ. I knew the two of you were acting weird. I should have guessed you were sleeping together. It's about damn time."

Ainsley slipped the sweater over her head and stood up, putting her arms into the holes. "You're not surprised," she stated, seeing Kenna's composed expression.

Kenna gave a one-shoulder shrug. "Why would I be? You've been spitting off sexual tension vibes for two years. I can't tell you the number of times I wanted to scream will you fuck her already. I seriously contemplated locking the two of you into a room overnight to see if it would happen."

I blinked. "The way your mind works scares me."

Kenna grinned. "Thank you."

I shook my head, flashing a side glance at Ainsley. She'd been relatively quiet, and I didn't know if that was a good thing. "Will you leave so we can get dressed," I said to Kenna.

"Under one condition. You tell Josie. She deserves to know that her brother is banging her best friend," Kenna said.

"Why?" I wanted to once again tell her it was none of her business because it wasn't.

"In case shit goes south, and knowing you..." she said, eyes narrowed on me. "...you'll fuck it up."

"There's nothing to fuck up," Ainsley piped in, drawing Kenna and my gaze. "Grayson and I are not an item. We're just..."

"Having fun?" Kenna supplied, her lips twisting. "Oh, I can see that. Still, you need to tell her. It'll be worse if she finds the two of you as I did."

Ainsley took a step to the side, away from me. "There's no point. I'm leaving."

"What?" Kenna and I shrieked at the same time, our heads whirling toward her simultaneously.

"I'm going back to school," she informed like it was no big deal. And maybe it wasn't...for her. "Right after Christmas."

Anger flared within me. Her running away wouldn't solve her problems but was exactly what it felt like she was doing. I was one of those problems. "And you decided this when?"

She met my burning gaze. "I was going to tell you."

Kenna put her hand on the doorknob. "This seems like a conversation I don't need to be a part of. But hurry up, unless you want Josie to walk in and find you half naked arguing about a relationship that apparently doesn't exist."

"Kenna," I growled. "Get out." Besides, Ainsley and I were fully dressed now.

The door closed, leaving me once again alone with the little devil.

She shoved her hands into her pockets. "We both knew this thing between us would end. It was a fling, but I need to get back to my life."

"You think you'll be safe at school?"

"Does it matter? I'm not safe anywhere."

I wanted to argue. Wanted to demand she would be safe with me, but that hadn't been true up to this point. "Fine, have it your way." The words came out rough as if I'd swallowed a mouthful of sand.

"We can still be friends," she offered.

Why did that phrase piss me off so much? Maybe because that was my fucking line. "Turns out, I don't want to be your friend."

She took a step toward me. "What are you saying?"

My fingers shoved into my hair. "I don't know." And that was the truth. I just knew I didn't like the idea of her leaving—of her being two hours away. Why was it different now than it had been three weeks ago?

Had things changed that much between us?

Had I changed that damn much?

No. Not really. I still didn't want a commitment. Not to her. Not to any girl.

Right?

"Are you saying you want to date?"

Something happened inside my chest. A compression. A piercing pain. A gasp of breath. "You're right. It was just a fling. Better we cut it off now than get anyone else involved."

She swallowed. "Exactly."

18

AINSLEY

I left the library before Grayson to avoid any questions. It would be best if I didn't walk in with him. As soon as I was out of the room, I exhaled, hoping the tightness in my chest would fade.

Holy shit. I slept with Grayson. Again.

What is wrong with me?

I was leaving in two days. The plan had been to tell him the friends-with-benefits shit was finished, not screw his brains out. At least I finally did tell him even if it was after the fact. I should be relieved—feeling lighter now that I'd ended things. Yet the pressure squeezing my heart remained, and I felt like crap.

I felt low.

I felt like I wanted to turn back around and tell Grayson we could play by his rules. That I wanted just sex from him. Truth was, I enjoyed it far too much. And oddly, I enjoyed Grayson in and out of bed, and that was precisely why I had to stop sleeping with him.

Stay strong.

Get through the next two days.

And you won't have to see Grayson's damn handsome face every day.

Avoiding him completely was out of the question.

But daily...that was too damn much for even the strongest of people.

It wasn't lost on me that he made me forget about the drama with my parents for a short time, and for that, I was grateful.

But now, I needed to pull myself together so it didn't look like I just had sex and find Josie. Like every problem in my life, I had to bury it for now. Falling apart a second time was not an option because, this time, there would be no Grayson to catch me.

Josie found me as I turned the corner a few steps from the kitchen. "Hey, I've been looking for you."

"Yeah, I—" I started to say. "Sorry, I needed a moment to myself."

"What happened?" Instant concern touched her face.

I couldn't pretend with Josie. She would see right through my facade, and I didn't see the point in trying. She would worry about me regardless. "*He* was there."

"Shit," she replied, no other context needed.

I slumped against the wall. "Yeah."

"Okay, first we need a drink." She took my shoulders and steered me into the kitchen. "I'm sure there's something in the kitchen we can get into."

No surprise, but I could really use a drink, so I was game. Josie put her arm around me as we entered the kitchen, and I wasn't completely sure, but I swore I smelled booze on her breath. "Have you already been drinking?"

She pinched her index and thumb together. "Just a little bit."

Josie day drinking wouldn't have been a big deal a few years ago, but now... "Did something happen I should know about?"

She started opening cabinets, searching for something strong. "Nothing specific. Just all the shit with Sterling possibly not dead. I thought we'd put that behind us, and I guess with what's happened to you it's stirring up old shit."

"I get it." Josie, like the rest of us, had trauma, and the thing with trauma was it never really went away. We could heal, feelings might fade, and the pain could remain dormant for years, but then you get hit with a trigger, and it put you back into the dark space.

We couldn't undo the past. We could only keep trudging through the present, treasuring the good days, and weeding through the bad.

"Open the damn bottle," I said, holding out my hand. A drink sounded fantastic all of a sudden. If we couldn't forget our tortured pasts, better to drown them in booze. I needed that printed on a T-shirt. "I never did get my mimosa this morning." Or breakfast I realized.

Drinking on an empty stomach. Fun!

She unscrewed the bottle, taking a sip before passing it to me. "Merry Christmas Eve."

Kenna moseyed her way into the kitchen during our second toast, and I avoided her gaze, feeling my cheeks flush. Less than ten minutes ago, she'd caught me in a compromising position with her brother. "Pour me one," she said, plopping down beside me.

"No glasses," Josie said, sliding the bottle across the counter.

"Glad you've hung on to your roots," Kenna replied, taking the wine.

Josie rolled her eyes at the dig about her past. To Kenna drinking straight from the bottle was a crime. "Are you going to tell me what's going on between you and Grayson?" Josie directed the question at me, catching me off guard.

Well, hell.

Kenna choked on her drink, and I shot her a pointed glare. She better keep her mouth shut. This was my secret to tell.

"Nothing," I replied, taking the bottle from Kenna and lifting it to my lips.

Josie's brows went up. That was all it took for me to cave.

"Nothing anymore," I amended, drinking.

Josie shook her head. "Don't tell me you fell for my brother?"

"Please," I snorted, sounding offended. "I don't fall for guys."

"You also don't sneak around either," she was quick to point out.

She had me there.

Kenna snickered, and I pinned her with another glare, which Josie noticed this time.

"You knew," Josie said to Kenna and then turned to me. "How the fuck does she know before me?"

"I had my suspicions but only confirmed it about..." Kenna looked at the fake watch she didn't have on her wrist. "Ten minutes ago."

Josie took the bottle of wine and slammed it back.

"We both agreed it shouldn't have happened. It's over," I quickly said, hoping it was true. If there were any feelings on my part, I would deal with them once I got back to school and miles away from temptation.

"Okay. At least shit makes more sense now. Do I even want to know for how long?" Josie asked.

My elbows rested on the counter, and I leaned my chin into my hands. "It doesn't matter."

"Your words aren't matching up with your face. I think you need this more than I do." Josie handed me back the wine, only for Kenna to snatch it from me.

"Screw that. After what I just witnessed, I need it more than both of you." Kenna hopped off the stool, took the bottle with her, and left.

Josie blinked, her lips forming a pouty frown. "Did she just steal our alcohol?"

I didn't bother to move. "Looks that way."

My best friend spun, opening a cabinet. "I'm sure there's another bottle in here somewhere."

Josie handled the news about her brother and me as expected but also better. I hated keeping shit from her. After finishing off a bottle of wine between the two of us, we were both feeling good. All those problems I had were floating somewhere far off in my head, just out of reach. To keep them away, I needed more booze.

The idea of a party became more appealing. The buzz warming my insides would eventually wear off if I didn't nourish it with more drinks. That was the nature of the beast.

I finished applying my final coat of mascara when I got the dreaded text. Talk about a buzzkill, though I shouldn't have been taken off guard. My intuition sensed it was coming, and my stalker didn't disappoint.

Who will it be tonight? Mrs. White in the library with a candlestick, or Miss Scarlett in the kitchen with the dagger? I told you to leave. Now someone will die. Who doesn't love a little murder mystery party?

This fucking asshole.

Was he really turning a Christmas Eve party into a game of Clue?

If anyone would die tonight, I'd make sure it was the jackass behind the anonymous number. To do that, of course, I should be sober, which might be difficult. I stared hard at my phone.

The devil on my shoulder wanted to say fuck everyone and enjoy the party. Drink with my friends. Forget anything bad existed outside this massive house.

The weaker angel who often got stomped on by the devil whispered for me to seize the opportunity. If this guy was really going to show his face tonight, I needed to be clearheaded, smart, and one step ahead of him.

Two seconds later, a knock came at my door. Mads walked in with two cocktails in her hand. One for me. One for her.

I could see how this night would play out.

Cheers, motherfucker.

The party was only a small gathering. Just the closest friends of the Edwardses. Maybe fifty people including the Elite.

Josie giggled when she saw Brock and flung herself into his arms. "Firefly," he greeted in that growling way of his. Did I find the nickname cute? I hated to admit I did. He looked down, keeping Josie in his arms. "Are you drunk already?"

"Just a bit tipsy," she replied with a smile. The little flared red dress she wore lifted slightly, showing off more of her legs covered in black tights.

Since I didn't have any sparkly or festive dresses with me, I borrowed one from Josie for tonight.

Brock glanced my way.

I shook my head. "Oh, no. This one is not my fault." But I wasn't very convincing seeing as I was on my way to being sloshed.

"Where's Grayson?" Brock asked me, a dark scowl forming on his lips.

"How should I know? We're not joined at the hip," I retorted dryly. I wasn't Grayson's keeper.

"They're fucking," Josie said, leaning into Brock, her smile still fully in place.

Brock lifted a brow, his arm secured around his girlfriend. "Is that so?"

"*Were*," I added, emphasizing the word. "Are you going to tell everyone?"

"They're going to get married. I'm predicting it now," Josie whispered or more like tried to.

Brock's lips twitched.

"Who's getting married?" Micah asked, coming up behind Brock just as Josie made her psychic announcement.

My arms went up in the air. I give up. "No one's getting married. Certainly not me," I mumbled.

"You want me to hook you up with someone?" Micah asked with a wink of his sparkling light-blue eyes. He shouldn't be allowed to do that, not when he had a girlfriend.

"God, no," I declined quickly. "No setups. No blind dates. I can find plenty of guys on my own."

Josie glanced at Micah, and I knew what would come out of her mouth. "She's hooking up with Grayson."

Micah's lips twisted. "I love drunk Josie."

"Me too," Josie giggled and flipped off her heels, kicking them one at a time across the room. No one was injured thankfully.

"Good luck," I said, shaking my head, and went off to find some food. And a damn drink.

I lingered around the buffet table, nibbling on bits of cheese, crackers, and sausages. I popped grapes and strawberries into my mouth. Ate canapés, dips, and chips all while washing it down with some spiked holiday punch.

Brock babysat Josie most of the night, and I left him to it, hanging out with Mads and Kenna. Most of the guests were older, friends of Liana and Chandler's.

As much as I wanted to enjoy myself, the text I received earlier constantly nagged at the back of my head. So much so that I scrutinized every guest, wondering if they could be the one. Would he really show up here? Did anyone look out of place? Uninvited?

My gaze passed over Grayson in the corner of the room talking to Fynn. Since my announcement, he'd avoided me.

Or maybe it was me avoiding him.

Regardless, I saw very little of him through the night despite being keenly aware of his presence. It drove me to keep the holiday punch full in my cup.

I looked down into my empty glass. Time to top it off.

Heading to the punch bowl, I smiled and shook my head at the sight of Brock trying to wrangle Josie off the coffee table. I don't know when she decided to climb on top of it, but seeing her in her black stockings with a drink in hand brought back fond memories. That girl was normally me up there. Well, Josie and me. I was half tempted to join her.

But first, that drink.

I had the ladle halfway to my glass when I felt someone come up behind me. I didn't think much of it, just another guest looking for a snack, until a voice whispered in my ear.

"Who will it be? Josie? Or perhaps Kenna?"

Something pressed into my back, and I was afraid to guess what it might be. Like perhaps a knife.

Fear kept me frozen, my hand clutching the ladle. "You have a lot of nerve showing up here," I said, my voice thawing.

"The risks are what makes it fun." His deep voice jogged a harrowing memory.

It made my heart pound against my ribs like a caged animal hitting the cell in a frantic attempt to break free. "What do you want?"

"A name."

I couldn't see his face, but I sensed his lips curling in a terrible cruelness. Slade didn't have morals or possess remorse. "What?" I uttered, shock bolting through me. Where was all that bravery and gumption I promised I would have? It abandoned me at the first sound of his voice.

"The name of who you want to die tonight."

He couldn't possibly believe I would give him a name.

Be courageous. Be bold. Be fearless.

I sucked in a shuddering breath and whirled around, a scream at the tip of my tongue, ready to unleash. The bastard was gone. Not gone as he vanished from the room but concealed himself with the guests. With frantic eyes, I searched for Slade, but I had nothing to distinguish him from Jane or John. No color of clothing.

All I had was his voice and a fuzzy memory of his battered face.

Suddenly sober as fuck, I scanned the room looking for Grayson. Or any of the guys for that matter. My gaze went to the corner of the room where he still stood, our eyes connecting, and unlike the other times, he didn't look away. Perhaps he saw the loitering panic in my eyes or the washed-out color of my face.

Regardless, with just that glance, he knew something was wrong.

His eyes hardened. His shoulders straightened. And he tore his gaze from me, scouring over the party.

I set my glass down on the table and rushed over to him, surprised my legs were as steady as they were. "He's here," I hissed, my fingers holding on to the side of his arm.

Grayson's attention was fully on me. "Who?"

"The guy from the race."

"Slade?" he asked, the name nearly guttural.

My head bobbed desperately up and down.

Grayson attached his hand to my arm just as a scream pierced over "Santa Baby" currently playing from the speakers. My heart dropped out of my chest. I knew that scream.

Josie.

"Josie," Grayson murmured, echoing my thoughts.

Where had I seen her last? It was the room adjacent to the dining room, where all the food was set up, near the couches.

The party went silent as everyone tried to figure out what was happening. Me included.

Without a word, I darted out of the corner, weaving through a small crowd, and when I broke through, Josie was on the floor, holding her ankle, looking up at Brock who was crouched beside her.

"What happened?" I demanded.

Grayson, Fynn, and Kenna had followed and stood gathered around.

Brock scrubbed a hand over his face. "She fell off the fucking table."

"That's all? Nothing else happened?" Grayson asked, lowering his voice.

"What's going on?" Brock prompted, aqua eyes darkening.

Grayson's eyes lifted, spanning the faces who were returning to the party. "Slade's here."

Brock stood, leaving Josie on the ground, holding her ankle. "He wouldn't dare."

"He approached me," I said quietly.

Brock gave me a hard stare, the tension in his jaw tight, before he said, "Split up. Find this bastard."

"I'll get Micah," Fynn said and went to find him.

Brock and Grayson shared one of their silent looks. It was sometimes maddening the way they communicated without saying a word. "I need to get her to bed before she actually hurts herself." He bent down and scooped Josie up. She rested her head on his shoulder.

I watched Brock carry her out of the room, comforted by the knowledge he would keep her safe.

"Stay close," Grayson ordered, his attention focused anywhere but on me, and I could accept that, knowing, regardless of our fight earlier, he would still protect me.

I frowned, mostly at myself. "Do you really think you're going to find him?"

"No," he retorted honestly. "If he was smart, he'd be gone. The last thing he needs is for us to get our hands on him again. What did he say?"

"Same threats, except now it's my friends who are going to die."

Or you.

I left out that little detail. Grayson wouldn't give two shits about a threat to his life. A threat on his sisters? Now those were worthy of a man's life.

Grayson's prediction was right.

Nearly thirty minutes later, every inch of the property was combed, and not a single sighting of Slade, except on the cameras. He was good, avoiding clear shots of his face by walking in with another couple, but the second before they were out of the frame, he flashed a smile. It was Micah who caught it.

By the time I went upstairs to bed, it was closer to morning than it was to night. Only a few hours left until the sun crested over the horizon. For the first time in days, I went into the guest room alone. I stared at the door, unable to decide if I should leave it open or closed. My eyes were, of course, drawn to the room across from mine.

Unease had me scowling.

With a confused heart, I left the door partially open.

I wanted to sleep in Grayson's bed. It would be too easy to sneak across the hall and climb in, and despite what happened earlier, something told me he wouldn't turn me away.

Yet, I didn't. I forewent the comfort of his arms to stare at the ceiling. My eyes avoided the window at all costs. I couldn't yo-yo with either of our emotions. My decision had been made, and I had to stick with the choice.

Sleep was overrated.

It was Christmas Eve.

Who the hell slept the night before Christmas anyway?

19

GRAYSON

Ainsley left the day after Christmas without so much as a goodbye. We'd barely spoken at all on Christmas, and I ignored the glares aimed at me from Josie and Kenna. The secret was out of the bag. I had nothing to say for myself.

The gift I'd bought Ainsley never made it under the tree. It still sat tucked away in my desk drawer. I don't even know why I'd been compelled to buy her anything. I'd never gotten a girl a gift. Not for a birthday. Not for Valentine's Day. And sure as hell not for Christmas.

It had been a spur-of-the-moment purchase.

Now she was gone. My life could go back to normal, and in theory, it shouldn't be a problem. The thing with theories was you always had to account for a margin of chance or error. We'd been friends before. I'd slept with plenty of girls I'd gone back to being friendly with. Maybe not as close as Ainsley and I were, but in theory...

Then why did it feel like from the moment she told me she was leaving all the color drained from my world?

Was this what that feeling was? The urge to run after a girl?

I didn't like it.

It was easy to rationalize what I felt by believing it was her safety I worried over. Part of it might have been. But if the threat was still out there, she wasn't free from danger.

What Ainsley didn't know was I had a guy watching her, security from a distance. She might think leaving would put an end to this nightmare.

She was wrong.

Whether it was Slade or the person behind the mysterious texts, they'd gotten a taste of what it was like to instill fear in another person—the power it gave you. They weren't done yet.

But the Elite would find a way to put an end to it. Hopefully tonight. Or at the very least, give us an edge.

I pulled up to Brock's and parked my car behind Micah's Hummer. They were outside, waiting on me. Fynn. Brock. Micah.

We were headed to King Street. Reno expected me.

He was getting the Elite.

Brock drove us to the lower side of Elmwood and into the Wolves' territory. It was weird to think Josie and Ainsley grew up only a few blocks away. Brock pulled his Land Rover off to the side of the road, one street to the right of King. Despite it being a rather chilly night, his Wolves were out, working the streets, hanging around, and generally waiting for trouble.

The weight of my gun pressed into my lower back, secured inside my jeans as we walked onto King Street. We pulled more than a few wary glances from Reno's guys. A couple nodded at Brock. The strip housed multiple businesses. All of which Reno got a cut of. It was the price of real estate in the Wolves' territory. From the laundromat to a Chinese restaurant to a convenience store.

Flickering neon red lights hit the side of my face as we approached Little Rice. Except the sign read Little Ice, the R burnt out. The best way to figure out where Reno was at any given time was to look for the security stationed outside.

Two of the beefiest guys I'd ever seen stood on either side of the glass door. "Reno's expecting me," I said, drawing up to my full height. Even big guys could fall.

The one on the left stiffened, folding his python arms over his chest. It looked uncomfortable. "He's busy," he mumbled through his bushy beard.

I stepped forward. "Maybe you didn't hear me."

He glanced over my shoulder, eyeing Fynn, Micah, and Brock. "You were to come alone."

I gave him a wry smile. "Plans change."

Still, neither of them immediately jumped to let us pass. The two guards continued to size us up. Finally, the bearded guy gave a jerk of his head and opened the door. The other held out his hand. "Weapons are left at the door."

My jaw tightened, but I was expecting this. I pulled out the Glock and placed it in his fat hand. Micah added a knife to the pile and his gun.

Inside the restaurant, dim lighting cast a solemn atmosphere. Only one table was in use. Reno sat alone, a plate of half-eaten food in front of him, platters of beef and chicken along with a bowl of rice. He didn't stop what he was doing. Didn't look up. Didn't acknowledge that four guys crashed his solo dinner plans.

Not until we hovered directly in front of his table did his eyes glance up from his plate. His gaze showed no emotion, observing each of us before landing on me. "You brought the crew. It's been a while," Reno greeted, kicking back in his chair. His hand gestured to the empty seats across from him.

Brock and Fynn sat at the table while Micah and I stood behind them, keeping tabs on Reno's men. They darkened the corners of the dining room, monitoring the exits, undoubtedly all armed.

Reno reached for his beer. "Can I get you something to drink?" he offered, putting the bottle to his lips.

Brock shook his head, impatience etched into his body. "Not tonight."

Reno set down the beer and folded his hands on the table, the silver wolf head flashing on his finger. "What brings the infamous Elite to my doorstep? I'm guessing it has more to do with than just what I have inside this black folder."

I hadn't noticed the folder until now. It sat slightly under his plate. "Slade," I said, my voice hard.

A flicker of surprise passed over Reno's ruthless eyes. "What of him?"

I clenched my fingers to keep from slamming them onto the table. Better yet, someone's face. "He broke into my house twice and attacked one of our girls. Why?"

Reno's shoulders tensed. "Slade?"

"Is there something going on that we're unaware of?" Brock asked, his body leaning off to one side.

Reno rapped his fingers over the table. "If what you say is true, it wasn't by my order. The only business I have with you is what's inside this folder. That's what we agreed on."

"He claims he was hired," Brock gritted out. "If it wasn't you, then perhaps you know who's paying him? That's something you keep tabs on, isn't it?" His tone purposely went condescending, a verbal slap on the wrist.

Reno didn't like being undermined. Not by his men and certainly not by outsiders. "I'll get you a name, but first, we need to settle up with this." He put a finger on top of the black folder and slid it to the middle of the table around a platter of beef and broccoli.

Fynn dropped a stash of cash on the table with a thud that shook the platters. He left it there in the center for Reno to take, but the boss only eyed the money.

Micah fidgeted beside me, antsy and ready to fight. I cast him a quick sideways glance.

Reno cut Brock a harsh glare. "It looks a little light." He nodded toward the stash of hundred-dollar bills.

"Until we have a name, this is the best we can do. And we want Slade taken care of," Brock said coldly without an ounce of compassion in his tone.

Reno knew precisely what Brock demanded. He wanted Slade dead, and he didn't give a shit how Reno made it happen, as long as Slade took his last breath.

Fynn crossed his arms and added, "We'll double your fee once both problems have been resolved."

Like all good businessmen, Reno's eyes brightened with dollar signs at the prospect of making more money. He didn't really give a shit about his guys. Not like the four of us did with each other. I'd die for Brock, Micah, and Fynn, and they would do the same for me.

Reno didn't have the same sense of loyalty, not when he looked out for himself first and foremost. It made him not just cutthroat but untrustworthy.

"This isn't how I do business," Reno said.

It was an effort to keep my voice from growling and snapping. "Slade didn't leave us a choice."

Reno mulled this over for a moment. "I'll talk to him. *And* I'll get you the name. You can take the file as a measure of goodwill. I think you'll be very interested in what my guys found."

"And Slade?" Brock pressed, not leaving here without an assurance Reno would make sure Slade would never be a problem again.

"If he did what you said, we'll negotiate," Reno pushed back.

Brock stared hard at him from across the table, the vein on the side of his neck protruding. "My price won't change."

Reno held Brock's glaze longer than most people would dare. "Understood, but mine will. Significantly."

From the side, Brock's lips curled in a cruel smirk. "That won't be a problem."

"Never is with you rich pricks." It was said without malice and hints of humor, but none of us took offense. The truth of it was, we were rich pricks and didn't give two fucks.

"Then we have a deal," Fynn stated.

Reno reached for his beer, his large fingers wrapping around the glass neck, flashing the silver wolf ring. "I'll be in touch."

Brock nodded and got to his feet. Fynn took the folder off the table and stood up beside Brock. Without a second glance, the four of us left.

"This is bullshit," Micah spat when we were outside. "I want that fucker dead."

I couldn't agree more.

"And he will be. Either by Reno's hand or ours," Brock assured as we hooked around the corner toward his SUV.

We weren't making the same mistakes.

I pulled the beanie down over my head and climbed into the back of the Land Rover, Micah on the other side. Once the four of us were situated, Fynn opened the black folder, and we all stared at the tiny SD taped to the thick paper. He peeled off the card and pulled out his phone, inserting it into a device plugged into his phone. We waited as he tapped the screen, pulling up the info on the SD. Micah and I inched forward from the back seat, leaning over his shoulder.

When Fynn had the information, he held the phone out for all of us to see. A photograph filled the screen, and as I stared at the picture, every doubt I had over the last year became justified. Sometimes your gut instincts don't just get it right. They slam-dunked it.

"Mother. Fucker," Micah hissed. "I knew that asshole wasn't dead."

We were all thinking it. Every one of us. And the silence that filled the car after Micah's declaration hung between us while we processed what the hell we'd learned. A hunch was one thing. Proof took it to new levels. Proof changed things. Proof made me want to kill him. Again.

Josie's number flashed across Brock's phone. Well, her nickname. Firefly. He answered the call, and the phone automatically connected to the car's speakers. Before he could even say hey, Josie's panicked voice rushed out, filling the car.

"He broke in, Brock! He's here inside the house! He's looking for Ainsley!"

In seconds, the whole demeanor inside the car shifted. My fingers dug into the back of Fynn's seat.

Brock leaned forward, his jaw rock hard. "Where are you?" he demanded.

"Upstairs." She sounded rattled, and that was difficult for Brock to hear, particularly since we were at least twenty minutes away. Fifteen if Brock blew most of the red lights between here and my house.

"Are you hurt?" Brock prompted, something I rarely heard hitching in his voice. Fear.

"No, but..." The hesitation made my heart stop.

"But what, Firefly?" Brock growled, his fingers tightening against the steering wheel.

"I shot him," she said, and the whole car flattened into another bout of deadly silence.

Brock's gaze met mine in the rearview mirror, and we shared a look, our expressions mirroring each other. Beside me, Micah chuckled, his head falling back on the seat. Leave it to Josie to handle shit herself. I raked a hand through my hair.

"Good," Brock said, the engine of his Range Rover ripping to life. "We're on our way. Don't let him leave."

I got Brock wanted to run to Josie, make sure she was safe, and take care of Slade. I wanted to do that as well. But I also wanted to storm my ass back into Little Rice and start a fucking war.

I should jump out of the car, drag Reno's ass to my house, and give him his proof, but the SUV was already moving.

"Uh, he's not going anywhere. Kenna and I tied him up," Josie informed.

These fucking girls. But really, what did we expect? They were *our girls*.

"The bastard is bleeding all over the floors." Kenna's voice came through, sounding far calmer than Josie's, which didn't surprise me. Kenna had a penchant for revenge that worried me. Not to mention, she hadn't been the one to pull the trigger. Shooting someone for the first time, regardless of whether it was a fatal wound or not, messed with you. It only made sense Josie was rattled to her bones.

Micah sat back in his seat, an amused, slightly eager expression on his face. "Why couldn't I have sisters?" he muttered.

I punched him on the arm, making him grin more. *Twisted asshole.*

"Stay on the phone," Fynn ordered, his hand braced on the dash as Brock took a turn at least thirty miles over the speed limit.

This motherfucker is dead.

* * *

Micah stayed downstairs to check the grounds and the first floor of the house. Who knew, there might be an accomplice or a lookout hiding in the bushes. Fynn, Brock, and I raced inside, flinging the front door open and bolting straight for the stairs.

I envisioned what we would find the entire car ride home; however, I wasn't prepared. I stumbled a step when we rounded the corner. Brock cursed under his breath at the sight of blood splattered on the stairwell wall and trailing up the steps. I didn't have to be an investigator to guess Josie shot Slade as he came up the stairs toward her and Kenna. At the top of the landing, Kenna and Josie were watching their bleeding prisoner.

The smell hit me. The sharp scent was like rusted iron. Blood. Slade groaned on the floor, a pool of dark liquid seeping out from under his body. He lay on his side, hands and feet bound.

Josie's eyes flicked to Brock's, but she didn't flinch. Her fingers stayed wrapped around the gun pointed down at Slade. If he so much as tried to get up, Josie would have put another bullet in him. The concentration mixed with anger and terror shone in her eyes.

Brock took the gun from Josie's hand. She didn't immediately let go, not until he murmured her name. She blinked before really focusing on him, recognition clearing the darkness clouding her eyes. Once the gun left her fingers, the tension holding her body rigid dissipated.

Frowning, she crossed her arms over her chest. Most girls might crumble against their boyfriend or start crying. Josie only stared at Brock and said, "I need to warn Ainsley."

I reached out and took hold of Josie's wrist. "Don't call her."

She gave me a confused expression. It was clear she was worried for Ainsley and still shaken from the break-in despite how strong of a front she maintained. "Why the hell not?" she argued.

Brock's hard eyes glared unapologetically at Slade. The asshole's head slumped off to the side, barely clinging to consciousness. I knew what was coming. I grabbed Josie, and Fynn took Kenna, and as Brock lifted the gun, we turned them away, shielding their eyes and covering their ears.

The shot rang out over the house.

Josie jumped in my arms, her breathing quickening. None of us moved for a moment, and the room became almost as still as the body now lying on the floor.

"Because he's dead, Firefly. He can't hurt her now," Brock said flatly.

Josie shoved out of my arms, pushing hard on my chest. Her attention went right to Brock. She didn't flinch at the sight of blood splatter on him. Most of it hit his clothes, but a few drops touched his neck. "You think this ends with his death?"

Brock's face stayed impassive. Any emotions he had were buried. There was no place for feeling to do what he'd done.

I answered for him. "No. I don't, but she doesn't need the stress. If she believes she is safe at school, I'd rather let her feel the security a little longer."

She tossed her hands up in the air. "How does that make any sense? She needs to be prepared. This guy was only the middleman." She pointed at the dead body. "We still don't know who the real threat is."

I met Brock's gaze over Josie's head. My sister was no dummy. She caught the exchange.

Josie's eyes volleyed between us. "What's going on? I'm done with the secrets. One of you better start talking, or Kenna and I will start busting some balls."

Kenna was still tucked against Fynn's tall frame. "I mean, we did just shoot and capture an intruder," she said.

For the love of everything unholy. Why did God stick me with not one but two of them?

I was most likely going to Hell, but being their brother was damn near hell on earth—a punishment within itself.

I couldn't believe we were standing in the hallway, blood all over the walls, having *this* conversation. "First, I have security detail watching Ainsley at school," I revealed. "It's only been, like, a damn day, but she hasn't left the dorm."

"And secondly," Brock chimed in. "Sterling's not dead. We can't be sure he isn't the one behind the attacks."

"Took you long enough," Kenna said snidely, neither girl reacting at the mention of Sterling's name.

The three of our gazes flicked from one another. "You knew," Brock said, his eyes narrowing at Kenna and Josie.

Josie ran a frustrated hand through her hair, and it was then I noticed she had blood in it. "We knew you were looking into the matter and that you believed he wasn't dead. So, I'm guessing you got proof tonight."

"Ainsley," I growled. She was the only one with this information and was how the girls had found out we'd been looking into Sterling.

Kenna shook her head, taking a step away from Fynn. "It doesn't matter how. You should have told us."

Micah bound up the stairs and looked at Slade. "Pity I missed it."

Brock ignored him. "I wanted to be positive before I said anything."

Josie stiffened. "Because you don't think we can handle the hard shit?"

Flipping the safety on, Brock shoved the gun behind his back and reached up to take Josie's chin between his thumb and finger. "We're not going to argue about this right now. We have business to attend to first. Let Grayson take care of Ainsley. Can you do that?"

Josie's lips firmed into a straight line, but she nodded. "If anything happens to her, the four of you are responsible, and I'll never forgive you."

We had quite the damn mess to clean up before my parents got home in less than forty-eight hours.

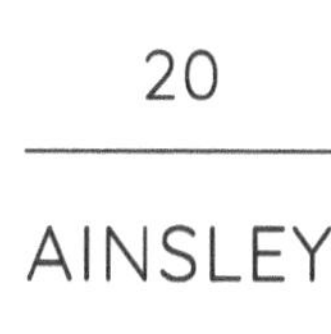

20

AINSLEY

I left for school without so much as a goodbye to Grayson. It was better this way. Let him be pissed at me.

Did loneliness and a sense of guilt follow me the entire time back to KU?

Damn straight.

I spent my first night in my dorm tossing and turning. The familiarity I hoped would comfort me didn't. I'd forgotten how noisy the old rowhouse could be, but without anyone else living in it, the place was too damn quiet. I rarely stayed here alone, and now that I was, every tiny sound was escalated. The floorboards creaked. The roof moaned. The wind howled. Tree branches tapped on the windows. It was nearly an eerie orchestra haunting me to sleep.

When I couldn't take it anymore, I grabbed my laptop and booted up my favorite comfort series *Tokyo Ghoul*, turning the volume up. Only then, with the voices of Ken and Touka filling my ears, did I drift off to sleep. No dreams. No nightmares. But that didn't mean my sleep wasn't fitful.

Grayson might have escaped my dreams the first night, but when

I woke up, I reached across the cold bed for a guy who was miles away. He wasn't mine to miss.

And yet I did.

Painfully so.

I soon discovered the waking hours were the worst. I'd been afraid of my dreams when I should have been fearful of my memories.

A pang stabbed me in the heart, and with tired eyes, I rolled over onto my back, staring at the sun-patterned ceiling reflecting off the mirror.

What was wrong with me?

Since when did I ever pine after a guy? That was not my style. I made them pine after me, not the other way around.

This was fucked up. I didn't like it.

Tossing the blankets aside, I sat up. "It was so much easier being alone," I muttered to the empty room.

I got dressed, peed, brushed my teeth, tossed my hair up into a bun, and decided to grab coffee at Break Zone. The fresh air would be good for me, and I didn't feel like brewing coffee my damn self.

An eerie emptiness settled over the campus in a way I wasn't used to. This place normally bustled with activity. Dozens and dozens of people at any given time walked the campus. This morning, on my way to get coffee, I only passed one other person.

I walked out the door of Break Zone, remembering the last time I'd been here and how I'd run into grumpy Grayson the morning after puking on him. My lips curled at the memory. I could picture his scowling face too easily.

And it was in that moment, with my caffè mocha in hand and my heart beating wildly in my chest at the conjuration of his face, I concluded...

I was in love with Grayson Edwards.

Holy shit.

I loved the asshole.

I did exactly what I told myself I would never do. Not just fall for him but fall *in love* before I found myself.

The shock of it kept me rooted in place. How had I not known until now? How had I let my heart get involved?

I didn't know a lot about love, but maybe I was finding out I couldn't control my feelings as much as I wanted to.

With feet that didn't seem to touch the ground, I started walking again toward my house. I went twenty feet when a different emotion took over the jolt of realizing I was in love. This new feeling was darker.

A prickling sensation danced over the back of my neck, making the arm hairs under my hoodie stand up. I glanced over my shoulder to prove no one was behind me, let alone following me.

And there wasn't.

No one that I could see, and yet the feeling of being watched remained.

The sidewalk was vacant except for a few frozen leaves blowing about. No one hid in the bushes. No one loitered on the sides of the buildings. No one pretended to jog through campus in the guise of stalking me.

Or any of the other million overactive scenarios my mind conjured on the spot.

You're being silly. And paranoid as fuck.

But could I blame myself?

No matter how I downplayed the feeling of being watched, it never went away.

I snuggled deeper into my oversized hoodie and increased my pace, skipping the walk around the campus I had planned to indulge in. Instead, I headed straight for the house, locking the door behind me. I checked the deadbolt and handle twice to make sure it was secured. Then I went through the house room by room, checking the windows including those on the second floor. Why I hadn't done this the night before almost sent me into a tailspin, especially when I discovered more than one window had been left unlocked.

I shuddered to think about what might have happened if the stalker had followed me to school.

Taking my coffee, I curled up on the couch and scrolled through my phone. I had another missed call from Mom, which I ignored like all the other previous calls. I wasn't ready to talk to her. There was also a text from Josie checking in.

I'm fine. Don't worry. See you soon.

I had already phoned Bea yesterday and let her know I was sorry but I had to go back to school early. Most employers would be pissed or fire me on the spot. Bea and Ralph didn't just sign my paychecks. They cared about me, and Bea knew I was having a hard time at home. She didn't question my decision to return to school early, only wished me luck, and made me promise to come back during summer, which I gladly did.

I spent the first week holed up in my dorm, binge-watching anime and K-dramas while scarfing down copious amounts of takeout from my favorite places. Honestly, it turned out to be my ideal vacation. But at some point, I had to get back out into the world. Classes started in a week. I had to pull myself together.

Sure, I made it through the first week without losing my mind or being murdered. The time away cleared my head, putting things back into perspective, but for a social creature, being alone sucked ass. I missed my friends. The keg stands. Heck, I even missed the lectures, just being in a room surrounded by people.

But...I was at college for a purpose, and being back reminded me of all I worked for the last year and a half—how grateful I was for the opportunity.

Not necessarily all the books, homework, and studying, but the lab work, the real nitty-gritty stuff of my major. That I loved.

But I would go stir-crazy if I had to spend another week holed up inside. I had to do something with my time or lose my freaking mind, so I went to the lab, testing and experimenting with scents. Being a perfumer was my career goal, but I dabbled in other things as well.

Extracting oils. Candles. Soaps. Anything that could be infused with scent. It helped to be well rounded in a field.

By the end of those seven days, when the scent I'd been working on was nearly finished, I realized what I was doing. Recreating the way Grayson smelled. I nearly scrapped it right then.

But I couldn't.

Not when the scent provoked such strong emotions inside me.

We hadn't spoken since I left, but my heart ached for him. I missed the jerk more each day that went by, and in a messed-up way, the longing made me work harder to forget him.

As if that was possible.

Grayson had gotten to me without me being aware of it until it was too late.

My heart desired to be in his arms.

My head wanted no man.

And my body aligned with my heart.

To war against both heart and body was no easy obstacle to overcome. The endless pain reminded me why I never wanted to be in love. Grayson had the power to hurt me. I was tired of people hurting and disappointing me.

Most days I wanted to give in and call the asshole just to hear his voice.

Especially the days when I felt unsafe, which unfortunately was more days than not. Particularly if I left the house. I couldn't shake the feeling someone was lurking on campus watching my every move. It kept me on edge when I'd hoped to be settled before classes started.

That didn't look to be the case.

Peeking through the blinds, I glanced at the road. *Am I being paranoid thinking someone is out there?*

Possibly.

Or my worst fear was true. The stalker *had* followed me to school.

My saving grace was tomorrow Josie and the others were coming back. Winter break was over, and we all resumed classes on Monday.

I sat in front of the TV, doing my best to ignore the window behind me and its closed blinds. More than once tonight, I swore something moved in the shadows. But the longer I stared into the darkness, the surer I became my mind played tricks on me.

* * *

As much as I wanted to grill Josie on all things Grayson the second she and Brock walked through the door, I did something difficult for me. I bit my tongue. It was harder than waiting for the next book in my favorite manga series. Like I wanted to blurt out all my questions without taking a breath and then dive right into my paranoia of being watched.

But it didn't matter. She took one look at me and knew.

I wanted to talk to my best friend. But this was also her brother.

Should I tell her everything got messed up? That I think I fell for him?

I smiled at her weakly.

Her reply was a hug and then to drag me into my room, and she closed the door. We sat down on my unmade bed. As I glanced around, it occurred to me I hadn't done a single load of laundry, and it showed. Dirty clothes were piled in corners, but Josie didn't notice. Her gaze stayed focused on me. "If it is any consolation, he's a wreck too," she said.

It did bring a bit of consolation hearing I wasn't the only one suffering. I drew my legs up and folded them into a pretzel. "Really?" It was hard to believe Grayson ever looked miserable. Grumpy, all the damn time, but not forlorn.

She nodded, a chunk of pink hair falling over her shoulder. "Yeah. I honestly thought he was going to drive down here and haul you back home."

"He didn't," I replied flatly, a spark of anger lighting inside me. At myself. At Grayson. At the fucking world.

"No," Josie agreed and then added, "He was waiting for you to text or call him."

I swore with colorful creativeness. "I didn't."

"That's because you are both stupidly stubborn."

With chipped black nails, I picked at a loose thread on the hem of my blanket. "It doesn't matter. This is where I need to be. Not distracted by a brooding guy with sexy lips and a firm ass."

She wrinkled her nose. "Is this what it's like when I talk about Brock?"

My lips twitched. "Probably not. I can actually appreciate Brock being hot."

"This doesn't have to be weird." I couldn't tell if she was convincing herself or me.

Regardless, I appreciated her effort. "It already is."

"You should call him."

My face tightened at the mention of reaching out first. "There's no need. I have you now."

Josie rolled her eyes and grabbed one of my pillows to cuddle. "You're already my sister, but I can't deny I wouldn't really love it if you were my sister legally."

I pinched her under the arm. "We are not talking marriage. Not ever."

Her lips curved up, but the smile didn't last long. She bit her lip, and concern tiptoed inside me. I'd been so preoccupied with my problems and feelings I hadn't paid close attention to her. Something was bothering her. She had a shadow in her eyes, one that hadn't been there when I left.

"Is there something wrong?" I asked.

This time, I was paying attention. The smile touched her mouth again but not her eyes. "Everything is okay," she assured, contradicting the sadness she hid behind smiles.

I didn't believe her. Why would she lie? To protect me? "Did something happen after I left?" I pushed, the flutters of worry growing.

"Fuck it," she muttered under her breath, stuffing the pillow into her lap to lean on. "I was going to wait to tell you later tonight. I didn't want to ruin our first day home."

"Ruin how?"

"Maybe ruin is the wrong word. Slade's dead," she blurted, coming right out and saying the thing she'd been avoiding.

I blinked, processing her words. "What? How?" Slade was a name I hadn't been able to forget no matter how much I tried.

"Brock." That was all she said. No details, but did I really want them? Just his name I realized was enough.

Brock killed Slade.

Holy shit.

Not that the bastard didn't deserve punishment, and truthfully, I fantasized too many times about killing him. I could admit a sense of disappointment it hadn't been me.

Perhaps I should feel a sense of compassion for a man losing his life.

I didn't.

I wasn't sure what that said about me, but I also wouldn't overanalyze the lack of empathy.

Exhaling a deep breath, I rested my head on her shoulder. "I'm sorry," I said quietly, all the energy in my body depleting.

She lay her cheek against my head. "You have nothing to be sorry for. This isn't your fault. Sterling isn't dead."

"I'd like to say I'm surprised, but I'm not." The bastard was like a pesky fly who wouldn't die no matter how many times you hit him.

"I know," Josie muttered, her feelings echoing mine.

My jaw clenched. "They think he's responsible, don't they?"

"You don't?" Despite the question, I sensed she doubted it as well. Perhaps she was looking for someone else to share her misgivings with.

"I'm not sure," I admitted. The Elite might have dispatched one threat, but danger was far from over.

* * *

Classes resumed, and I began the mundane task of waking up, attending lectures, taking notes, going to labs, scrambling to get to the cafeteria before it closed, studying for hours, and working part-time at the bookstore before dropping into bed utterly exhausted. And then I did it all over again.

Day after day.

This was what I wanted. My life back. Normalcy.

Then why did I feel so empty inside? Why was I so tired all the time? Why didn't I have much of an appetite after burning so much energy? A professional might diagnose me with depression.

The thing was, I knew myself. I wasn't depressed. Sad? Sometimes. Lonely? Again, sometimes.

The days flew by, and with each week, it was easier to forget all the things that happened in Elmwood over the break. I hadn't received one single threatening text.

I also hadn't heard from Grayson. No messages. No emails. No calls.

Not that I expected him to contact me.

It was better he hadn't.

We both had to get on with our lives.

It was the end of the first week of February, and I just finished my last class. Slinging my bag over my shoulders, I trotted down the stairs of the chemistry building.

"Ainsley," someone called from behind me.

I paused halfway down and glanced over my shoulder to see Kate McGuire. My first thought was to turn and keep going, pretend I hadn't heard or seen her even though I clearly had. It wasn't above me to be that rude, yet I waited for her.

"I wasn't sure I'd catch up with you," she said breathily as if she'd run down the hallway, her apricot cheeks flushed. She followed me as I started walking again, not wanting to cause a roadblock on the stairwell.

Plus, I really didn't want to talk to her. I honestly didn't know what she could possibly have to say to me. It wasn't as if this bitch and I were friends.

"Did you need something?" I asked, turning the corner to the second set of stairs that took us to the main floor.

"Are you going tonight?"

I didn't like the crafty lift of her lips. Smug. Like she had a secret she was dying to tell me. I took the bait. "Where?" I asked because it seemed like the response she was looking for, regardless that I couldn't care less, and it showed in the bored tone of my voice.

Kate and I couldn't have looked any more different. She wore a cream knitted sweater that accentuated her golden eyes and a short plaid skirt with tights underneath. "The party. Grayson and Fynn are here."

And there it was. The bomb she'd been dying to drop on me. Grayson was on KU soil, and apparently, I was the last to know. What bothered me was how the hell did Kate know Grayson's presence would be any concern of mine?

The only people who knew about what happened between Grayson and me were the Elite, which technically included the girls now—just the eight of us.

I narrowed my gaze at Kate as we started down the hallway toward the exit. "I thought you actually had something worthwhile to say to me. Instead, you've just wasted my time." I refused to let Kate think she had unnerved me in any way. It was what she was looking for. The girl didn't have a nice bone in her body.

Pleased, her smile twisted into something cunning. "Then I guess I'll have him to myself tonight."

Oooh, she knew what buttons to push. She was lucky I didn't react like I wanted to and slam her pretty head into the nearest wall. For a split second, I could see myself grabbing a fistful of her blonde hair. Unholy anger licked through my veins.

We about reached the doors, and I halted, turning to face her. "Again, I don't see why you think I would give a damn where Grayson sticks his dick."

Her eyes lit up faintly, a wicked twinkle of someone without a soul. "Who said I was talking about Grayson?"

The whore got me.

But she also met her match. This time, I smirked and replied without blinking, "Everyone knows about your little obsession and that he'd rather fuck a duck than touch you. None of them would. I bet that stings. I can tell you from firsthand experience Grayson's goddamn magic in bed. Best orgasms of my life."

Her mouth dropped open, and it was the most glorious sight. Me, one. Kate, zero.

Walking backward toward the exit, I flipped her off. "See ya, Kate. Have fun tonight chasing dreams." Then I pushed through the doors and left her standing there gawking after me, a flash of ire springing into her gaze.

The slap of cold on my cheeks felt good. I needed it to cool my blood. Storming across campus, I barely felt the biting breeze. The ground was fully covered in snow from a snowstorm last week, and despite days of cloudy gloom, the sun found a small break in the sky to peek through today. I was too lost in my head to appreciate the glittering snowy campus and how it looked as if we were living inside a settled snow globe.

I burst inside the townhouse, finding Josie in the kitchen, scrolling on her laptop, a notebook open beside her. She glanced up as I plowed into the room. "He's here?"

21

AINSLEY

ontext wasn't necessary. Only one *he* on this planet could get me this worked up. I didn't give her a chance to confirm. Words continued to tumble out of my mouth with no concern about anyone else being home. "Why didn't anyone think to tell me? How else am I going to ignore him?"

Josie tucked the highlighter in her hand behind her ear. "You're not. Friends don't ignore each other."

But that's exactly what we'd been doing. Ignoring. Avoiding. Rejecting. Discarding. It didn't matter how you described what Grayson and I were doing to each other. It all boiled down to the same thing. I sunk into the chair across from her at the table.

Josie closed her laptop, realizing this wasn't going to be a quick conversation. "You said things wouldn't be different. That everything would go back to being the same as before."

In theory, that shit always sounded good but never worked out. I wasn't in the mood to be reasonable. "Then why didn't you tell me he was coming?" I reiterated my point.

"To prove things aren't the same. And so you couldn't run away and escape again. The two of you need to talk whether you want to or not. I can't have my best friend and brother at odds."

I dropped my chin into my hand, propping my elbow on the table. "You tricked me."

She rolled her eyes. "Just tell him how you feel."

I snatched her cup of coffee and took a sip, pleased to find it still warm. "So he can rip my heart out and stomp on it? Fuck no."

"Ainsley," she reprimanded like she was my mother.

"Where is he?" I asked, suddenly noticing how freaking quiet the house was.

"The guys went out to get something to eat."

My lips pursed. "Uh-huh. You mean they went to scheme."

We grinned at each other. "Same difference," she retorted.

I fumbled with the coffee cup, spinning it in my hands. "Are you going to the party tonight?" The one I just found out about from the campus bitch, but really, there was a party somewhere on campus every night. It was not surprising, nor did I need to be invited to every single one.

Josie drummed her fingers over the closed laptop. "I think so. Are you coming with us?"

A yawn pulled at my lips. "I haven't decided yet, but if I do go, I'm going to need a nap." It would take more than a cup of coffee to keep me awake. School was kicking my ass lately.

"You feeling okay?" Josie asked after my second yawn.

"I swear I could lay my head down on the table right now and pass out. But not getting enough sleep is what college is about, right?"

The frown forming on her mouth didn't suggest she thought my excuse was valid. I didn't want to worry her more than I already did.

"Go take a nap while it's still peaceful around here. I can wake you up in a few hours if you want," she offered.

The suggestion was too good to refuse, and the thought of my bed made my eyes droopy. "Just for a little bit," I agreed.

"And promise you'll talk to Grayson tonight. I want you guys to work this out. You're both too important to me."

I didn't want to make such a promise, and yet, I couldn't deny the thrill that twirled inside me at the idea of seeing him.

It had been too long.

I didn't even know what I would say.

I probably wouldn't say anything and would just fuck his brains out. Actions often spoke louder than words. I'm not sure sex was what I wanted to say, but my body was so on board.

Crawling into bed, I yawned. All the blinds in my room were closed, submerging the room into darkness and tricking my body into thinking it was later than it was. I dropped off into sleep moments after laying my head on the pillow, but it wasn't Josie startling me awake hours later. Nor was it the guys coming back or anyone in the house for that matter.

It was my phone.

Half asleep, I picked it up, too tired to have any thoughts about threatening messages until I saw the text.

Guess who's back? Miss me? Our favorite boy is in town. See you tonight. Unless you're scared.

I hated this plunging feeling inside my chest, the return of all those emotions I'd wanted to leave in Elmwood. It had been too good to believe my stalker just vanished or that Slade hadn't been only the hired gun but the mastermind. It didn't matter that Slade being the culprit behind the threatening messages made no sense. My mind was quick to accept any reason if it stopped the madness.

It hadn't.

I turned my phone off and discarded it on the bed, leaving the device tangled in the sheets as I got up. After two steps across the room, I came to a halt. My heart raced in my chest.

Fuck this.

This was my turf. My campus. I refused to spend the rest of the semester trembling in my room, living in fear of a predator who used other people to do their dirty work. Unless this prick wanted to face me, he could take his threats and shove them up his ass.

Come for me.

This time, I won't cower. I won't fall apart. I won't break.

I'll strike back.

That was the kind of girl I was.

Perhaps all this bad girl energy came from knowing I was surrounded by the Elite for at least the weekend. Or maybe I just remembered who the hell I was.

I spent more time than usual getting ready. Yes, a part of me wanted to look damn good when Grayson saw me.

The nap helped, but even after getting dressed and finishing my makeup, I still wasn't feeling a hundred percent me. It could be I needed to eat. My last meal was hours ago when I nibbled on a piece of toast for breakfast.

My gaze swept over my reflection in the mirror, and I turned side to side. The fishnet leggings wouldn't offer much warmth against the cold, but I added a layer of black thigh-high socks. The high-waisted skirt hit above the knees, flashing a. peek of my stomach. I readjusted my bra underneath the cropped graphic hoodie I wore and narrowed my eyes.

God, why do my boobs hurt so much?

A knock sounded on my door, and I twisted away from the mirror as my door opened. Mads poked her head inside. "You ready?" she asked.

Did she mean ready to see Grayson or ready to go? *Don't over-think this, Ains.*

My lips curved. "For a party? Always."

With a deep breath, I followed Mads out, leaving my phone behind. No one was going to ruin my night. And if the stalker wanted to keep harassing me, they were going to have to do so in person.

Our house sat only a block from Greek Row where all the good parties happened. Walking made sense, and then we also didn't have to worry about a designated driver, one of the best things about college. The campus also offered safety shuttles, which were just golf carts volunteer students drove.

Grayson, Brock, Josie, and Kenna were already at the Gamma

Zeta house, a fraternity at KU. They left thirty minutes ago. I don't know why I expected Grayson to hang back with Micah, Mads, and Fynn, but he didn't. The disappointment was real.

Perhaps we could go the entire weekend without seeing each other.

What a pathetic thought.

And a worry I didn't need to have.

As I climbed the three steps onto the porch of the frat house, weaving around a group of girls who thought it would be a good idea to stop and have a conversation, my gaze lifted and collided with Grayson's.

He didn't look away.

Neither did I.

I usually scoffed or laughed at those scenes in the movies where the couple locked eyes from across the room and the world just stopped.

That shit actually happened. At least it did to me at this moment.

My eyes drank up the sight of him from his dark wash jeans all the way up to the white tee under a zip-up hoodie. He looked good. Too damn good. I'd always thought Grayson to be attractive, but now I knew what he could do with his hands and mouth, it escalated his status to smoldering hot.

The door to the frat house was propped open. He stood on one side and I on the other. His signature frown touched his lips, making me want to smile. I'd never seen a single person scowl as much as he did. I couldn't even take him seriously.

"Excuse me," a girl behind me said, sounding miffed I was in her way. Tough shit, but her interruption broke the eye contact between Grayson and me.

When I stepped inside, he was gone.

So, he is going to be like that. Fine. Two could play this game.

But first, I needed a drink.

Mads, Micah, and Fynn had gone in ahead of me, and it wasn't a big surprise to find them grabbing drinks at the frat bar. Grayson was with them, leaning against the side of the bar, a beer bottle dangling between his fingers.

I stared back at him, not saying a word until the guy serving drinks asked what I wanted. My usual drink of rum and Coke sat on the tip of my tongue, but it wasn't what came out of my mouth. "A Sprite please with a twist of lime."

The guy behind the bar blinked. "You don't want any Tito's with it?"

I shook my head.

"You're not drinking?"

For the love of everything unholy. Even the sound of his voice did funny things to me. I tilted my head toward Grayson. "No. Not tonight." Of all the things I imagined he would say to me, it was sort of poetic it would be in reference to alcohol.

"What's wrong?" he asked, too perceptive.

The bartender set my sad excuse of a drink on the table. "Nothing. Just not in the mood," I replied, taking the glass.

Grayson didn't budge. "Then what are you doing here?"

Exactly. Now that I was in the crowded house, it was the last place I wanted to be. Everything annoyed me. The crowd. The music. The smells. The only thing I didn't find irritating was Grayson's face. Maybe I should just go home. "I'm asking myself that very question," I mumbled.

He arched a brow. "You never called."

"Neither did you," I snipped back.

"Have you gotten any more threats?" Why did his voice have to sound like it was drenched in sex? He hadn't even said anything sexy. Just the opposite. Something had to be wrong with my hearing.

"No," I lied. If he would have asked me earlier in the day, my answer wouldn't have been a fabrication.

A pretty girl with glossy red hair came up behind Grayson, sliding her arms around his waist. "Hey, I wondered where you'd run off to." She had a sultry voice that would make any guy hard.

I didn't want him to see the hurt spearing into my chest, which he might have seen if he hadn't been distracted by the redhead. Small favors. It gave me enough time to mask the flare of heartache with anger. I snorted. "I see it didn't take you long to move on. Enjoy your date." Heavy sarcasm coated my tone.

Did I sound like a jealous ex-girlfriend?

Yes, but I was too pissed off to care.

Grayson's brows furrowed, and yet he didn't remove the girl wound around him, nor did he stop me from leaving. He made it clear I needed to close this chapter of my life. I was the one who went and caught feelings. I couldn't blame him for not feeling the same.

Wanting to be anywhere but in the same room as him and the girl he picked to screw tonight, I whirled on my heels and stormed deeper into the house, losing myself in the crowd of bodies.

I instantly regretted not adding a shot of vodka to my drink, regardless of how much the thought churned my stomach.

Josie spotted me a few minutes later, and she could tell by my face something happened. "Grayson?" she assumed.

A huff breezed through my nostrils. "Your brother is an asshat."

"I concur," she said, linking her arm through mine.

My forehead wrinkled. "Why didn't anyone tell me he brought a girl?"

Josie whirled and scowled at me. "What girl?"

I sipped on my Sprite; the ice had mostly melted and watered down the drink. "Some fucking redhead."

Her lips pursed as her eyes darkened. "Should we kill her?"

I snickered, but the not-so-funny thing was death or near-death experiences hung around us like a giant storm cloud. At any minute lightning and thunder could strike. "Don't tempt me. The mood I'm in, I *could* kill someone."

A shadow darkened her brown eyes. It wasn't the first time I'd seen it since she returned to school, and despite her assurances everything was fine, I knew something was wrong. My suspicion told me it had to do with Slade's death. I wished she would tell me.

"I know he's my brother, but I'm going to give you the same

advice I would as if he was just any other guy." She paused a breath and then said, "Get revenge."

"Like hooking up with another guy?"

She shrugged. "Why not?"

I couldn't believe she was telling me to have a one-night stand. That was the kind of advice I would give. For weeks she'd been so pro-date-my-brother, and now she was like fuck a stranger. "Maybe I will. Got a target in mind?"

"Does it matter? Take your pick." Her eyes swept through the room of people. "The moment he sees you with someone else, shit will hit the fan."

Okay. So that was her real motive here. Not for me to get over Grayson but to make him jealous, make him realize what he'd let go. "Devious." My lips curled. "I like it."

Brock appeared at Josie's side and pressed a kiss to her lips before eyeing us. His brows drew together. "What are the two of you plotting?"

Josie leaned against Brock, her lips twisting into a secret grin. "Just how to end Grayson."

"I'm going to assume that's a joke," Brock grumbled, his aqua eyes sharpening.

Taking a long swig of my Sprite, I handed my glass to Josie. "Watch and find out."

The great thing about college parties was there were a lot of desperate guys looking to get lucky. It was no difficult feat finding someone to dance with. Talking was impossible the farther inside the house you went due to the music being so damn loud. The drunker the DJ got, the louder it pumped.

But I didn't want to talk to anyone. I wanted to dance.

And that's what I did for the next half hour with every guy who was willing. The back of my neck was warm and damp despite the doors constantly swinging open.

"You look hot," the guy swaying against me yelled into my ear. His hands went to my hips.

I didn't want him to touch me, but I also didn't remove his hands, not even when they skimmed up my sides. The point was to put on a good show. Grayson had been watching me from the moment I zigzagged my way into the middle of the makeshift dance floor.

Finding him in the corner of the room near the sliding doors leading to the backyard wasn't hard, not when I'd been keenly aware of his presence all night. A beer bottle dangled from his fingers as his eyes devoured me, and the heat radiating in the centers made my body flush.

It was hard to ignore that, even in a house full of over a hundred people, Grayson was the hottest guy here.

I was so caught up in him I didn't notice my dance partner leaning close to my neck, not until his lips grazed my skin.

What the fuck?

I jerked my eyes away from Grayson, my hands going to Mr. Touchy-Feely's chest, readying to shove the asshole away from me. I never got the chance.

"Keep your lips to yourself, dickbag, unless you want to lose them." Grayson had the guy lifted by the front of his shirt, glowering in his face.

The guy put his hands up, contradicting the smart-ass smirk on his face. "Sorry, dude. Can't help it your girl would rather suck me off than dance with you tonight."

I groaned. Not because of what this idiot said. I couldn't care less. What I didn't want was Grayson killing someone tonight, which was exactly what was about to happen.

I needed to step in, but no sooner had the thought crossed my mind than the dumb frat boy's head snapped back, thanks to Grayson's fist flying. Even over the pounding bass, the crack of his knuckles connecting with the fool's nose was audible.

Blood gushed from the impact, and Big Mouth couldn't seem to know when to shut up. "What the fuck! You broke my nose." His hand flew directly to his face.

The crowd on the dance floor backed away yet stayed to watch, sensing the fight wasn't over.

Grayson hit the guy again, knocking him flat on his ass. "Touch her again, and I'll break more than your nose."

"Grayson!" I yelled, putting my hand on his shoulder as he loomed over the idiot. This was my fault to some degree. I hadn't invited the dumbass to put his lips on me, but I'd also been using him. I had to stop Grayson from doing any more damage.

I tugged on his sweatshirt, but he didn't move, and I didn't stand a chance of forcing Grayson to leave if he didn't want to. The man was an immovable force.

A shadow appeared at my back.

"I wouldn't get up if I were you, buddy," Micah told the guy with the broken nose as he struggled to push himself to his feet.

The jerk finally listened and stayed seated. He'd be sporting a black eye tomorrow, and perhaps he should go to the hospital to get his nose checked out.

My hand dropped away from Grayson's shoulder. I was relieved Micah could deal with him. And then I had another thought. He could also team up with Grayson. Regardless, I'd had enough of the Elite for a single night.

Shaking my head, I glared at Grayson. "I need some air." The sharp metallic scent of blood made my stomach queasy.

I sensed someone trailing after me. The tingles on my neck told me who it was. People whispered and stared as we pushed by, most of them stepping out of our way to let us pass. Josie caught my eye for a second, Brock frowning beside her, but neither of them did anything other than watch us leave the house.

A gust of wind slapped against my cheeks, crisp and icy, but it felt good. The air inside the house had gotten too stifling. We weren't alone outside, but at least here, under a slice of moonlight, I could hear myself think. A couple sat on the porch banister drinking, paying little attention to us.

I went to the opposite side, looking out into the shaded yard, and drew in a breath. The air cooled my lungs, and I turned around, facing Grayson. He had his hands shoved into his pockets, watching me with cold eyes. Despite it only being weeks since I'd last seen him, his height floored me. I'd forgotten how tall he was.

My neck craned backward as I glanced up.

Grayson backed me into the corner of the porch, my butt pressing into the wooden railings. "What are you doing?" he growled at me.

This conversation was long overdue. Better to hash it out now. "Isn't this what you wanted? To go back to being friends? That's what I'm doing. This *is* what the old Ainsley would do."

"Are you drunk?" He leaned in closer as if to smell for any traces of alcohol.

My body came alive at his nearness. Like a live wire during a storm, one of us was bound to get shocked. I lifted my hand, torn between shoving him away or pulling him closer. He caught my hand, taking the option from me. The pad of his thumb rubbed along the inside of my wrist and I nearly sighed but managed to cover it with a laugh.

Drunk? Fucking funny since I hadn't had one drink other than a Sprite, and it did little to settle my rolling stomach. I sort of felt drunk. Or sick. I couldn't tell which.

Perhaps both.

But something was definitely wrong with me.

"I wish I was," I mumbled, holding his gaze. My head tilted to the side. "Where's your *date*?" I spat in return.

"I don't date," he retorted in a cold, quiet tone.

I didn't need the reminder. "Your fuck for the night then." The words lashed out of me, and I didn't care how crude they sounded. I hurt inside. I wanted to hurt him.

He took a step closer, his warmth seeping into my bones. "You're being ridiculous."

"I'm not the one who broke some tool's nose," I fired back. I hated my feelings being discarded regardless of how irrationally I might be behaving.

Grayson's smirk was nothing short of lethal. "At least you admit he was a tool."

My breath caught. Smiles of any kind were rare, but when he unleashed them, I swear my world stopped. "You can't go around hitting every guy who looks at me. We're not together, Grayson."

"Maybe that's why I'm here," he said, shocking me.

I gasped. I didn't want to read too much into that statement, but my mind when off in a hundred different directions that all lead back to the same hopeful conclusion. He wanted *me*. "You have a funny way of showing it."

He took another step closer, his chest touching mine, all humor evaporating. "I wasn't going to sleep with her."

"It doesn't matter." Or it shouldn't matter, and eventually, what Grayson did would stop hurting me. Time. I just needed time.

"Ainsley." His hand went to my waist. I loved the warmth penetrating through my clothes. My body wanted him closer, my heart more so, but my stomach was doing all kinds of weird somersaults. Not the good kind.

And still, I leaned into him, a breeze carrying his scent, and I inhaled, missing the way he smelled. Except...the usual sea with hints of something citrus caused a confounding reaction.

My hand flew to my mouth, and I spun, barely clearing the banister as I threw up the Sprite. I hadn't eaten much today, so the only thing in my stomach was liquids. It burned up my throat, stinking my nose.

God, what a fucking time to get sick.

I waited for a beat to make sure another bout of vomit wasn't about to make a sudden appearance. Wiping the sleeve of my hoodie across my mouth, I turned back around. The intensity of his expression softened, concern touching his dark eyes.

He gave me a bit of space, no longer crowding me into the corner. "Are you okay?"

I shook my head. "No. I need to go. I can't be here anymore." He didn't stop me as I pushed past him, dashing down the porch steps into the night.

Why am I always throwing up around him?

Fuck. My. Life.

Grayson caught up to me in a few strides. He wouldn't let me walk back home alone regardless of what happened. I didn't want another reason to like him, but it was just the guy he was.

Drunk puke somehow didn't embarrass me as much as whatever this did. The flu, perhaps. Was the universe working against me? Grayson and I were finally talking, and then I spewed in the bushes.

Silence stretched between us on the path back to the rowhouse until I couldn't take it. "Don't you have a redhead waiting?"

"Why are you always throwing up on my shoes?" he asked, a tinge of amusement in his deep voice.

I shouldn't laugh.

It wasn't funny.

But I couldn't suppress the giggle, and once I started, I couldn't seem to stop.

My eyes glanced at his feet, but in the dark, I couldn't get a clear picture of them. It was possible a bit had splattered on his kicks, but at least it hadn't been a direct hit. I lifted my gaze. His vexed expression only amused me.

A small smile played across his lips. "I'm glad one of us thinks this is hilarious, little devil."

"Fuck," I muttered, running a hand through my tousled hair. "I'm going to be indebted to you for life trying to pay off the number of shoes I've ruined," I said after catching my breath. My chest hurt from laughing so hard. I hadn't even minded that he called me little devil. In fact, I liked it.

Fuck my life.

God, it had been weeks since I'd laughed to the point of pain.

"Feel better?" he asked.

My lips hurt, and for once, it wasn't because someone hit me. "Shockingly, I do." Our footsteps clattered over the sidewalk as we started walking again, my laugh fit having passed. "Why are you avoiding me?" I asked, feeling bold and brave.

"I could ask you the same thing."

I swallowed. I would regret this, but it had to be said. We were getting to the nitty-gritty. "It's too hard seeing you," I admitted. I'd gone and done the worst thing. Caught feelings for him.

I'd been focusing on the path in front of us, deliberating avoiding Grayson's face, and then in my next breath, I was staring into his eyes, my back pressing against the rough bark of a tree trunk just off the sidewalk.

His expression was hard and unreadable. "You think it's easy for me? Seeing that guy touch you, put his lips on you... It's safe to say I lost my shit."

My veins flared with anger. "And you think it was any easier for me seeing that girl sidle up to you? Wrap her arms around you as if you were hers?"

The fingers on my arms gentled. "You were jealous."

"As if you didn't know," I snarled. "I'd never been more jealous in my life. She's lucky I didn't rip her hair out."

Grayson chuckled and pressed a kiss to my nose. "Jealousy looks cute on you, little devil."

I dropped the back of my head against the tree. "I can't keep doing this with you. I thought I could keep things casual. It's never been a problem before, but with you it's different. Maybe it's because we were friends first."

"Perhaps," he considered, the lines of his body relaxing against mine.

My temper was morphing into something I desperately wanted to crush. Desiring him would so not help the situation and only compli-cate matters more. "So, what are we going to do about it?"

His gaze darted to my lips. "I want to kiss you. God, do I want to kiss you right now."

My head shook. "You can't. I threw up."

His hands wound into my hair, grabbing a knot and pulling my head back. "I'm clearly aware of that fact. Still doesn't change how much I want your mouth."

Oh shit.

He was turning me up inside. He couldn't do that.

"Grayson," I murmured, wishing my stomach hadn't chosen tonight of all nights to go topsy-turvy because there was no doubt in my mind I wanted Grayson in my bed. Sleeping with him no matter how good it might feel wouldn't solve our issue, which was I loved him. And he... "Oh God, I'm going to be sick again."

I turned my head as Grayson jumped back, and sure as shit, what little contents left in my stomach came up. Dry heaving was the worst.

Grayson's hand rubbed circles at the small of my back until I finished. "Come on, let's get you in bed."

* * *

I thought for sure I'd spend the night in the bathroom with my head in the toilet, but once I got under the covers, I passed out. The last thing I remembered was Grayson holding my hand. He was gone when I woke.

Not long after I stretched the sleeping kinks from my muscles, my bedroom door squeaked open. Josie popped her head in, checking to see if I was up, and when she noticed my eyes open, she jumped on the bed.

I groaned as the mattress jiggled and rolled over, burying my head under the covers. My stomach protested at the movement of the bed.

She pushed lightly at my shoulders. "Get up. You can't avoid him the whole weekend."

Peeking out from a corner of the blanket, I glanced at Josie. She wore a pair of sweats and a sports bra the same color as her hair. "I'm not avoiding him. I don't feel good," I mumbled.

"Hangover?" she guessed.

"No, and that's what's so messed up. I didn't drink at all yesterday."

"You threw up breakfast the other day too."

I flopped on my back, a hand pressing to my forehead. "Ugh, don't remind me. I can't even think about food."

Josie stared at me. I could feel her gaze and practically see the wheels grinding inside her brain. She was working through a thought. "Holy. Fuck."

"Now what?" I exclaimed, wondering if I could get her to bring me a cup of coffee. I needed something to settle my stomach. Tea would probably be better, but I wanted coffee.

Straightening her back, she pulled her legs up on the bed, fully facing me. The serious expression on her features made my gut clench. "Ainsley, when was the last time you had your period?" she asked.

"Why are we talking about my cycle?" I groaned, sitting up slowly. Blood was another topic my stomach rebelled against.

"We are usually only a day or two apart, which means you should have gotten yours last week," she proceeded to explain.

And like I'd been snapped with a rubber band, she suddenly had my full attention. I started to do the math in my head, counting back the days. "Where are my pills?" The first stirrings of this can't be happening squeezed my chest.

Josie opened the drawer of my nightstand and pulled out the little credit card–style pill container. Her brows drew together as she studied the birth control packaging. "You didn't take the brown."

The brown pills were the inactive ones. "I never take them."

Holding out the little pack for me, she looked at me with wide eyes. "You're late, aren't you?"

22

AINSLEY

My head shook, a pesky buzzing of disbelief vibrating in my ears. "I can't be pregnant," I whispered, staring at the pills as the possibility started to sink in.

You can. You might be." Josie's voice sounded so much calmer than mine.

I gave myself two seconds before I started to freak out.

One. Two.

"What am I going to do? I can't have a baby." I took the package of pills and hurled them across the room as if it was their fault I might be pregnant. It was wholly on me and my lack of responsibility. "Holy shit. It's your brother's baby."

The situation had no amusing qualities, yet this statement made a hint of humor sparkle in Josie's eyes. "I know. I put that together already."

Hopping out of bed, I paced the small room from one wall to the other. "This can't be happening to me." The sudden fear gripping me overtook the nausea I'd been battling.

Josie leveled me a look. "He never used a condom?"

I shook my head. "I was on the pill."

"Ainsley," she reprimanded.

I had no excuses. My head dropped into my hands. "I know."

Chewing on her lower lip, she toyed with the ends of her ponytail, eyes brimming with both worry and disbelief. "Do your boobs hurt?"

They had been a little achy and fuller. "I guess. They're more sensitive, but I figured it's because I'm getting my period!"

"There's only one way to be sure. I'll go to the store," she said, taking control of the situation. "Stay here."

As if she had to convince me to stay in bed. I was never leaving.

Less than fifteen minutes later, Josie came back with a white bag carrying a small box and a bottle of juice. Our campus had a convenience store that sold everything from snacks to medicine and apparently pregnancy tests.

"Here, drink this." She handed me a bottle of apple juice. I couldn't remember the last time I drank juice that wasn't being used as a mixer. "Then pee on this." Next came the dreaded box and the stick inside that would determine my future. How insane to think about how a little strip of compressed fibers and pee would impact my entire life from this point forward.

I stared at the box, clutching tighter to the juice bottle.

Right now? We were doing this now? I wasn't sure I was ready to find out. There was something settling about being blissfully unaware. Once I took this test, I had to face the truth regardless of the outcome.

Panic clutched my chest. "Is everyone home?"

She shook her head. "They went out to breakfast. I told them you were still sick."

"Thank you," I replied, taking a sip of juice.

The process of peeing on a stick was the easy part. The hard part came after. Three minutes didn't seem long until you were counting each second. Then it was like a lifetime. The longest three minutes of my fucking life.

Together, we stared at the digital white stick, willing it to read not pregnant. At least, that was what was happening inside my head.

Not pregnant. Not pregnant. Not pregnant.

The digital screen flashed.

Pregnant.

Son of a bitch.

My eyes closed, and I prayed I could will it away. Blink and the screen would change, but the word pregnant flashed behind my eyes as if the letters were burned into my mind. *This can't be real. No. I'm not pregnant.*

And then Josie said, "Holy shit, you're pregnant."

I barely heard her over the humming growing louder in between my ears. My back hit the bathroom wall as her eyes rose from the white stick to mine, and we just stared at each other.

My world crumbled. I thought I would be sick. Again. "I can't be a mom. Look at me. I'd be a shit mom."

Josie leaned into the counter. "We both know that's bullshit. We've always taken care of each other. But whether you want to be a mom is entirely up to you."

Tears pricked the backs of my eyes. "I can't do this. What about your brother? I can't be the one who ruins his life too." Because I'd already made up my mind a baby would destroy my future.

"Having a baby doesn't mean they will ruin either of your lives. Change? Fuck yes. Ruin? Never. Not you, Ainsley Fisher, you're too damn stubborn, smart, and determined to let anything or anyone stand in your way."

The tears I'd been holding at bay threatened to spill. Overwhelmed, I slid down the wall to the floor, dropping my head into my hands. "I can't deal with this."

Josie's hands came to my shoulders as she crouched down in front of me. "Yes, you can. I'll always support you. No matter what."

Pregnant. Pregnant. Pregnant. The word spun around in my head on an endless loop. I dropped my hands and met Josie's gaze. "Don't tell anyone. Not yet. I need to figure my shit out first."

It might be a lot to ask considering her brother was involved, but I needed time to process this. "Okay," she quickly agreed. "But promise me you won't tackle this alone."

What else could I say but, "I promise."

Josie sat down beside me on the floor. "This might not be the best time to tell you, but I feel like you should know. If the roles were reversed, I know you would tell me."

My face went blank. I wasn't sure I could handle anything else, and judging by her somber expression, I assumed this wasn't good news. "What is it?"

"Grayson has a security guard protecting you," she informed.

Fucker.

I clenched and unclenched my fingers, trying to feel something other than numb. I should be fuming. All those times I felt as if I was being watched hadn't been in my head. Someone was spying on me. Grayson had hired a bodyguard.

"You might not think he cares about you," Josie rushed to defend her brother's actions. "Hell, he might have even convinced himself he doesn't care about you, but I know my brother. He would never go to such lengths if feelings weren't involved."

My head hit the back of the wall, and I let out a long, slightly ragged breath. "I know he cares about me."

"But you think it isn't the same way you love him?" she asked quietly, trying to understand.

I groaned internally. She just said *love*. She knows I'm in love with him. Heat warmed my cheeks. "I can't believe I fell in love with your brother."

She crossed her arms over her propped knees, a ghost of a smirk drawing on her lips. "There are worse guys you could have fallen for."

"Like Brock Taylor," I said jokingly.

She snort-laughed. "Yeah, that would have been a problem."

"What a fucking mess." If there had been any chance Grayson might want to get serious with me, something I never thought either of us would want, telling him I was pregnant would surely send him running for the hills.

I refused to use a baby to trap someone into a relationship. Hell no. Never. That wasn't me. I'd rather be a single mom.

The truth was, I didn't even know if I wanted to be a mom at all. Kids were something I didn't think about. Ever.

This wasn't a decision I could take lightly or make rationally.

* * *

The clock on my nightstand read nine thirty-eight in the evening. I didn't remember setting an alarm before lying down for a quick nap. I hadn't meant to sleep for so long, nor did I have anywhere to be, yet an insisting buzz kept going off.

It took me another minute before I realized it was my phone.

My hand fumbled on the bed. I followed the vibrating until I found it, bringing the device close to my face as I groggily glanced at the screen. It was a message from Grayson asking me to meet him at Demon's Park, what used to be the old amusement park a few miles down the road from the Kingsley campus. He was racing tonight and wanted to talk to me beforehand. The last line I read twice.

Be there at ten.

It was just like Grayson to ask me to meet him and then in the next line give me no choice. Such an Elite maneuver.

I rolled my eyes and looked at the time again.

Shit.

Getting to the park by ten meant I had to leave in like five minutes. Not a lot of time to pull myself together. Did I even want to go? I didn't have great track records lately with street races, but if Grayson really did have someone tailing me, then at least I wouldn't be alone. As weird as the thought of having a guy watch me was, it also gave me a sense of security I never expected.

Besides, I couldn't deny I wanted to see Grayson. He left tomorrow. Tonight might be our only chance to talk. I needed clarity after our last conversation. He left me conflicted and confused. It almost sounded as if Grayson wanted something more from me than a hookup. He made it clear he wanted me. That part I didn't doubt, but was I reading something I desperately wanted him to feel?

I had only enough time to run a brush through my hair, scrub my teeth, slap on some deodorant, add a spray of perfume, and rush out the door in a pair of jeans and a chunky sweater.

Grabbing a Sprite from the fridge along with a sleeve of crackers, I dashed out the door and into my car. The queasiness never seemed to subside. Whoever coined the term morning sickness either had never been pregnant or was a guy. This shit could happen at any time of the day and often hit me out of nowhere but particularly on an empty stomach.

Like now.

Suppressing the urge to throw up, I munched on a cracker as I guided my car onto the road. Once I cleared the campus grounds and got on the main road, Demon's Park was only a few minutes away.

To keep my mind from dwelling on the last two times I'd seen Grayson race, I thought about my current predicament. Did I tell Grayson tonight about the baby? I'd barely thought about it myself.

My mind whirled while I tapped my thumbs against the steering wheel. Nerves fluttered in my ribs.

I couldn't have a baby. What about school? How could I possibly go to school and take care of a baby? What about money? Babies weren't cheap. How many jobs would I have to work just to pay for diapers, daycare, and all the other millions of things babies required? Even if I managed to overcome all those worries, I had to find a place to live. College housing wasn't an ideal place for a kid.

The city lights whirled past. Every few minutes or so, I glanced in my rearview mirror to see if I could spot someone following me. Through campus and on the main road, it was difficult to tell, but when I turned off onto Demon's Circle, I didn't see a single headlight behind me. Either this guy was extremely good at being invisible or no one was tailing me tonight.

I didn't have too much time to mull it over as I approached the gated run-down fence leading to the park. If I continued to take the curve of the road running along the perimeter of the park, it would take me to the side lot. Demon's Circle wound around the park like a racetrack, and eventually, I'd end up back at the entrance.

Where the hell is everyone?

I spotted only one other car outside the entrance gate. I didn't recognize the vehicle, but that meant little seeing as Grayson drove a different car every week. And the ones he raced he drove little.

Were they all at the side parking lot?

Leaving my car on and the door opened, I stepped out to look around. The wind howled, blowing through the not-so-stable metal fence. My creepy radar went up a thousand notches. Everything about this place looked as if it came straight out of an Alfred Hitchcock movie. I read somewhere his catchphrase was *always make the audience suffer as much as possible.*

That's what this place was...a torture park.

Squeak. Squeak. Squeak.

A rusted sign hung over the gate and clanged against the bars, adding to the eeriness and fraying my already frazzled nerves. Every bone in my body told me to get back in my car and leave. I turned to do just that, but then I heard voices.

Faint.

Like they came from inside the park.

The headlights from my car beamed straight ahead into the entrance, but they helped little for me to actually see anything.

"Hello!" I called out. "Grayson!"

I waited for what felt like a reasonable amount of time for him to holler back. He didn't. No one did, and yet I swore I heard...laughing.

Well, as if that wasn't scary as shit.

My fingers looped around the metal bars, and I peered inside the park, half expecting a crow to fly down and peck my eyes out. Or shit on me. I'd take a crow over a fucking clown any day.

This place closed more than ten years ago for remodeling and never reopened. Lack of funds or unable to secure any financial backing. Something along those lines, but the empty years hadn't been kind. The grounds, the rides, and the buildings were all run-down and in desperate need of some TLC.

Or an exorcist.

Nothing about the park enticed happiness or fun. It was downright spooky. *Why do I feel like the main character in a horror film about to be hunted by a psychopath with a bloody butcher knife?*

"This isn't funny!" I yelled, moving away from the gate and toward the other car. Peeking through the tinted windows, I looked to see if anyone sat inside. From what I could tell, the seats were empty.

It wasn't like Grayson to play games with me. Not like this. He was an asshole not sadistic. With all I'd been through, he wouldn't lure me to a place like this for tricks and not show up.

But someone would.

My stalker.

I thought back to the text I'd gotten from Grayson. What if he didn't send the text? What if something happened to him? The idea someone could hurt Grayson seemed implausible, but the reality was, he wasn't invincible. He wasn't a superhero.

With rushed hands, I fished my phone out of my back pocket and unlocked the screen. It was still opened to the text app, and I reread Grayson's message, this time paying closer attention to details. The text was short and didn't give me much information other than a time and a place to talk.

Screw this. I'm leaving.

My fingers tapped over the screen as I opened the phone app. It would be quicker to call him. I turned back toward my car, about to hit the Sunshine contact in my phone, and came face-to-face with another person.

I screamed, a freaking ear-piercing shriek that rang over the park.

It died off when I recognized the face.

My hand flew above my heart. "Kate?" I gasped. Confused, my heart continued to jackhammer in my chest, about to break through my ribs. I could hear it pounding in my ears. I absolutely hated the intense adrenaline of fear that surged through your body after getting the shit scared out of you.

"What are you doing here?" I asked, leaning back against the car I realized was probably hers.

Kate's hand tightened around something, drawing my gaze. Her arms were at her sides, but there was just enough light from my headlights behind her for me to see the glint of steel. "I'm giving you my final message," she said, glimmers of hatred cooling her cat-like eyes.

A dozen thoughts ran through my head at once as I pieced together what the hell was going on.

What the—

Holy shit!

It couldn't be.

She's the one behind the texts?

It was no surprise Kate didn't like me, but her expression went deeper than dislike.

And this bitch had a knife.

My gaze latched on to the blade in her hand, and I took a step back with nowhere to go, my ass already pressed up against the car.

Shit!

My widened eyes narrowed. "You're the one who's been sending me all those messages?"

She took a step closer like a vulture circling its prey. "Why does that surprise you?"

"I'm not sure. I guess because I assumed you were a dude." I inched slowly toward the door, careful to keep my movements subtle.

"How can he like someone so stupidly clueless?" she sneered cynically. "You don't deserve him."

My fingers slid to the door handle. "Who? Are you talking about Grayson?" I snorted, losing touch of my situation and knowing I probably shouldn't taunt her, but the idea she still harbored any delusions about Grayson came off as pathetic to me.

She clearly had problems. I wasn't sure how seriously I could take a girl who showed up in designer jeans and fur to...

Hell, I didn't know what her agenda was with me.

Why had she lured me here?

If Kate was behind all the shit that happened to me, if she'd hired Slade to hurt me, she could be more dangerous than I was giving her credit for.

It might not be smart to disregard her yet.

"Don't say his name," she hissed, raising the knife like an escaped mental patient about to go on a killing spree.

I attempted to open her car door, but shocker, it was locked. *Fuckity fuck.* "Let me see if I'm understanding. You think if you get rid of me you'll have an opening with Grayson?" Thinking like a lunatic took brain power I didn't possess under this amount of duress.

Kate smiled with a kind of joy that meant bad things to come for me. "So, she has a brain after all."

She wouldn't really kill me, would she?

I was no longer certain of anything other than the fact I needed to get out of here. If I could reach my car, I might stand a chance of escaping before she tried to hack me up with a blade.

"You left me little choice," she said, pointing the knife at my throat.

I could think of a few other options. Checking into a psychiatric hospital was at the top of the list. Or prison. Prison was a high alternative.

We were feet apart, but I was unsure if I'd be able to move fast enough and avoid getting sliced. I stared at the weapon, noticing something familiar about the hilt. "Is that my knife?"

Kate leveled me with a dark look that made me shiver. "My brother gave it to me before he went missing. You killed him, didn't you?"

Her brother was unalive? Who was her brother? "Hate to break it to you, but I haven't killed anyone. Yet," I added because this bitch was so dead. "I don't even know who your brother is." I took a moment to look for another solution out of this mess. If I wanted to get away, it was imperative I kept my wits about me.

She laughed, a manic sound matching the evil in her eyes. "Who do you think I got to sneak into your room or attack you during the race?"

My eyes snapped back to her. "Slade's your brother." *Holy shit. No wonder he wouldn't give up her name.*

"*Was*," she spat, waving the knife in my face. "You and your fucking friends took him from me. You ruined my life."

I jerked my head back, but I had no space left to retreat. I had to run. It was my only shot. If I could distract her for a few seconds to give me a head start, I might make it to my car. Regardless, I had to try because the alternative wasn't an option. "You're sounding a little crazy, Kate. Okay, perhaps that isn't out of character for you, but I fail to see how my friends had anything to do with how unhappy *you* are about *your* life."

Kate glared, a small tick flickering in the corner of her eye. "There's only one thing that would make me happy."

A low sickening laugh bubbled up my throat. "Let me guess, Grayson."

"That. And killing you," she snarled.

And that was my cue to run. She must have seen the panic leap into my eyes. Just as I shoved off the balls of my feet, her hand shot out, tangling into my hair. So much for a distraction.

"Let me go!" I shrilled, forgetting about the blade she held in her other hand. Pain erupted in my skull, her grip tightening. My hands flew to her wrists and arms, pushing at her fist, and when that didn't work, I started scratching her.

Stronger than I would have given her credit for, the psycho skank yanked my head forward and slammed me into the car window.

I was plunged into darkness like I'd fallen into a cold pool, sinking further and further into its depths.

* * *

Before I opened my eyes, a flare of agony registered on my back. Something rough and hard scraped through my sweater, digging into my skin. The world swayed as if I was moving, unsettling me. I forced my eyes open seeing my feet were above my head. The bitch was dragging me across the ground.

The nightmare gushed into my memory, triggering my fight-or-flight response. I started to kick and twist my body. The one thing I had going for me was Kate hadn't noticed I woke up until I started to fight, giving me an edge.

I got one foot loose and used it to kick her hand holding my other leg.

"You bitch," she hissed, cradling her arm against her chest and fastening me with a death glare.

I didn't plan to stick around and fight over who was the bigger bitch in this situation. She would clearly win.

Scrambling, I shoved to my feet, keeping my eyes trained on her, but my vision wavered as a sharp pain stabbed the side of my head. Stumbling, I winced, my hand pressing above my temples. The throbbing tenderness increased at my probing touch. Blood coated my fingers as I pulled them away.

"I bet that hurts," Kate said, the knife still in her grasp.

And I was still weaponless and at a disadvantage. I backed up, putting distance between us. "You knocked me out."

"Don't try to run," Kate warned.

Yeah, sure. But at this point, I'd say anything to get her to stop waving the knife in my face. "I won't run," I lied. First chance I got, you better believe my ass was running. "You can still let me go. It's not too late," I tried to reason, regardless of how slim a chance it would work.

"Shut up. Just shut the fuck up and move." Still cradling her arm against her chest, she waved the knife in the air, indicating the direction in front of her.

I had two choices. I could go along with Kate and pray she didn't actually kill me.

Or I could run.

I chose option two.

I mean, she'd told me to move. I just went in the opposite direction with no plan, no layout of the park, and no idea what I would do next short of running until my lungs or legs gave out.

Pivoting, I took off into the dark, my feet hitting the pavement at full force. Not a single light flickered throughout the park, and I hoped that worked to my advantage. If I could put enough distance between us, perhaps she would lose me in the darkness.

Kate let out a berserk shriek that pierced through the night like an animal being skinned alive. I didn't risk my momentum by looking over my shoulder but kept my focus on moving and not falling. Besides, I could hear her shoes clattering behind me as she gave chase. Who the fuck wore platforms to a murder?

I dashed off the main pathway, bolting between rides and ducking under the Ferris wheel. I clipped my shoulder against a support bar. Pain shot down my arm, but I kept going, pushing farther into the park. It seemed as if I moved deeper into the grounds when I should be searching for an exit.

The signs didn't help. Most of them were turned around, broken, or faded, not that they would have assisted much. The darkness made it impossible to read anything, particularly while running.

My breath came out in clouds of cold puffs, faster and faster as my heart raced from exhaustion and fear. Cursing my lungs and legs, I regretted not taking advantage of the college's gym. The treadmill wasn't looking so bad. I'd have more stamina than I sadly had now.

This had to be a joke.

I really was being stalked in an amusement park.

My first thought was don't go anywhere near the funhouse. No one ever came out of the fucking funhouse.

Seconds turned into minutes as I flew past the carousel. I could no longer hear her steps chasing after me, but I wasn't stupid enough to believe Kate had given up. The bitch would stalk me. Somehow not knowing where she was in the park scared me more than when she had been in front of me with a knife.

I contemplated jumping onto the carousel and hiding among the shabby horses, but if she could still see me, it wouldn't be much of a disguise.

How the fuck did I end up being chased at Demon's Park?

This was unreal. Like I was living a nightmare, unable to wake up. My mind had trouble wrapping around the idea of Kate being the devious evil behind all the threats. It was no secret she was labeled as trouble, but she was more than just a spurned girl who wanted to slash someone's tires.

She was dangerous.

I spun around in a circle, trying to decipher which way was the exit.

How the hell do I get out of here?

I didn't have time to linger and took off toward a concession stand. The pain in my head tripled from the rise in my blood pressure, but it was the least of my worries. I darted behind the food cart and hunkered down, pressing my back into the wall. My bones and muscles screamed, and I didn't know how much longer I could keep running.

Hummmm. Click. Click. Click. Click.

My gaze lifted at the sounds suddenly echoing throughout the park, moving from one section to another. Lights flickered, generators hummed, and off-speed carnival music crawled out of the speakers. The park slowly came to life, zone by zone, and I no longer had the darkness to cloak me.

But neither did she.

I peeked out from behind the concession counter, scanning for movement. If she turned the electricity on, she had to be in the control room. Wherever the heck that was. And assuming she was here alone. Unknown factors were loose ends, and I hated dangling questions.

Surveying the park, I tried to get my bearings and figure out which direction would get me back to my car. Left or right? I had a fifty-fifty chance to get it right. Or wrong.

Taking a few moments to catch my breath, I straightened to my feet as an ear-piercing shrill shrieking resonated from the PA system. Grimacing, I jumped, my hands covering my ears.

Kate's voice came through once the shrieking stopped. "You can run, but you can't hide forever."

The fuck I can't. And I didn't plan on hiding until she got bored. We both knew that would never happen. I reached into my back pocket. *Son of a bitch.* She took my phone.

I searched the buildings near me, looking to see if I could locate something like a maintenance office, and Kate's voice came through the speakers again. "You should just give up now. If I don't kill you today, there's always tomorrow."

Kate gave crazy a new definition.

"Ready or not, here I come," she sang into the mic like a little girl at Disney World.

I needed to get out of the open. The lights would make it too easy for her to spot me. There had to be somewhere I could hole away. Find a weapon. A phone.

I spotted the funhouse.

Shit. Shit. Shit.

I was so going to be that girl.

If I died, so help me, I would come back and haunt this bitch so hard.

GRAYSON

Tomorrow I left to go back to Dalton's campus, but I couldn't leave until I said what I came here to say. Nothing about this weekend went as I'd envisioned. It all went wrong, but it wasn't too late to fix it.

That's why I was here. To fix things with Ainsley. If I could only find her.

When we got back to the rowhouse, her car was gone. Disappointment made me impatient. I hoped to spend what little time I had left with her, convincing her what an idiot I'd been.

I checked my phone. No messages.

My foot tapped on the floor as I silently cursed myself.

Had I blown everything? Would she give me a chance? Would I be able to tell her what I barely came to understand about my feelings? Last night on our way home, I'd been so sure what I saw in her eyes and heard in her voice mirrored what I felt.

A part of me wondered if I was capable of love. Sure, I loved my family, loved my friends, but I'd never been *in* love. Never come close.

And I still wasn't positive what I felt for her was love. But it was more than I'd ever felt for another girl. I hadn't wanted her to leave after Christmas. I missed her. I hadn't grown tired of kissing her, of exploring her body. I longed for her in my bed.

What confused me was whether it was desire or love burning inside me. I'd spent years keeping my heart protected, hardening it from everyone. After losing my brother, Sawyer, I vowed to never feel the pain of heartache again.

Being with Ainsley unlocked the chains wrapped around my heart, and now they were freed, I didn't know how to close my heart again. She got inside of me. There was no going back. There was only her.

This gaping ache in my chest was her fault.

And I needed to see her. *Where the hell is she?*

The longer she was gone, the higher my restlessness grew. Something was wrong.

My skin crawled with tiny prickles of unease.

Standing up, I charged into the other room, unable to quelch this urge to find her. Kenna was laying on the couch watching a movie. "Where's Ainsley?" I demanded.

"I don't know," she snapped, annoyed I interrupted her concentration. "I don't keep track of your girlfriends. Go ask Josie."

I didn't bother to correct her. It was a waste of breath on Kenna. "Where's Josie?" I asked.

Shifting on the couch with a huff, she glared at me. "For fuck's sake, Grayson. Call her."

"You don't think I've tried? It goes straight to voicemail."

Kenna pointed the remote at the TV and paused the movie. "Her phone's probably dead."

"Maybe. It wouldn't be the first time."

The annoyance in her features softened as she realized I was genuinely concerned. "Josie's upstairs with Brock. You can guess what they're most likely doing."

My nose scrunched. "How do you live with that?"

She shrugged. "Why do you think the TV is so loud?"

Leaving Kenna to her movie, I took the stairs two at a time to the second floor. Josie and Brock shared the first room on the left. Mads and Micah had the one across the hall. Both doors were closed.

I rapped my knuckles on the door. If my gut feeling was right, I didn't feel bad about interrupting something.

Josie opened the door fully dressed, thank God. Her cheeks were a bit flushed, strands of pink messy hair framing her face. "Hey," she greeted, letting the door swing all the way open. Brock lay on the bed, his shirt and dark hair rumpled.

I got straight to the point. Instincts propelled me to not waste time. "Have you seen Ainsley?"

"Did you check her room?" Josie suggested.

"Her car is gone," I stated.

Brock turned down the TV in the room as Josie said, "I hadn't noticed."

"She isn't picking up her phone."

My intention wasn't to upset Josie or worry her, but I could tell she was headed in both directions. "Did you check with the guy you have watching her?"

I silently cursed, wishing I hadn't sent him away. "I gave him the weekend off when I got here."

"Let me try her. Maybe she's just avoiding you."

I waited as Josie went into the room and grabbed her phone. "Voicemail," she said, standing by the bed and glancing up at me from her phone, frowning.

A series of F-bombs went off in my head. I whirled, heading down the hall.

Josie chased after me, following me down the stairs. "What are you doing?" she asked.

I went right to the kitchen to grab my car keys. "Going to look for her. I need to talk to her before I leave."

"You're starting to freak me out." I could see the concern swimming in her eyes.

I raked a hand through my hair and glanced at Brock who came into the kitchen behind Josie. "Something's wrong," I told him.

Brock nodded, putting a hand on Josie's shoulder. "Okay, we'll find her. Fynn?"

"He went out to get us food," Kenna informed from the couch. "He should be back any minute."

Josie grabbed my arm. "We need to talk."

"I don't have time—" I began to protest, but she was insistent.

"Grayson, it's important."

She knew something. My eyes narrowed as she dragged me into Ainsley's room. It was the closest place for privacy, and whatever she had to say to me, she didn't want anyone else to hear.

The door closed, and she spun to face me, her expression serious. "Do you love her?"

The question took me back. "What?" I blinked, feeling like I'd been zapped by a stun gun to the chest. I shouldn't have been surprised. Josie, like Ainsley, said what was on her mind.

"Do you love her?" she repeated steadier.

Yes, I'd been contemplating the question for weeks, but I wasn't ready to expose those feelings to anyone but Ainsley. "I fail to see why that's relevant right now."

She folded her arms. "Grayson, answer the damn question."

"I don't know. Maybe. Yeah. I think I do." The admission tumbled out of me in a bumbling mess of uncertainty.

Josie nodded. "If you really believe something happened to her, then I need to tell you this. She's going to be pissed, but it's important you know. She was going to tell you, but she only just found out today."

"Josie." Her name rumbled in my chest, a flare of haste spurring me to hurry. "What is it? What did she find out?"

Josie stared at me, and I could see the struggle in her eyes. She gnawed on the bottom of her lip, and I was about to order her to spit it out when she blurted, "She's pregnant."

This time, a bomb went off inside me. "What did you say?"

"She took a pregnancy test this morning. She's pregnant. It's yours in case you haven't put it together. She hasn't been with anyone since you."

I'd only just barely accepted the fact I probably loved this girl, and now my sister was telling me Ainsley was pregnant.

Kids weren't something I contemplated in my life. Like ever. That was old people's shit, and I'd just entered the best years of my life. "The test is wrong." That was one mistake I'd been careful never to make, but even as I said the words, I remembered breaking my condom rule, and once I'd been inside her, felt what it was like to be free of all barriers, it had been all too easy the next time and the next.

"It's possible," she conceded, indulging me. "But if it isn't..."

I couldn't deal with this. Not right now. "I need to find her." That's what mattered. That's what came first.

"Agreed. I'll try her phone again."

Fynn walked through the front door just as I grabbed my keys off the kitchen counter. He lifted his brows when he saw my face. Setting the bag of takeout on the table, he picked up on the weird tension in the room. "What happened?"

"I need you to pin the last location on Ainsley's phone," I told him.

He could see how important the request was from the expression on everyone's face. "Okay. Is there something I need to know?" he asked, moving into the family room where his laptop was charging on the coffee table.

"She's missing," Kenna said, her movie forgotten in the background.

No other details were necessary. Fynn got to work. "Give me thirty seconds."

Unable to sit still while I waited, I paced the length of the couch, clenching the keys in my hand. Brock put a hand on my shoulder. "We'll find her," he assured.

I had to believe him because the alternative of something bad happening to her would send me into a black hole.

Fynn's fingers stopped tapping on the keyboard. My eyes flew to him, and his gaze connected with mine. "Fynn?"

"She's at Demon's Park," Fynn said.

"What the hell is she doing there?" Brock asked what everyone in the house was thinking. What was she doing there of all places?

"I'm going to find out." I ran out the front door before anyone could speculate more.

"I'm coming with you!" Josie shouted, quick on my heels, but Brock was quicker.

He snaked an arm around her waist, hoisting her off her feet as I reached my car.

"Brock, put me down!" She shrilled lowly, like an angry baby bobcat.

The engine roared to life, drowning out her further protests. I gave one last glance in her direction before I took off. She would give Brock hell, but I trusted him to keep my sister safe. Brock would get Micah and Fynn. They would meet me there.

Demon's Park wasn't far. It wouldn't take me long to get there, especially the way I drove. A crack of lightning speared across the night sky. Ten seconds later, a rumble shook the earth. I blew every stop sign and ran a few red lights, ignoring the horns honking at me.

I yanked my car off the road at the sight of Ainsley's car parked in front of the gate. The Accord wasn't alone. Dread pitted in my gut as I recognized the car. Kate McGuire.

Dots started to connect.

Holy fuck. That bitch.

I'd always believed Kate to be a vindictive person. Her sweet-as-honey charm never worked on me, which pissed her off. I'd seen those coppery eyes flash with venom when she didn't get her way. Oh, the bitch was good at hiding her true nature, but as someone who also wore a mask, I saw through her bullshit.

The truth was, the more she attempted to get my attention, the more turned off I got to the point where I grew to abhor her. I thought after high school she'd let her obsession go.

Now I'm guessing that was a big fat no. She upped the stakes by messing with Ainsley.

Reaching into my glove box, I took out my gun and checked to make sure it was loaded. I didn't know how dangerous Kate might or might not be, but if she touched Ainsley, I'd kill the bitch with my own hands.

I prayed this would all turn out to be a big misunderstanding and I was wrong about Kate, but as I stepped through the gate, the sinking feeling in my gut grew heavier.

For an abandoned park, this place looked as if someone was trying to breathe life back into it but coming up short. Trash, cigarette butts, beer bottles, and other crap littered the streets. Teens and college kids had been sneaking into this place for years to drink, get high, and party. I'd been here a time or two myself. If I recalled, we'd had an Elite party here that I was almost damn sure Kate attended back when we were juniors, pre-Josie era.

Colored lights flashed and flickered in random patterns. Music filtered from the speakers, echoing over the graveyard-silent park. I couldn't remember the last time I'd seen this place functional. The sounds and music made it difficult to hear anything. I didn't know which way to go.

Her name rose in my throat, and I wanted to call out, but perhaps the element of surprise would work in my favor. Kate didn't know I was here.

Behind me, headlights beamed through the iron bars of the gate. The Land Rover's tires spit up gravel as the car came to a skidding halt. Josie rushed out the door, and I groaned. Micah bolted out after her, grabbing her arm. "Hold up, Josie Jo."

Kenna popped her head out next. A fierce scowl marred Brock's lips as he and Fynn joined Micah. I should have known Josie wouldn't stay behind. When it came to people we cared about, nothing would get in our way.

"It's fucking Kate," I said as my friends walked through the gate. I lifted my brows. "What are *they* doing here?" My eyes indicated to my sisters. Sometimes being a triplet was a pain in the ass, and keeping them safe... They made it a damn struggle always inserting themselves into trouble.

Although, one could argue they wouldn't find themselves in half as much trouble if they weren't associated with us.

I didn't ask where Mads was. It was a relief to have one less person to worry about.

Brock scanned the park, his expression grim. "They refused, and I didn't have time to lock them in a room."

Josie hit Brock on the arm. "Let's split up and search."

"You're crazy if you think I'm letting you walk around this place alone," Brock said. "We'll go in pairs. Micah and Grayson can split up if we need to cover more ground."

Micah turned his steely gaze to me. "Surely, we can handle Kate."

And that's when we heard her voice over the megaphone system. "Time's up. Ready or not, here I come."

Micah's brows furrowed as he glared up at one of the park's speakers. "Anyone else think she isn't playing a friendly game of hide-and-seek?"

Kenna rolled her eyes, tucking a switchblade into the back pocket of her jeans. "No shit, Sherlock."

Cool air blew against my back. I didn't want to know what Kenna planned to do with a knife. "She's hiding."

Brock nodded. "Let's find her before Kate does."

"And if we find Kate?" Fynn asked.

I gave Fynn a look the four of us knew well. Secure her until we located Ainsley. Knock the bitch out if we had to. "Let's go before the bitch decides to switch games on us," I ordered, taking off to my right at a jog.

Fear was not an emotion I felt often. I cared little about consequences. In racing, you had to have a certain amount of carelessness and recklessness. But this was the first time I'd ever been in love and had someone to lose. Josie and Mads had been different.

This felt more extreme.

I refused to lose what I hadn't had the chance to fully gain.

Micah took one side of the path while I took the other side. With the weight of the gun tucked into the back of my jeans, I proceeded through the park.

Lightning slashed wildly across the sky, illuminating the few dark corners of the park. I caught a flash of movement.

My breath snagged as the shadow darted by the shoot-the-duck carnival game. I crouched behind a bench, waiting to catch a glimpse of their face. I couldn't tell if it was Ainsley or Kate.

Another bolt of lightning lanced.

Kate. Her name roared in my head as a few droplets of water fell. It would only be a matter of time before the sky opened and poured rain.

I didn't have time to gesture to Micah who continued to move in the opposite direction Kate headed. Creeping along the carnival game stand, I kept my eyes on her. She could have possibly spotted the others, but it didn't appear so. Kate seemed to know where she was going, and it made me wonder if this place had cameras. Had she figured out where Ainsley was hiding?

She cut through the park, staying off the paths and maneuvering between rides before coming to the funhouse. I closed the distance separating us, contemplating if I should tackle Kate to the ground.

"You can stop following me now." Kate spun toward where I stood, the centers of her eyes reflecting the amusement park lights.

As I straightened up, my shoulders remained tense. "Where is she?" I demanded, the question coming out like a threat.

"You like to play with odds. The first one to find the prize wins."

I wanted to whip my gun out and shoot her, but Kate bolted into the funhouse, and I raced after her. Utter darkness blinded me for a few seconds once the door swung shut behind me. I paused and listened, having no idea where Kate was. My breathing became the only audible sound, moving in and out of my lungs.

I took a step farther into the funhouse, using my hands to guide me along the walls. Then she giggled.

"This isn't funny, Kate. Don't make me hurt you." I wouldn't hold back this time. Kate had gone too far.

"Like you did to my brother?" she taunted.

Her voice was close. I whirled my head in the direction it had come from. The floor was purposely unlevel under my feet as I continued to walk. My eyes slowly adjusted to the lack of light. Pulling out my phone, I activated the flashlight, shining it down the narrow hallway. I mulled over her reply. "Your brother was Slade." *Why hadn't I put that together until now?*

"He was my best friend, and she took him from me," she hissed.

"This isn't Ainsley's fault."

The pitter-patter of rain hit the funhouse roof. "You're wrong."

Kate believed every deluded word she uttered. We weren't dealing with a sane girl. I kept walking, twisting and turning through the maze. "What's the plan here, Kate? I'll kill you before I let you touch her."

Her laugh mocked me. "I guess we'll see." I couldn't see her, but the clatter of her shoes echoed as she sprinted down the corridor.

I took off after her, following the sound. The deeper I advanced into the hallway, the smaller the walls became, caging me in.

Fucking funhouse.

For someone like Ainsley or Kate, the narrow passageway wouldn't pose a problem, but for me, it was growing damn uncomfortable. Squeezing through, I entered the next level and halted, my phone flashing over my reflection. This was the hall of mirrors. Fucking fun.

I propelled myself forward, twisting through the puzzle until I saw a dozen versions of Ainsley materialize in the mirrors. My heart clobbered in my chest. I glanced from one image of her to the next, having no clue which was real or if any were her. It could all be an illusion meant to confuse.

"Grayson?" Ainsley called out, her voice trembling and tentative. Terror made her eyes huge.

"Ainsley!" I put my fist through the reflection, shattering the thin sheet of glass in front of me. I had no time to mess around with mirages.

Holding up my phone, I shone it into the space where the mirror had been. Kate stood behind Ainsley, a smug grin on her lips. "Looks like I win."

"Grayson," Ainsley whimpered, her eyes latching on to me.

"Don't move," I told her. "Everything's going to be okay. She won't hurt you." I shifted my gaze to Kate, my jaw hard. "If you want any chance with me, you'll her go," I said to Kate. I would utter a thousand false truths to get her to leave Ainsley alone.

Kate shook her head, seeing through my bald-faced lie. "I can't trust you, Grayson. And besides, she needs to pay for what happened to Slade."

I saw it then. The reason Ainsley stood so frozen, not moving a muscle and barely breathing. Kate had a knife pressed to the side of her throat.

My fingers reached behind my back, touching the grip of my gun under my shirt. "If you hurt her, I promise you'll die too. I won't let you walk out of here alive."

Kate adjusted her stance. "You think I care whether I live or die? What's the point? Do you know what it's like to love someone who won't love you back? It's a pain worse than death."

I angled my head to the side, my fingers secured around my gun. "I guess you'll find out if you don't put your knife down."

She whispered something in Ainsley's ear. I considered pulling out my gun and shooting Kate in between the eyes, but it was risky with Ainsley so close to her and the funhouse lights completely out. I was a good shot, but I couldn't take the chance. Not yet.

Ainsley took a step backward and then another, Kate doing the same. This bitch had another thing coming if she thought I would let her just walk out of here with my girl. I followed, moving a cautious foot forward.

Kate tsked. "Someone needs to stay behind."

"Not going to happen," I growled, my face muscles tight.

Ainsley gave me a look, and I could tell by her expression she was about to do something stupid. I narrowed my gaze to convey what a bad idea whatever she had in her head was. In Ainsley fashion, she argued. Only she and I could hold a silent argument with our eyes.

"Move," Kate hissed, nudging Ainsley.

Ainsley obeyed, but it wasn't her feet that moved. She pulled back her arm and sent her elbow flying into Kate's gut. Kate wheezed, her hold on Ainsley loosening. Ainsley didn't waste the opportunity. She shifted, shoving her shoulder into Kate and pushing her back. Kate rammed into a mirrored wall.

Spitting mad, Ainsley glared at Kate. "No one threatens me with my own knife."

"Run!" I shouted at Ainsley, wanting her as far from Kate as possible but also wanting to wrap her up in my arms. I whipped out my gun.

For once, Ainsley didn't argue and took off.

Kate scrambled after her, gold hair flying out behind her. I pointed the gun at her back, my finger on the trigger. Kate turned a corner after Ainsley.

Motherfucker.

She was only a step or two behind Ainsley, but my legs were longer, and I'd catch her before she got to my girl.

I burst through the door, thrust into the night and the chaotic circus of lights and carnival music. Rain cascaded from the ominous clouds covering the sky in a drizzle, not yet fully coming down in buckets. Lunging straight at Kate, I tackled the bitch to the ground, not giving a second thought to the knife in her hand.

She went down hard, a vicious thud disorientating her long enough for me to knock the blade out of her grasp, sending it skidding over the slick blacktop. I straddled her, keeping her pinned to the ground. "It's over."

She shook her head, catching her breath. "It's not over for me. Don't you see I love you? I've loved you since high school."

"This isn't love," I seethed, my fingers moving to the base of her neck. "Let's get one thing straight, Kate. I don't love you. Never will. I'm in love with someone else."

Kate's face tightened. "That bitch doesn't deserve you. She's trailer trash," she spat. "I've been watching her."

"Oh, I know."

Damp strands of hair plastered to her face. "She's trying to trap you. Just like the gold-digger friend."

Eyes sharp and blistering, my control snapped. Unchained rage flowed through my veins as I wrapped my hands tightly around her neck. I squeezed, fury taking over. My mind clicked off. Kate's fingers flew to my hands, scratching and clawing at my skin. I didn't feel the sting. I felt nothing but the hot fire of my frenzy.

Her body bucked underneath me, legs kicking as I continued to cut off her air supply. My only thought was to make the bitch stop talking—to silence her forever. Subconsciously, I might have wanted to do more than that. She was a threat. The best way to deal with a threat was to extinguish it.

Somewhere in the haze of red consuming me, I thought I heard my name, but it was faint and seemed insignificant.

Kate struggled to breathe. I was past fucking caring.

I sensed her before I saw her. My gaze lifted off Kate, and I looked up into Ainsley's face. She was crouched down by my side, staring at me with wide eyes. Her lips moved, and I could tell she spoke my name, but I couldn't hear her voice, not over the roaring in my ears.

Her hand touched my shoulder, and the noise in my head receded like all the wind was sucked out of a tunnel. "Grayson!" she called, and this time, I heard her.

Staring at her, I blinked, and the pressure applied by my fingers pushing into Kate's throat slackened a fraction.

"Stop," Ainsley said. "Grayson, you're going to kill her."

I failed to see how that was a problem. If I didn't kill her, she would only try to hurt Ainsley again. I couldn't let that happen.

"Grayson," she pleaded, her eyes glistening, drops of rain running down her cheeks. "Don't."

After everything Kate had done, how could she be merciful enough to let her live?

Ainsley touched the side of my face, and I inhaled, releasing my hands. Underneath me, Kate greedily gulped breaths of air, filling her depleted lungs. At some point, she stopped fighting me, but her condition wasn't of my concern.

"Grayson," Ainsley sighed, relief brimming in her mossy eyes. She took my hand and stood up, tugging on my arm. I climbed off Kate, leaving her lying on the ground.

"You're okay?" I murmured, realizing I had a weakness. Ainsley was my Achilles' heel.

She nodded. "Of course, I am. I knew you'd come."

With the same fingers that had been ready to kill, I cupped the side of her face, moving into her hair. Touching her sent a curl of calm through me, slowly overpowering the anger vibrating in my bones, and then I wrenched her against my chest. "Don't ever do that again."

Her arms came around me, and she nuzzled her nose into the crook of my neck. "Being stalked once in my life is more than enough for me. I don't plan on going through it again."

"I'm sorry," I murmured, brushing my lips over her forehead.

She glanced up into my eyes. "This is hardly your fault, sunshine."

I never wanted to let her go. The ground could open and swallow us whole, and I wouldn't release her. "We can argue about whose fault it is after I get you home."

Her lips began to curve, but the full smile never made it to her lips. Ainsley's mouth dropped open, a mad moment of wild panic widening her eyes and sending alarm bells thundering inside me.

Whirling, two thoughts ran through my head. Kate wasn't alone. Or the bitch was dumb enough to get up and not give up.

It was the second.

I had no time to assess the situation. Kate had picked the knife up off the ground and came toward us. No. Not us.

Ainsley.

Kate let out a horrible shriek seeded with deep rage, pain, and violence, lunging straight for Ainsley at my side.

My blood turned to ice. Fear spiraled inside me.

I didn't think.

I reacted, immediately putting myself in front of Ainsley like a human shield.

"No!" Ainsley screamed behind me, but my fate was already decided.

Kate flinched at the last second. It wasn't enough to change her course. Her body's momentum was already in motion, and the blade sunk into the left side of my stomach, right under the ribs.

The pain didn't register at first. My brain knew I'd been stabbed, knew the knife was embedded in my flesh, but I was numb. I cringed, my fingers going to the hilt. It was better to leave it in place than to rip it out and risk doing more damage or bleeding all over the place.

I released a breath as Kate faltered back a step or two, horror radiating in her eyes that had been filled with nothing but malice seconds ago. Kate never meant to hurt me. I hadn't been her intended target, but what Kate failed to understand was hurting Ainsley caused me pain, agony far worse than a stab wound.

Ainsley screamed. She scrambled around me, her eyes going to the knife jutting out of my side. "Oh my God." Her hands lifted to touch me, but they halted in midair as if she was afraid or didn't know what to do. "Oh, shit, Grayson. She stabbed you. The bitch stabbed you," she repeated, disbelief strung in her tone.

"I'm aware, little devil."

"Grayson!" Brock bellowed my name as he dashed toward me.

Another scream followed. This one came from Josie.

Micah was on their heels. "Oh, shit," he said, taking in the sight of me and the blood staining my shirt. "Damn, Grayson."

I kept my fingers around the knife, making sure it didn't move. "Get her," I rasped at Micah, directing him to handle Kate.

"With pleasure." Micah grinned, moving toward the vixen.

"You should have killed me." A feverishness coated her words as simmering hysteria swam in her gold eyes.

Josie had her phone out, fingers fumbling on the screen as she called for help.

Ainsley's head twisted toward Kate. "Don't fucking talk to him," she spat.

Kate smiled with terrible sadness, ignoring Ainsley and looking only at me. "It didn't have to be this way. If you had picked me, I would have loved you more than her, given you so much more."

A lunatic as a girlfriend.

No, thank you.

"You don't get to pick who you fall in love with," I rasped, my fingers stained with blood.

Micah reached for Kate's arms. The bitch jerked, slipping through his reach, and sprinted off in the direction of the Ferris wheel. I had no energy to go after her, but Micah didn't think twice. He took off, swearing under his breath.

I almost told him to let her go, but the girl in my arms trembled, and I remembered the feeling of being on the edge of losing my mind. Kate was responsible.

"Why did you do that?" Ainsley stared up at me with tears pooling in her eyes.

I gave her the truth. Words I should have said months ago. I no longer wanted to live with regret. For too long, I'd regretted shit from my past. "Because I'm in love with you."

Tears streamed down her cheeks. "How can you say that now? If this is some on-the-verge-of-death confession, I don't want to hear it. You can't leave me, Grayson. You can't die on me."

"I'm not going to die." I winced, the pain fully making itself known. It hurt to breathe, the in and out motion piercing the wound again and again.

"How do you know? You could bleed out," she argued. I wasn't sure if we would ever have a conversation where she wasn't contradicting me, and I was damn okay with that.

"The knife is plugging the cut." Well, mostly. The puncture spot was still bleeding a lot, the front of my shirt soaked with blood, but the rain also washed some of it away, making it difficult to tell how much I'd lost. As long as I wasn't woozy, I took that as a good sign.

Brock came over, a critical eye surveying my injury. His scowl deepened. "The paramedics are on their way. Let's get you to the entrance." He slipped an arm around my waist.

I wanted to argue, but the look he gave me told me not to even try it. He would help me whether I wanted it or not. Brock would make sure I got the care I needed. Our safety came first.

We took maybe three steps with Ainsley stuck to my other side, careful not to touch the knife, and she blurted, "I'm pregnant."

Brock stumbled. The man never missed a step, but hearing Ainsley's sudden announcement knocked him off balance for a second. I understood the feeling well.

I glanced sideways at the girl who stole my heart. "I know."

She blinked a couple of times, processing my response. "I think I'm in love with you."

I frowned, and it had nothing to do with the pain or the blood still seeping from my wound. "You think? I want to hear you say it, little devil."

Her nose wrinkled, the bridge damp from the rain. "You have a knife sticking out of your stomach, and you're still demanding shit from me."

Brock huffed as if he agreed with Ainsley, but I needed to hear it.

"Say it, little devil," I rasped, not caring that every time I talked, pain sliced through my side.

Her hair was dripping wet just the way I liked it. She shook her head. "I love you, Grayson. I don't know why, but I fucking love you."

My lips twitched. "Now I can die."

Outrage descended on her features before darkening into something fierce. "Don't you dare."

I chuckled but quickly stopped at the pain slicing through my side from the rumbling.

Hobbling toward the exit, I let Brock support my good side, taking some of my weight. Josie and Ainsley cast worried glances at me with each step. My sister was still on the phone with 911, pleading with the operator to hurry up and demanding to know where the hell the ambulance was. The four of us approached the Ferris wheel, which was close to the entrance. Through the misty rain, I spotted Micah staring up from underneath the ride. Fynn and Kenna were beside him.

I didn't see Kate, and that struck me as concerning.

Where was she?

Had Micah lost her?

A flurry of panic swirled within me, only to be fractured by a scream piercing through the night, just barely audible over the carnival music still playing.

Not even ten feet in front of us, a body plummeted to the ground with a sickening thud. Flesh smacking. Skull cracking. Bones crunching.

Brock and I jerked at the same time, startled by the sudden sound and appearance of a body. It lay in a contorted mess, arms and legs bent in ways that weren't humanly possible. I didn't need a clear picture to identify who it was.

Kate.

Blood quickly pooled around her, soaking and staining the ground. Her eyes were opened, staring blankly up at the sky as rain pelted her lifeless face.

"Holy shit," Brock muttered. His eyes quickly found Josie's, needing to make sure she was okay. My sister stood motionless, gaping at the body. A moment later, the phone slipped from her fingers.

I stepped in front of Ainsley, pushing her behind me with one hand. She buried her face into my back. "You don't need to see this." I glanced over my shoulder at her, but the image was more than likely already imprinted behind her eyes.

Micah, Fynn, and Kenna jogged over to us, gaping at Kate. Shock and disbelief shimmered in their expressions. "She jumped," Micah muttered, his eyes fixated on Kate's as he shook his head. "The crazy bitch jumped."

"We need to go," Brock said in a harrowing growl. "There's nothing we can do for her now."

Kenna dipped down, collecting Josie's phone and handing it back to her. In the distance, sirens slowly sounded over the falling rain. A zap of lightning lit up the sky as we left Kate behind. Her phone had landed a few feet from her body. Fynn scooped her phone up and shoved it into his pocket.

Death hung in the air, its cold essence washing over the park. I shivered, and it felt like a ghost had passed through my soul. It could have been the loss of blood, but either way, I wanted to get the hell out of here.

The sirens grew closer when we reached the main gate, red and blue lights swirling down the stretch of road. A young police officer was first on the scene. Brock nodded at him in greeting and calmly explained the situation. Micah volunteered to lead the officer to Kate's body.

Two EMTs attended to my injury, immediately checking my vitals, while the police officer contained the external building. Ainsley insisted on riding in the ambulance with me and staying by my side. Her fingers interlaced with mine; neither of us cared they were covered in blood. I brought the back of her hand to my lips. "I love you." The words I'd been so afraid to say to a girl freely fell from my mouth. Perhaps part of it was due to what happened tonight, a reminder of how quickly life can be taken from us that made me not want to waste a second of it.

I loved her.

Sister's best friend or not, Ainsley was the only girl I wanted to be vulnerable with. The only girl I wanted to argue with. The only girl I saw a future with.

She smiled, dark mascara smeared under her eyes and running down her cheeks.

As I was wheeled into the ambulance, I met the eyes of my friends. My gaze shifted to the shadows, and I squinted, swearing something was out there. *Someone.* I couldn't be sure, but it looked like a face.

Kate hadn't come alone.

Ice coated my veins, and I tried to sit up, but the EMT at my side pushed me back onto the stretcher. I glanced back at the dark corner just inside the park, searching for a glimmer of that face, but I saw nothing. No sign anyone was there.

I was wheeled up the ramp into the ambulance, and the door closed.

My increased breathing slowed as Ainsley squeezed my hand. She was here. She was safe.

I wanted to believe what I saw was a hallucination—that my mind was screwing with me, but the truth was, Sterling Weston still lived and breathed. We'd seen the proof.

And that meant the nightmare wasn't over.

Not yet.

EPILOGUE

GRAYSON

I shifted the Bugatti's gear stick, the engine purring as my foot pressed down on the gas. Everything about this car was sexy. From the sparkling black paint to the aqua leather interior. What's sexier was the girl sitting in the passenger seat.

Strands of Ainsley's recently dyed deep-purple hair blew out the window, twirling in the spring breeze. A pair of dark shades concealed her eyes. "Are you seriously racing today of all days?"

We just left the doctor's office where she had her five-month ultrasound, the one where they could see the sex of the baby. "I need to do this. For Sawyer." Today also happened to be the anniversary of my brother's death. Every year on this day, we held a race in his honor. It had become a sacred tradition in Elmwood and among surrounding street racers, the only race where half of the prize pot went to charity.

It was our little way of giving back for all the illegal activity and havoc we created. It was also the one time of year the cops turned a cheek the other way despite the number of complaints they might get.

Ainsley slipped her sunglasses down the bridge of her nose and peered over them at me. "And I get that. I really do. But I need you. And so does she." She rested a hand on her tiny bump, but it wouldn't be small for long. She had just recently started to show.

My brows arched as I turned the corner onto Field Road. "She?"

Her plum-colored lips curved. "I'm not sure. Just a hunch."

Another girl in my life to protect. *Fuck*. How could I handle that?

The first few weeks after the Kate incident had been rocky. A mess of emotions and uncertainty. I had a bit of time to think in the hospital.

A baby.

What the hell was I going to do with a baby? How could I be a father? As long as there were people out there who wanted to hurt me, it wasn't safe for a kid. Could I be that selfish?

Sterling was out there.

When Ainsley told me she was thinking about keeping the baby, something flipped inside me. I would die to protect them both. I would destroy anyone who dared harm them. I would make them happy with every breath I took.

And I wouldn't do it alone. I had an entire crew who would do the same.

Family.

We were family.

And now the Elite was going to have a fucking baby.

I wasn't sure who was more excited, Kenna, Josie, Mads, or my mother. This baby was so loved and spoiled already. Even the guys were gushing over the pregnant mom-to-be. I couldn't imagine what it would be like once the little bundle arrived.

Yet, the future wasn't without challenges. We were young and still in college. Ainsley worried too much, but I also understood where her concerns stemmed from. Having our baby would alter our lives, but I made a vow to her that I had every intention of keeping.

She would finish school. She would have the career she dreamed of. I would make sure her dreams came true. Most of all, she would be an amazing mother.

She was mine.

They both were.

I downshifted as we approached a stoplight.

"Why is that so hot?" Ainsley asked.

I had no freaking idea what she was talking about and glanced over to see her watching me. "What?"

A shameful glint sparked in her green eyes, and she grinned. "Watching you shift the car. Do it again."

My lips quipped. "Watching me drive turns you on, and yet you want me to stop."

She leaned across the seat, and her breath teased my ear as she murmured, "I want you to keep driving and skip the race so I can have sex with you while you're shifting the car."

My cock swelled. An old dirty trick, using sex to get her way, but damn, if my dick didn't give a shit. I still wanted this girl as much as I had months ago. Hell, years if I was being honest. The wanting never stopped.

I glanced at the dash clock. "I have time to squeeze in a quickie."

She scrunched her nose. "Romantic." Folding her arms, she sighed. "Fine. If you're racing, then so are we."

My jaw flexed. "No. Absolutely not."

"Sunshine, I wasn't asking."

Just a flash of her in the car as I sped down the road at speeds that would mess a person up if I lost control made my fingers tighten on the steering wheel. "Still not happening. I won't take risks with you."

"Only yourself."

I veered the car into a parking lot not far from Burnout Bridge. It was already congested with cars and people. More than previous years by the look of it.

The Bugatti glided over the blacktop, weaving between cars as people moved out of my way. I parked the car alongside Brock's SUV before killing the engine and popping the door open. I went to Ainsley's side of the car and lifted the handle. Rusty came over.

"Grayson Edwards, the man of the hour," he greeted, clasping my hand. "Nothing keeps you down. Not even a stab wound."

I'd specifically asked Rusty to coordinate the event this year for one reason only. Information. He didn't know it, but later, we were going to have a *friendly discussion*. If we were going to close in on Sterling before the bastard made another move, we had to find a way to be one step ahead of him. As of right now, we were playing catch-up.

Ainsley brushed a hand on my arm, and my eyes followed her as she went to join the girls. "Is everything set?" I asked Rusty, my gaze lingering on my girl for another few seconds before glancing at him.

"Yeah, man. We good."

"Anything?" I asked, shoving my hands into my pockets and giving him a hard stare.

Rusty shook his head, the stupid grin on his lips slipping. "Radio silence, man. Haven't gotten wind of anything."

The news should instill relief. I didn't want trouble today of all days, especially with Ainsley here, and yet, the continued silence from Sterling made me antsy. "Make sure you keep your ears to the ground."

"My guys are on it," Rusty assured. "We stick together."

Recruiting Rusty had either two outcomes. The first, he sided with us, bringing in numbers, people to look out and listen for whispers of Sterling. The second, he led us directly to Sterling. I was ninety-nine percent sure Sterling was the culprit behind the shooting from Rusty's last race. If he contacted Rusty again, I would know.

My features darkened and chilled my voice. "For your sake, you better hope so."

An engine revved at the edge of the parking lot, flashing its headlights to signal the five-minute warning. Rusty left to get things set up, and I joined the others, coming up behind Ainsley and wrapping my arms around her waist, my fingers lacing over her little bump. "I love you," I murmured in her ear, my lips grazing over the numerous piercings.

She spun in my arms, facing me. "Because of this," she said, placing her hands on the small bump on her belly. This had become a bit that we did. What first started as doubt and insecurity had turned into playful banter.

My hands stayed looped around her, keeping her close. "I loved you before, and I'll love you after. Both of you."

"You better," she said, twining her arms around my neck and pressing her lips to mine.

I didn't let her off with a quick kiss, taking full possession of her mouth. The taste of her, the soft lushness of her lips, the little shivers that trembled over her skin at my touch, none of it dulled.

"All right, Grayson, enough with the PDA," Kenna groaned, interrupting a perfectly wonderful moment. "You already got the girl pregnant for Christ's sake."

I didn't want to stop, but I pulled back, keeping my arm secured around Ainsley's waist, and glared at my sister. "Jealous?"

"That you get to kiss Ainsley? Maybe," she teased. "I always wondered what it would be like. She's a little nerdy for my tastes."

"Hey," Ainsley protested and laughed. I loved the sound. It twisted me up inside. "Nerds are hot. Look at Fynn."

"Fynn is not a nerd," Kenna argued.

Fynn only grinned as he leaned against his Infiniti, arms folded over his broad chest.

Micah tossed Brock a beer. "What happened to no glove, no love?" the former playboy heckled, continuing to pass out drinks and bypassing me. He knew I didn't screw with alcohol when I raced.

My lips twitched. "Some rules are meant to be broken. Isn't that our motto?"

Micah's dimples appeared. "Fuck yes." He popped the top of his can, foam spilling over his hand. "I'm going to be the best damn uncle."

"An Elite baby. The first." Brock shook his head, lifting his drink. "You better hope it's not a girl."

Ainsley smiled. She was so damn sure it was a girl.

Josie noticed the way I glanced down at Ainsley, shaking my head. "What secrets are you keeping now?" she demanded.

I grinned. "She had her ultrasound today."

"Oh, shit," Mads squealed. "Don't tell me. It's a girl."

Ainsley and I might have a ton of shit to still iron out. The future wouldn't be without challenges and hardships, but we had an entire crew of friends who supported us and already loved this baby.

Ainsley plucked an ice cube from the cooler and popped it into her mouth. "You'll have to wait for the gender reveal party this weekend."

Kenna's expression contorted into a thing of displeasure. "Hell no. Tell me now. I can't put off shopping any longer. It's literally killing me."

I snorted. "You can't keep a secret worth shit. Besides, Josie's the only one who knows."

I let Ainsley deal with this one and moved to stand by the guys. I only had a minute or two before I needed to get back in my car. "Any luck?" I asked Fynn.

Since the night at the amusement park, Fynn had been combing through Kate's phone. He had extracted her deleted messages and gone through her apps. Most of it was not useful information. Kate and the mysterious contact called Baron had only communicated through encrypted texts. They never met up in person. Never exchanged their real names or sent pictures of themselves. We couldn't prove Sterling was the real mastermind behind Kate's game, but fuck me if he wasn't. My gut told me it was Sterling who put the idea in Kate's head and fed into her delusions.

Fynn shook his head. "Not yet. But I will. He can't hide behind his cryptic texts forever."

"I can't take any chances he might hurt Ainsley."

"We won't let that happen," Brock promised.

My only worry wasn't Sterling. Ainsley's father, Jett Fisher, also weighed heavy on my mind. She hadn't gone home since Christmas break but had talked to her mother. She told her about the baby under one condition, her mom couldn't tell her father. Not yet. Hell, Ainsley might never tell him, but the choice was hers to make.

Not that Jett would hurt his daughter again. I'd make sure of it. Jett and I had a nice little chat after Ainsley informed me she wanted to keep the baby and asked if I was okay with that. I'd been more than okay with her decision. It didn't matter to me how young we were, how difficult the next few years would be, or that everything was happening so fast.

The moment I realized I loved her, Ainsley became mine. Mine to protect. Mine to love. Mine to treasure.

Despite Jett's sloppy apology, he probably wouldn't remember our conversation, seeing as he'd been lit off his ass, but I'd go back again and again until he got the message.

If her father ever hurt her again, I would do more than break every single finger. Ainsley and I agreed our child wouldn't be a part of the mess her father created. Bree was more than welcome to see her grandchild whenever she wanted for however long, but as long as she lived under the same roof as Ainsley's father, our baby would never step foot into the toxic house.

I breathed in the air polluted with gas and oil, loving the smell. The endless chatter of people, the revving of engines, the music flowing in the background—there wasn't a part of this I didn't relish in.

I sought out Ainsley when I reached my car. She smiled and walked over to me. My fingers went to her hips, boosting her against the side of the car. I pressed into her and brushed my lips over hers. "A kiss for luck?"

Her fingers curled into my shirt. "You better win, sunshine. I don't date losers."

A low chuckle left my lips, my breath curling against her parted lips. "I never lose, little devil."

"I love you."

Those three words lit up something within me. It didn't matter to me whether I won or lost today. I had everything I needed right here, and for once, the restlessness inside me was quiet.

My lips sealed over hers with a searing heat that had me wishing we were anywhere but in a parking lot full of people. I wanted her alone. In my bed. And naked.

"I love you, little devil."

"You better. I'll see you at the finish line, sunshine." She stepped out of my embrace, and I opened my door.

A vibration rumbled in my pocket. I unearthed my phone, glancing at the screen, and when my eyes darted up, Fynn, Brock, and Micah all had out their phones. We stared at each other, knowing we'd all received the same message.

You won't find me. Not until I'm ready to be found. Let's hope history doesn't repeat itself. Every race must come to an end.

My fingers squeezed, crushing against the phone. This fucker was going down.

THANK YOU FOR READING!
I hope you enjoyed Ainsley and Grayson's story.
The conclusion to the dorm series is coming soon...
Book Six: BROKEN
Kenna and Fynn

ELITE OF ELMWOOD ACADEMY
(New Adult Dark High School Romance)
Turmoil
Disorder
Revenge
Rival
Unchained

DIVISA HUNTRESS
(New Adult Paranormal Romance)
Crown of Darkness
Inferno of Darkness
Eternity of Darkness

DRAGON DESCENDANTS SERIES
(Upper Teen Reverse Harem Fantasy)
Stealing Tranquility
Absorbing Poison
Taming Fire

Thawing Frost

THE DIVISA SERIES

(Full series completed – Teen Paranormal Romance)
Losing Emma: A Divisa novella
Saving Angel
Hunting Angel
Breaking Emma: A Divisa novella
Chasing Angel
Loving Angel
Redeeming Angel

LUMINESCENCE TRILOGY

(Full series completed – Teen Paranormal Romance)
Luminescence
Amethyst Tears
Moondust
Darkmist – A Luminescence novella

RAVEN SERIES

(Full series completed – Teen Paranormal Romance)
White Raven
Black Crow
Soul Symmetry

BEAUTY NEVER DIES CHRONICLES

(Teen Dystopian Romance)
Slumber
Entangled
Forsaken

NINE TAILS SERIES

(Teen Paranormal Romance)
First Shift

Storm Shift
Flame Shift
Time Shift
Void Shift
Spirit Shift
Tide Shift
Wind Shift
Celestial Shift

HAVENWOOD FALLS HIGH
(Teen Paranormal Romance)
Falling Deep
Ascending Darkness

SINGLE NOVELS
Starbound
(Teen Paranormal Romance)
Casting Dreams
(New Adult Paranormal Romance)
Ancient Tides
(New Adult Paranormal Romance)

For an updated list of my books, please visit my website:
www.jlweil.com

Join my VIP email list and I'll personally send you an email reminder as soon as my next book is out! Click here to sign up: www.jlweil.com

ABOUT THE AUTHOR

J.L. Weil is a USA TODAY Bestselling author of teen & new adult paranormal romance, fantasy, and urban fantasy books about spunky, smart mouth girls who always wind up in dire situations. For every sassy girl, there is an equally mouthwatering, overprotective guy.

You can visit her online at: www.jlweil.com or come hang out with her at JL Weil's Dark Divas on FB.

Stalk Me Online
www.jlweil.com
jenniferlweil@gmail.com